RITU SETHI

His Hand In the Storm

Gray James Detective Murder Mystery and Suspense

Author website:
www.rituwrites.com
Facebook: @ritusethiauthor
Twitter: @ritusethiauthor

ISBN: 978-1-9995609-0-4

To Isabelle

Contents

CHAPTER 1

April 1, 5:30 am

MORE NUMBING PAIN.

At precisely five-thirty am on April the first, Chief Inspector Gray James tucked his cold hands into his pockets, straightened his spine, and looked up.

He breathed out through his nose, warm breath fogging the air as if surging out of a dragon and tried to dispel the mingled hints of flesh, cherry blossoms, and the raw, living scent of the river.

The drumming of his heart resonated deep in his chest – brought on more by intellectual excitement than by any visceral reaction to murder. Because of this, Gray accepted an atavistic personal truth.

He needed this case like he'd needed the one prior, and the one before that. That someone had to die to facilitate this objectionable fix bothered him, but he'd give audience to that later. Much later.

A car backfired on le Chemin Bord Ouest, running east-west along Montreal's urban beach park. A second later, silence ensued, save the grievous howling of a keen eastwardly wind, and the creak of nylon against wood, back and forth, and back and forth.

Heavy boots tromping through the snow and slush came up from behind. A man approached. Tall, but not as tall as Gray, his cord pants and rumpled tweed conveyed the aura of an absent-minded professor, yet the shrewd eyes – not malicious, but not categorically beneficent either – corrected that impression.

Forensic Pathologist John Seymour looked up at the body hanging from the branch of a grand oak, gave it the eye and said, "Well, I can tell you one thing right off."

"What's that?"

"You wouldn't be caught dead in that suit."

Gray sighed. "What do you suggest? That I refer the victim to my tailor?" To which Seymour shrugged and got to work.

With every creak of the rope biting into the bough, Gray half-expected the swinging shoes to brush the snow-laden grass; each time the cap-toed oxfords narrowly missed. A grease stain marked the bony protrusion of the left white sock (with a corresponding scuff on the heel – from being dragged?), above which the crumpled brown wool-blend fabric of the pants and ill-fitting jacket rippled in the wind – like the white-tipped surface of the river beyond.

Dawn cast a blue light on the water and snow. A damp cold sank through Gray's coat and into his bones. Amazing how the usually peaceful beach park took on a menacing air: the St. Lawrence choppier than usual, swirls of sand and snow rolling like tumbleweeds, the sky heavy and low. But a children's playground lay behind the hanging body, and its red swings, bright yellow slide, and empty wading pool offered a marked contrast to the swaying corpse.

With every flash, Scene of Crime Officers photographed the body and documented what remained: only an exposed skull, framed by sparse hair on top, ears on either side, and a wrinkly neck puckered in a noose. A red silk tie under the hangman's knot accentuated the complete absence of blood. Blood would have been preferable. The features were stripped to the bone, with eroded teeth set in a perpetual grin as if the skull were enjoying a joke at everyone's expense.

"White male in his early fifties," Seymour said. "Well off, by the look of him. Only small bits of tissue left on the cheekbones, lips, and around the eyes. Notice the distinctive gap between the two front teeth."

That could help with identification.

The custom ringtone on Gray's cell played "She's Always a Woman." Why was she calling him so soon? He stabbed the phone and tucked it back into his cashmere coat pocket before circling the body several times.

"What killed him?" Gray asked.

"The facial trauma preceded the hanging."

That much was obvious since the rope wasn't eaten away like the face.

"We can't know the cause of death until I get him on the slab," Seymour said. "And before you ask, the time of death is hard to say. Parts of him are already frozen. Maybe four to seven hours ago. I'll have a better window after I've checked the stomach contents and what's left of the eyes."

Seymour crouched and felt the victim's knees and lower legs. "Rigor mortis has set in, probably sped up by the cold." He rotated the stiff ankles. "Look at these tiny feet. Can't have been too popular with the ladies."

3

Gray closed his eyes and counted to five.

All around, professionals bustled gathering evidence, clearing onlookers and photographing the scene. The park lay sandwiched between the beach and parking lot leading to the main road. On one side, the river flowed eastward in a blue-gray haze, blurring the line between water and sky. On the other, traffic going into downtown Montreal grew heavier by the minute. The road led to his neighborhood, where Victorian and Edwardian homes, bistros, and cafés crunched together for ten hipster-infused blocks.

This park held memories of weekends spent with his wife and son. A lifetime ago. *Why did it have to happen here, of all places?*

"Did some kind of acid cause the burns, Doctor?"

"Yeah. Parts of the eyes are still there. Almost as if they were left for last. I wonder why."

Gray could think of a reason but didn't elaborate.

A gust of wind swung the corpse's legs sideways, narrowly missing an officer's head.

"What the hell." Seymour grabbed the ankles. "The sooner we cut him down, the better."

Which couldn't be soon enough. Gray bent down and held the lower legs. He gripped the ankle awkwardly with his right thumb and little finger, the middle three immobile these last three years since the accident, and a snake-like scar running from his palm to his wrist blanched from the cold.

Despite his hanging on tight, the corpse danced in the wind. "Don't rush on my account, Doctor."

Finally, attendants cut the victim down and laid him on a stretcher. Seymour hunched over, his blond hair parting in the breeze, revealing a pink, flaky scalp, the grinning corpse powerless to refuse examination.

"Definitely acid," Seymour said. "Going to be hard for you to trace, since it's so easy to get. Impure sulphuric acid's available at any mechanic shop. You find the purer kind in pharmaceuticals." He flashed a penlight into the facial crevices and probed them with a long, needle-like instrument.

The victim couldn't feel it, but each stab and scrape made Gray flinch. "Must you do that?"

"Look at these chipped bones," Seymour said. "Here, next to the supraorbital foramen, and here on the left zygomatic arch. They're edged off, not dissolved by acid."

"Torture, right?"

"Could be."

Gray paced his next six words: "Was he alive for the acid?"

"I'm going to have to brush up on vitriolage. If he were, he'd have breathed it in, and we'd see scarring in the esophagus, nostrils, and lungs."

Looking around at the flat, deserted beach park, the ropy ebb and flow of the water, Gray said, "He didn't die here, did he?"

"No. From what I can see, livor mortis indicates he probably died sitting and was strung up later. I'll let you know after all his clothes are off." Seymour pushed himself up with his hands, his knees popping like the report of a firearm. "What could the poor bastard have done to deserve this?"

Gray didn't answer. As someone guilty of the greatest sin of all, he considered himself wholly unqualified to make any such judgment.

His cell played "She's Always a Woman," again, and he pulled it out. Images from the previous night played in his mind: her hands flat on the mattress, his palm encircling her belly from behind. And those unexpectedly strong martinis she'd made earlier.

Putting away the phone, he spoke brusquely. "When will you have something ready?"

"Preliminary report probably later today. And I'll send remnants of the acid for analysis to determine the type and grade."

As the body was carried to a van and Seymour followed, second-in-command Lieutenant Vivienne Caron approached Gray carrying two cappuccinos from a nearby Italian cafe. Wonderful steam rose from the opened lids, and the dark, nutty aroma drifted forward, the first hint of comfort on this bleak morning.

Her chocolate brown eyes exuded warmth – eyes both direct and shy, their color perfectly matching her short, straight tresses now whipping about in the wind and framing gentle features.

"Chief Inspector." She addressed him formally, despite their longstanding friendship. The sound of her nearly perfect English was pleasant and familiar, beautifully accented with the musical intonation characteristic of certain Québecois.

Even though she held the coffee before his left hand; he grasped it awkwardly with his right.

"Don't spill any on that thousand-dollar suit," she said.

It made him gag. "Why do you always add so much sugar?"

"Because I know that with a juicy case to solve, you'll be too busy to eat or sleep."

A moment of silence passed between them, pregnant with history he didn't want exhumed.

"I have to make sure you're okay," she said. "Even if you refuse to... She was my best friend."

He placed a hand on her shoulder. "You live with Sita's ghost more than I do. Enough time has passed for me."

"Maybe. It's changed you."

"For the worse?"

Vivienne stilled, her mouth open. "Non. For the better. That's the problem."

Her eyes were warm yet partly adversarial. He saw it as the conflicting desire for wanting him to be okay, but not to leave her to grieve alone. She'd once told him the same trauma that had disillusioned her had enlightened him.

"It doesn't matter what happens," he whispered.

"Doesn't matter?" Her voice took on an edge.

"As long as you can control your reactions – it doesn't matter. Freedom comes from living in grays – no black; no white. No convenient polarities."

Her eyes pierced his, but he knew, out of respect, she wouldn't directly say what she thought; that he oscillated between Zen and obsession, contentment and blackness.

She shuffled her feet. "I don't know how you made that leap, after the tragedy."

"The worst thing that could ever happen to me has happened. After that, I can either fear everything or nothing – I have nothing left to lose."

Vivienne didn't reply.

What right had he to preach when he still experienced unguarded moments which filled his insides with quicksand as that malignant though raced through his mind: what do I do now? How do I fill this day and twenty years of interminable days when everything is for nothing? When this life feels surreal, dissociated as though I'm on a foreign planet with strangers.

Those moments often occurred when he didn't have a case; they occurred before sleep and drove his nightly obsession.

"Living in Gray?" Vivienne shook her pretty head. "I believe in good and evil."

"Then where do I fall? Or will you make excuses for me?"

"Non. I won't make excuses for you. "

Her eyes hooded over; she took a step back. A door slammed between them, again.

"No cell phone, no ID," she said. "Any footprints or tracks are covered by snow."

"Let's have someone check with the occupants of the hospital rooms facing the river."

Westborough Hospital sat directly across the road. A magnificent feat of engineering, its four glass-walled buildings were connected by skyways. It had taken twenty years of fundraising to build (with its founding director recently fleeing to Nicaragua under allegations of embezzling some of those funds) and took up several square blocks.

Gray forced down the coffee. Already, warmth and caffeine coursed through his system, bringing life to his numb toes tucked inside the slush-soaked loafers. "Did you check with missing persons?"

"Only one recent report matches. Norman Everett of Rosedale Avenue in Upper Westmount. He's only been gone since last night and reported missing by his step-son, Simon Everett. And of note, Norman's a doctor at Westborough Hospital."

Gray's head shot up. "Missing since last night, and works at this particular hospital? The timing's perfect. Give me his details. I'll do the interview myself while you finish up here."

"D'accord."

She handed over the number, and he made the call to Norman Everett's house, reaching the missing man's wife, Gabrielle.

Before Vivienne could go, a Scene of Crime Officer jumped forward and handed Gray a transparent evidence bag.

"Found this by the tree over there, Chief."

"How recent?"

"It lay just under the snow. The city cleaned this area recently; hardly any debris around."

Gray thanked him and looked down at the four by six-inch identity badge, examined the photo, and read the identifying details, gripping it tight enough that his fist blanched. The image blurred for the briefest second before clearing.

Vivienne rubbed her hands together. "What's wrong?"

He didn't trust his voice yet. A shoal of uncertainties flooded his chest. The case suddenly became more raw, more urgent, but he'd handle it. He always did. Gray unclenched his jaw and fingers, and handed her the evidence bag.

"The killer?" she asked.

"A witness."

"Look at that ID. Look what it says. You can't be sure."

"Yes, I can." His tone came out harsher than he'd intended. He could guess her next words, and he'd deserve them. *Does anything matter, now? Will you be able to control your reactions?* But she didn't say it. Didn't point out the one circumstance that sliced his calm with the efficiency of a scalpel. Instead, she met his eyes in a gentle embrace before moving farther up the beach.

Bells sounded from St. Francis, the eighteenth-century cathedral up the road for the Angelus prayer. Quebec had the largest Catholic population in the country, and maybe as a result, the lowest church attendance and marriage rate. But the familiar ringing comforted and smoothed the sharp edges of his morning.

Gray left the cordoned off area, crossed the breadth of the beach park, and headed to the attached parking lot and his car; the black metallic exterior gleamed in the distance.

At one time, the Audi S5 had consumed a substantial chunk of his detective's salary, but he hadn't cared. Memories of countless family road trips lay etched within its metal frame.

Still twenty feet away, he pressed the automatic start to warm the engine, just as Seymour summoned him from behind.

The doctor jogged over sporting a wry smile, breath steaming in the cold air, and his long coat flapping. Behind him, the van carrying the body left the parking lot.

"I forgot to ask you earlier – about your next expedition," Seymour said. "Mind having some company?"

"I failed last time," Gray said. "Or hadn't you heard?"

"A fourteen-hundred-kilometer trek to the South Pole, on foot, is hardly a failure."

"It is if you can't make the journey back. Anyway–"

A boom drowned out his words. The earth shook, and air blasted towards them, throwing Gray to the ground onto his right shoulder, pain searing up his arm. Chunks of metal and debris flew from the newly obliterated Audi in every direction, denting nearby cars and clanging against the pavement. A puff of smoke shot upward, chasing the flames, leaving the smell of burning rubber and metal hanging in a thick cloud – while cars on the nearby road screeched to a sudden halt. The fire swayed as though alive, angry arms flailing and crackling, spitting sparks in all directions.

"What the hell!" Seymour lay in the snow, his mouth open, his arm up to ward off the scorching heat.

Gray's car lay mutilated, the black paint graying as it burned. People jumped out of their vehicles to take a look. Vivienne and some officers ran towards him, their feet pounding on the asphalt.

"Someone is damn pissed off at you," Seymour said, eying his own dented Mercedes. He turned to Gray. "What did you do?"

CHAPTER 2

April 1, 7am

ONCE AGAIN, GABRIELLE EVERETT couldn't find her husband. He hadn't come home the previous night, and she didn't know where he was. Truth be told, this was the second one she'd lost. As Oscar Wilde would have said: to lose the first could be attributed to bad luck, but to lose a second was surely akin to carelessness. No longer in the throes of romantic love (she remained open to it; it was love that did not return the favor), she nevertheless believed in keeping a hold on one's spouse. And here she was, having lost another one.

The first had gone missing ten years earlier in the Jean-Talon Market and never been heard from again. Gabi presumed he'd run away from his life as a lawyer, more than he'd run away from her, and could only hope it didn't reflect too harshly on her public image.

Despite her Francophone beginnings below the railway tracks, she now lived in the affluent Anglo neighborhood of Westmount, where one was expected to keep the front garden professionally tended, and one's reputation for austerity and predictability intact. Here, a four-way stop sign meant the grander car had the right of way, and scandal and discontent were best left blanketed under the carpet of one's Mercedes.

Gabi closed her eyes and took a deep breath. Entering the kitchen, she decided to make a cappuccino. The freshly ground beans scented the air. Today, she poured frothed milk in a simple leaf design, though, in her barista days, she could have favored a swan, a butterfly, or even the face of a bulldog.

The empty day stretched before her. As did the empty house. The living room looked staged, as though tarted up for a quick sale; so different from the apartment she had lived in when she was ten, where the air stank of dirty dishes and laundry drying on the radiator. Where the smell of mold and dead mice was the norm. Where on that fateful day, with a father who had recently died and a mother lying on the sofa in a drunken stupor, Gabi had frantically searched for the life-saving object – the medicine – that fateful moment when Gabi had learned what it meant to have nothing left to lose. And she'd never forgotten. Money helped. Becoming a monster helped.

Today, in her Westmount house, holding the steaming cup between cold hands, she stepped out onto the porch.

The crisp breeze gained momentum, carrying with it the sweet promise of spring as it swept across Georgian and Tudor-style manors lining the affluent hilltop. She breathed in deeply, washing away old memories and old remembered smells of mold and mice.

A figure caught her eye, emerging from behind a cherry tree. It bore an uncensored look of violence and contempt. The face seemed familiar, just at the edge of Gabi's recollection – familiar, yet changed.

She scurried back into the house, slammed the door, and snapped the bolt in place. Recognition just within reach, she peered out the window for another glimpse and saw that the figure stood still, seemingly chiseled in granite.

And then it came to her: her husband, Norman, had revealed something while drinking – something regarding the health-tech startup her son, Simon, had launched two years earlier, and in which Norman functioned as Medical Advisor. The company was poised to sell for hundreds of millions, and for Gabi, nothing mattered more than Simon. Nothing.

The links fit together in a chain of events. More were coming – it wasn't over. All the faces concerned flashed in Gabi's mind – of all the people involved, including the remembered face of her beloved frail little sister.

A shrill sound pierced the air and made her drop the cup. Coffee spilled onto the Persian rug. The phone kept ringing as the brown liquid spread and sank into the weave, the stain staring up at her, spoiling the perfection of her professionally decorated foyer.

She lifted the receiver. A baritone voice on the other end, smooth as cognac, eased her strain. Until he identified himself.

"Mrs. Everett?"

"Yes?"

"This is Chief Inspector Gray James of the SPVM. Your son reported your husband, Norman Everett, missing. Could I come and see you right away?"

Simon had done what? Already? Stupid boy. She swallowed the dry lump in her throat and pushed out the words. "Yes. I'm home now." Of course she was home. He'd telephoned the house, hadn't he? The policeman thanked her and said he'd be over shortly.

Ending the call, Gabi peeked out the window. The figure had gone.

Thick clouds scurried overhead, blocking the sun and darkening the sky. An arc of light streamed in through the foyer window onto the rug, gradually narrowing to a sliver until it finally disappeared and she could no longer discern the coffee stain.

Her thoughts flew to her son. How could she protect him? From violence, from failure, from the arid clutches of poverty Gabi had once known so well herself?

But Gabi understood that the most dangerous person in the world was someone with nothing left to lose.

And she knew, in that instant, that her second husband would never come home.

***

Smoke from the fire tore at Gray's throat; heat scorched his skin. Even the pain in his right hand and shoulder, where he'd fallen, barely registered. His car had actually exploded.

Seymour asked again, "What did you do?"

Gray couldn't answer. All he could do was stay on the ground and watch his beloved Audi burn – six years of memories, of himself and his family, disintegrating in the glow and hurling old feelings to the surface. From a time when his life had meaning – of wanting, needing things to work out a certain way. He'd worked hard to overcome those flaws. Three years of calm slipped, and rage mounted inside him, outstripping the draft from the inferno.

Vivienne had reached his side, her eyes wide, her face pale. Seymour stood and shook the debris from his coat.

The custom ringtone on his cell played Stravinsky's dark Concerto No. 1, which invariably meant one thing.

Gray got up and answered while circling the periphery of the blast. First and foremost, he had to make sure no one was hurt. Thoughts of how or why this happened charged through his brain. He swallowed the pebble in his parched throat.

"Bon matin, Directeur," he said.

"What's all that commotion?" Director Cousineau's voice battled the surrounding chaos. Beside Gray, Vivienne dialed emergency services.

"My car exploded."

A short pause. "You must be careful," Cousineau said.

"I'm always careful."

"Non, mon ami. You walk the line. Always have. Sleeping with your boss's mistress, especially a boss like Séverin, is not being careful."

"You hired him," Gray said, marching on feet that weren't his own, rubbing smoke-stung eyes. There were no casualties, thank goodness – but the debris had flown past the crime scene boundaries. Would it also contaminate the investigation? "I'm the one stuck dealing with Séverin."

"Gray, he knows you spent last night with Céline–"

"What's done is done."

"Then undo it."

Swirling around, he scanned the area for anyone suspicious. Lots of cars had stopped on the main road after the blast. Onlookers littered the sidelines, but no one stood inside the parking lot other than his men. No one. And his officers had secured the crime perimeter before his arrival. Which led to one inescapable conclusion.

"She's telling everyone," Cousineau said. "Why can't you control your libido?"

As if that could explain this attack. No one in their right mind did this out of jealousy – not to a fellow policeman. But was Deputy Director Séverin in his right mind when it came to his secretary, Céline?

"I will take you off the case," Cousineau said.

"No!" Gray needed this case, damn it. Idleness invariably provoked an all-consuming blackness he couldn't face.

"You've been compromised. I will assign Peter–"

"Absolutely not. I have to discover who killed this man. And I'm going to. Someone else can head the inquiry into the explosion, but the murder investigation stays with me."

"Who is the boss here, mon ami? I think you forget yourself, non?"

Gray brought his temper under control. Getting upset accomplished nothing. He now had two crimes surrounding him – the hanging corpse and now this bombing –with his life in danger.

A fire engine bellowed as it drew closer, drowning out Cousineau's words – Cousineau who would protect Séverin if push came to shove. Cousineau who had promoted Gray but often kept his true loyalties hidden.

Gray ended the call and watched the water fly onto the jumble, the answering steam rise from the flames. A distance up the beach, clusters of onlookers and press stood riveted, taking videos and photographs, documenting the attempted murder of a Service de Police de la Ville de Montreal detective.

The investigation risked being compromised, his hair and clothes reeked of smoke and rubber, and someone was trying to kill him. Gray took a moment to compose himself. After a few deep breaths, stillness came. He was where he was supposed to be, in the middle of chaos, surrounded by unsolved problems. Once again, he felt calm and in control.

Pulling out the ID found at the scene, he examined the photo, thinking about what Vivienne had said. That the person in the photo could be the killer. Now, she'd maybe suggest the same person rigged Gray's car to explode. But Gray couldn't get himself to believe it. The eyes in the picture, wide and wet like a puppy's, revealed something alarming. Institutional pictures – particularly those of Westmount Psychiatric, an institute for the criminally insane location adjacent to the main hospital – could be deceiving. But Gray was certain of one thing: the picture depicted a child, a boy of around twelve.

Gray brushed the grit off his suit. Somewhere out there was a vulnerable and unstable minor who had witnessed this terrible murder. And it was up to Gray to protect him.

***

This early and she'd already told everyone about last night. Gray wished only to change his clothes at home and slip out unnoticed. She might still be there – in the bedroom where he'd left her in the early hours of the morning – but he didn't want to deal with Céline at present, not with the complexities of the case now at the forefront of his mind.

Still, he couldn't go and speak to a witness in clothes that smelled like death and explosions. He parked the loaner police car in the rear parking pad behind his house on Leeson Avenue; it choked to a halt. The fabric interior smelled like dog and cigar smoke – intermixed with the acrid scent Gray carried from the explosion.

Unfolding his bruised and aching body, he stepped onto the crunching gravel, glad to still be in one piece after the morning's chilling experience.

A dog barked in the distance; no immediate neighbors currently worked their backyards or came out of doors. The narrow lots of detached and semi-detached Victorians and Edwardians crowded together on either side of his house.

Making his way across the modest rectangular backyard, he headed towards the back kitchen entrance, passing a grapevine which never gave sweet grapes, hosta of various sizes he'd planted himself, and a stone path in imminent need of repair.

The three-storey Edwardian satisfied his primary requirements: high ceilings and tall doorways, so he never had to stoop or crouch. With each step, the century-old pine creaked reassuringly under his feet, and he made his way towards his first destination: the sculpting studio at the back of the house.

The old lock turned smoothly with a click; the hinges moved silently.

Clay hung in the air, chalky, sweet, and reminiscent of petrichor, the earthy scent produced by rain on dry soil. An overhead skylight illumined two dozen busts lining the shelves against the wall – all of his son at various ages from nine to about twelve.

No matter how often Gray tried, he couldn't get the angles of the face right: the straight and short forehead inherited from his East Indian mother; the classic nose and delicate, high cheekbones; the thin lips trembling... as they had that last fateful day.

Capturing Craig's likeness at nine, from memory, was challenging enough – but Gray had compounded this task by also undertaking sculptures depicting Craig at ten, eleven, twelve: features imagined as they might look in maturity – with more determined eyes (maybe), a stronger, more masculine nose, the lips less afraid. As though these older representations could live the life his son had never been allowed to live.

Nothing stirred while he silently stood observing the room, meeting the complexities of the moment, in this most complex of rooms.

Coming here had become a nightly obsession, working on the busts by moonlight an overwhelming need without which sleep refused to come.

Here, Craig's moulded faces watched him reassuringly, and Gray stared back – but now, he should go. He turned and locked the studio behind him.

In the upstairs bathroom, he splashed cold water over his face and examined the lethargic-looking stranger in the mirror.

"Why didn't you answer?" A curt voice said. "I called you twice."

Céline Lapin stormed in naked and pushed her way past him. Without waiting for an answer, she stepped into the small clawfoot tub, equipped with an aftermarket hand shower, sporting a mug filled with instant coffee crystals and nothing else.

She turned the temperature knob to hot, filling the bathroom with steam and fogging the mirror. When the water turned sufficiently scalding, she held her mug under the shower head and filled it to the rim. Gray watched her combining two activities that should never be combined. She sniffed the dubious blend and then sipped it like a Chardonnay, her auburn hair clinging to her neck and the curve of her spine.

It was the first time he'd witnessed this absurd scene, and he decided it would be the last.

Gray walked out and headed to his bedroom. After easing into a crisp blue shirt, socks, and a clean suit, he returned to the steamy bathroom. Céline stepped out of the tub; a puddle expanded beneath her feet onto his bathroom floor. She grabbed Gray's robe and slipped it over her wet body.

"You didn't mention your personal involvement with Séverin," he said.

"You didn't ask. We both work under him; some of us more than others. Why? What's happened?"

"It doesn't matter."

"What doesn't matter?"

Damp fingers caressed his cheek, the long nails sharp against his skin. Her breath smelled of instant coffee. And he remembered another face, eyes softer, nails short and clean. The familiar stab still surprised him after three years. His wife's presence drifted in, and he imagined what she'd say about the woman in his robe.

Really, Darling? Another redhead? How many is that now? The last one, at least, was nice.

That final sight of Sita lay etched in memory, slim hips swaying under the fuchsia jersey-knit dress, backdropped by sand and choppy river, not blaming him, but not able to look at him, either. Disappearing off the face of the Earth.

"I like being with the Wonder Boy of the department," Céline said, popping the bubble of silence.

Thoughts of Sita receded, leaving the usual emptiness Gray never fought. A moment later, that too disappeared.

He lowered Céline's clammy hand from his face; it fell to her side in a fist. Their parting would result in no sorrow, no real loss whatsoever on either side. He thought nothing more damning could be said about any relationship, however brief.

"I have to go. You can leave the door unlocked on your way out." Gray felt the sharp eyes stab his back as he walked down the hall and descended the stairs. As Gray left, he hoped this minor chapter with Céline would now be closed.

He drove towards Westmount. Standing in front of Norman Everett's house, he admired the hilltop view overlooking downtown, Old Montréal, and the distant river. It was a pricey street, even for a prominent medical consultant.

A short, slightly plump woman around fifty answered the door. She wore a white linen suit with a bright red camisole that matched her lipstick exactly. The straight blunt hair, just skimming her shoulders, spoke of weekly visits to the salon. Even indoors, she wore dazzling high heels covered with multicolored jewels. Gabrielle Everett cared about her appearance and what others thought of her. So far, she matched her house perfectly.

Her deep-set eyes crinkled in the corners. Brow furrowed, she looked past him and down the road, signaling fear that surpassed concern over her husband's disappearance: she was scared of Gray being there, and he had to wonder why.

"Mrs. Everett, I'm Chief Inspector Gray James of the SPVM. Your son reported your husband missing."

She moved to one side. The fearful eyes rapidly relaxed and became less guarded. He felt an illogical urge to warn her, to remind her he was a policeman and not her friend.

Her living room, all white leather and glass, sparkled – everything except a large brown stain on the foyer rug which resembled spilled coffee. She noticed his gaze and rubbed at the mark with one twinkling shoe. The room should have been cold and uninviting, but it was saved by a wood-burning fireplace on one side.

She motioned Gray to an armchair opposite the sofa.

"You and Dr. Everett have a lovely home here," he said.

"The house is mine, from my first marriage. Norman couldn't afford this."

"About your husband, Mrs. Everett."

"Call me Gabi."

"Gabi. Could he be with someone else?"

"Husbands sometimes have girlfriends," she hedged.

"But not yours?"

"He had the ego, but not the energy," she replied.

Gray didn't miss her use of the past tense.

"You mean he's impotent?"

"In a word, yes. If you have to use a word."

"Does your husband have any other medical problems?" he asked.

"Norman has a bad heart. If he doesn't take his medicine, he gets an irregular heartbeat."

A heart condition? Would Dr. Seymour's autopsy confirm the same in the faceless corpse?

"Did your husband take his medication yesterday?"

"I don't know." She got up and brought over a bottle from the kitchen. Pradaxa. He asked if he could keep it and requested a picture of her husband. She went up to retrieve one.

While she was away, Gray took the opportunity to study the room. A family photo sitting on the grand piano spoke volumes – a contrived pose in a photographer's studio of mother, step-father, and son.

Everett stood behind the other two, his face stretched out in a forced smile revealing a small gap between the two front teeth. Gray's heart slammed inside his chest; he smelled blood. The acid-torn face loomed in his memory with its widely spaced front incisors. He examined the rest of the photo. Mother and son looked more comfortable, sitting on a settee holding hands. It was a sad picture in many ways – at least for the balding man standing stiffly in the back, and Gray felt sorry for Norman Everett, just as he had felt sorry for the corpse hanging from the tree.

Gabi came downstairs and handed over the snapshot.

He stood and placed it in his jacket pocket. "We've found a body. A victim of a violent crime. We need an identification."

Her hands flew to her face, a little too quickly. "You think it might be Norman?"

"Possibly. I'll have Detective Vivienne Caron drive you to the lab to make an identification. She can bring you back here afterward."

He waited for her to ask him about the dead man. She stood before him, open-mouthed, eyes lowered. No questions about where the body was found or by whom. No curiosity regarding how the victim had died.

"Where were you last night, for the record?"

"Here. I got home at six and stayed in all night. Norman often works late, and my son Simon has his own place. Simon has a healthcare technology company, and Norman is a major investor and medical advisor."

A health tech startup. Another possible link to the hospital near where the corpse was found, near where the presumed victim, Norman, worked.

"I thought you said Dr. Everett didn't have much money of his own. How could he afford to invest in a tech startup? Or was he a front-man for a silent investor?"

Gabi's face puckered up. She seemed to physically recede into her chair.

"There's also the matter of dental records. We can check your husband's against the body we found."

"He never went to the dentist. He was terrified of them."

Gray could tell when a suspect was holding back, and she was a suspect. She was also unknowingly serving her son up as one. He liked Gabi Everett, but if she'd killed her husband, she would come to regret her confidences. He now had a faceless corpse and a missing man with a heart problem. If Gabi positively identified the body, all that remained was Seymour checking the corpse for traces of the heart medication.

When it was clear that she wouldn't elaborate, Gray got up to leave. At the door, he turned around and asked:

"What's the name of your son's company, Gabi?"

***

Gray could just make out the yellow tape cordoning off the crime scene in the distance. Adjacent to the snow-capped trees, the St. Lawrence flew eastward, white tips rising and falling on its surface like countless anonymous faces submerging into the blue-gray depths while howling out into the wind.

Across the road, Westborough Hospital glittered shiny and new. But where Gray now stood, a hundred meters down the road, the architecture was a little older and more crumbly.

Gray clutched the ID found earlier in the beach park. The young face of a boy, no more than twelve, stared back and him, and the name of the institution had brought him here: to Westborough Psychiatric Institute, adjacent to the main hospital and crime scene. The Institute had a harsh reputation since it housed the criminals. With a little luck, the young witness had returned to his cage during the night. Or else, Gray might never find him.

The large Queen Anne two-story dated back to 1902. The towers, turrets, and rounded porches had a regal air, but they desperately needed repairs. Peeling paint, stained bricks, and graffiti all vied for attention. A nineteen-seventies five-story addition loomed directly behind, like a warty growth, its Brutalist-inspired cement walls littered with graffiti.

Inside, a security guard escorted Gray around the corner to Director Leblanc's ground-floor office. The slightly balding and pear-shaped Leblanc was pacing back and forth and yelling into the phone. Great. So it would be like that. Seeing Gray at the door, the Director ended the call and held out a red, eczematous hand with an alarming sheen. Gray didn't want to take it, but he did, and the clammy, calloused palm grazed against his. He needed another coffee.

"We detain many murderers," Leblanc said, leading the way to Étienne Cloutier's room in a stiff, slow stride that made Gray want to push him from behind. Here was a man who would get in the way.

"And the boy you are visiting is one of them," the director said. "He's sometimes violent and delusional."

Inside his room, Étienne stood looking out the window at the river. A branch grazed the outside of the old paned glass, scratching the surface with each gust of wind. The child moved to a single bed which stood beside a dresser, a guitar, and a stack of comic books. Otherwise, the room was depressingly bare. He turned two wet puppy-dog eyes in their direction.

Straddling a chair, Gray sat beside him. "We found your ID in the beach park. What time did you leave the Institute last night?"

His hair smelled of sour sweat. He merely shrugged.

"Did you see anyone or anything on the beach?"

Another shrug.

Gray leaned forward. He measured his next words, knowing the risk, wishing he could leave things alone. All the while acknowledging that murder contaminated everyone it touched. No one escaped, especially not the innocent.

"Someone died last night. I can't tell if you're safe from the killer unless you talk to me."

The small mouth fell open revealing crooked, yellow teeth. The pre-pubescent voice was heavily accented with a working-class Quebecois accent. "They make me take pills. I dunno if ze man is real."

Leblanc lurched forward. "There was no man. Only a hallucination."

Étienne stuttered. "He have no face. Like the moon."

"Who did this? What did they look like?"

"He rise in the air, like magic. The bad man hang him from a tree, I scream, and then he chase me."

Gray swung his chair around. "You ran back here?"

"Fast. I close ze gate, and he try and grab me with gray claws. But he can't."

The boy's hands shook; his lips trembled, reminding Gray of other small lips that had once trembled. Gray felt a kick in his gut, but Étienne looked nothing like his son, Craig, except for those fluttering lips.

The boy curled into a ball on the bed and rocked back and forth. Leblanc flew to his side, and the interview would soon be over; the doors of bureaucracy would slam shut.

"What did this person look like?" Gray said. "Man? Woman?"

Étienne shook his head, gasping and gurgling. "Cloth sack over ze face. Black robe."

"Tall? Short? Did this person speak to you?"

"The eyes. Oh God, the eyes—"

"This questioning is over, Chief Inspector. It's time for you to leave." Leblanc called out for a nurse.

A stern and starched-looking woman entered, reached the bedside, and efficiently loaded a syringe. No consolation, no reassurance. Just an aggressive stab of the hypodermic followed by Étienne's pig-like squeal.

A muscle jerked in Gray's jaw. His questions had brought this on. He'd done this to the child.

"He obviously made it up," Leblanc said. "To avoid solitary confinement."

"We found the body this morning. He made nothing up. If you punish him, I'll hear about it."

"Are you threatening me, Chief Inspector?"

"Call it what you like. You're not set up to protect witnesses. I'll assign additional protection."

"No. The boy's under my jurisdiction."

Control threatened to slip through Gray's fingers. Powerlessness, felt once before, would never again take a child's life. Not on his watch.

"He's a murderer." Leblanc said. "A little younger than most, but we're not funded to be a daycare. He killed another boy. Beat him to death with a rock."

So much for patient privacy.

A commotion in the hall sent Leblanc flying out of the room.

"Security here no good,' Étienne said, his voice groggy. "Doctor who take care of me last year say they get me out of here, but I no hear back. Doctor gone, and I want to get out. Please help me find 'im. At night, the boys come to get me, and I hide in cupboard, over there." He pointed to a small alcove in the corner of the room.

A three-foot door led to a storage nook that must have been sealed when the house turned into a psychiatric facility. Gray pulled the edges out effortlessly, and the door opened to reveal Étienne's sanctuary: a musty and damp alcove with a low, cracked ceiling angled to one side, making it impossible to stand inside. An old blanket lay on the pine floor with a pillow on top, the case yellowing and stained and hosting several carpenter ants.

Gray ran a hand through his hair and moved to the only window in the room, overlooking the choppy river and the snow-covered beach park. A view of sky, water, and openness, where the boy could see others living freedom while he was trapped in these unfair walls. Parts of the slush appeared moth-eaten and the struggling winter grass peeped out in yellows and green from below.

It was time to go. He said goodbye, promising to check in soon.

Taking one last look, he wondered what the years ahead held in store for this young witness. Étienne stared back, his wet, drugged eyes asking, searching – for something Gray was powerless to give.

Especially with Leblanc's promised interference. Gray could feel professional detachment slipping away, if indeed he had any to begin with, leaving in its place that personal raw core which erupted at the thought of failure and brought forth that caustic whisper: *what if you fail this child, too? How will you go on?*

CHAPTER 3

April 1, 10:30 am

GRAY PULLED THE car up at Westborough Hospital – where Gabi's husband, Dr. Norman Everett, worked – towards the colorful newly-constructed blocks of over two million square feet of eclectic glass and metal strung together by impressive skyway.

He had already taken the time to briefly research Norman, his work at the hospital, and his involvement with groundbreaking research. After examining Norman's office, Gray planned to visit the health-tech startup that Gabi's son Simon ran.

He drove through the lot, appreciating the hospital's attempt to make medicine less clinical: next to the pediatric complex stood a thirty-foot metal teddy bear. An even taller stethoscope sat at the center of the geriatric ward. And in the front, before the parking lot, was a gigantic abstract sculpture resembling an apple.

The temperature had warmed a couple of degrees, but the sky remained ashen. Freezing rain incessantly slammed the windshield. The engine choked to a halt. He pulled his coat more closely around him and stepped out of the car. Immediately, icy shards assailed his eyelids.

A woman in a bright red coat miraculously maneuvered through the lot on stiletto-heeled boots, the clicking echoing behind her; two men walked purposefully, chatting in French with their hands in their jeans pockets; cars flew past on snow tires crunching over ice.

Sighing, Gray let his shoulders fall. Séverin was getting to him, making him paranoid – and Gray had never, would never live in fear.

The automatic revolving doors stood ten feet away, past the slushy circular drive. To the right, the river gleamed a molten silver, next to oaks with swaying arms, lawns honeycombed with snow, and the snaking icy boardwalk. Here, the river's cleansing scent was mixed with the smells of the city and exhaust fumes from passing cars.

If only he could lay his weary head down on a soft pillow or put his feet up at home while nursing a tumbler of scotch – with Handel or Couperin playing in the background.

An object ricocheted past him, making the popping sound of a child's toy, which was followed by the sudden shatter of glass.

Sharpness stung his ear, and wetness slid down his neck and under the collar of his shirt. The world shifted while people and places tipped sideways and then back, blurring and clearing.

Gray pushed through the revolving doors and ducked. His heart drummed in his chest, and voices crackled around him, some shrieking, some yelling and pointing at the shattered front panel of the hospital entrance. Cold wind ripped through the hole into the hospital lobby while the square-tiled floor seesawed back and forth under his feet. Gray ran behind the black leather sofa and yelled:

"Police! Everyone down!" He dialed 911 and shot out instructions to the dispatcher. Faces lurched at him, then away, eyes wide, mouths gaping open. But now he was the lone figure in a vast expanse of open space – vulnerable and exposed, near agoraphobic, making him long for a small enclosed area he could control instead of this futuristic lobby. A gun might be aiming at his head this very second.

Gray herded everyone further back towards the double glass elevators. A security guard ran over, and Gray took him by the arm and shot off instructions: to keep everyone together and call for backup, to check the bystanders for a weapon, to let no one leave under any circumstances.

Wetness crept underneath his coat and soaked the side of his shirt. Blood dripped from his ear onto his wrist, the redness bringing back another time when blood sprouted out of his wrist like through an open mouth, when the tendons had ripped, and the worst thing imaginable had happened.

But this situation was different. Gray reined in his imagination and practiced the box breathing used by the military and police professionals in times of crisis. He turned his attention towards the dozen or so people by the elevators while breathing in for the count of four, holding his breath for the same count, and blowing out to the count of four. Calm descended. No one appeared suspicious or familiar. The assailant was nowhere in sight.

Sirens sounded from a distance and grew louder. Gray moved towards the front entrance, jumping over the shattered glass and small trail of blood dotting the tile and slush.

Two marked cars with flashing lights screeched to a halt before the doors, spraying snow from their tires. Gray ran outside to meet them; the wind stung his wounded ear and freezing rain slammed his lids. Four officers came towards him. He shouted for two to scour the lot and grounds and sent the other two to secure the lobby – all on autopilot, despite the world blurring and the slush and salt-ridden ground threatening to jerk up to meet his face. And now, he did what he had to do. Gray punched in the number using sharp, hostile stabs.

The phone connected in two rings. His boss, Deputy Director Séverin, answered.

"What the hell?" Gray said. "At a hospital, with all these people around? Have you lost your mind?"

"Calm yourself, Chief Inspector."

"Like hell, I will."

The rough Quebecois voice crackled over the cell. "What is the problem?"

"You just tried to kill me, again, that's the bloody problem."

"What? You are mistaken, or delusional. Why would I try and kill you?"

"You're obsessed with Céline. And you know we spent the night together. Maybe there's another reason I haven't uncovered yet. Trust me; I will."

Cold steel twisted in Gray's gut. He staggered back into the lobby and ground out the words. "I'm bringing charges of attempted murder."

Séverin laughed on the other end. "If someone tries to kill you, that's not my problem. They might be doing me a favor. Any sane man would have left the force by now. But you aren't sane, are you? You live in calm desperation, need a case to keep you occupied, non?" Séverin's voice rose. "Go after me, and I'll have you suspended for the remainder of this investigation.

I'll drum something up to tell Cousineau. He'll have no choice but to put you on leave until you can clear yourself of whatever I dream up. Clear?"

"Crystal. You're not what I'd call a subtle man." The lobby's leather sofa looked a long way away, but Gray made his way over and plopped himself down. His aching head fell into his hands.

"I never assigned this case to you," Séverin said. "You were next on the roster and got called automatically."

"Why don't you want me on this investigation?"

"This is a game of chess, my friend. And I will win. I am holding back, asking you to be reasonable. We don't turn against our own kind."

"Only bomb and maim them?"

"I don't know what you're talking about. You must learn to get along, Chief Inspector."

The line went dead.

Gray lifted his head from between his legs, embarrassed at his disorientation from receiving a simple bullet wound to the ear. His arms floated before him, pale and dismembered. Concussion? It was possible given the force of this morning's explosion. Knowing it didn't help the pain in his head.

He scanned the lobby. No one watched, but outlines and curves of familiar objects swiveled and zigzagged. He drummed down the impatience to go to Séverin's office now – to kick down the door, grab his boss by the throat, and shove him against the wall. Gray took a few deep breaths. He had to play this game smart, or he'd end up as roadkill. He had a plan regarding Séverin, and he wouldn't diverge from it, despite today's shooting.

A shape came forward and cast a shadow; a halo of light surrounded the blonde head and gentle eyes, a small nose, and a thin mouth. She leaned in close, her breath smelling of cinnamon. The lady from the lobby café. She held out an open bottle of orange juice. "This will help."

Gray gulped it down fast, and the sweet, tart liquid soothed his parched mouth and slid down his throat.

"Are you my Guardian Angel?"

"I'm a barista at the hospital coffee shop."

"Close enough," he said, squinting. "And lucky me, there seem to be two of you."

"I've called a doctor."

The dizziness began to fade. Lines and swivels took solid form and colors stabilized. Behind him, the officers took statements from the bystanders. A doctor wearing a white coat hurried over and knelt beside him, introducing himself, but Gray didn't catch the long name. He grimaced and counted to ten as the gloved hands probed his ear.

Gray answered his questions and endured the penlight blinding each eye in turn, all the while thinking about Director Cousineau – how he would advise Gray to give up the case, run with his tail between his legs. A hot flush ran up his face and burned his cheeks. No way. Never in a hundred years.

The doctor stood, his stern face resolute. "We have to go to the emergency department, now. You need sutures to control the bleeding and a full exam. Did you hit your head today?"

"No, something hit my head."

"Then we'll need an MRI."

Gray held up his hand. "Just patch me up. It's enough for now." He felt better, and feeling was returning to his limbs.

The doctor crossed his arms across his chest and tapped his foot. However frantic Gray's day might be, the man clearly felt his to be worse. "We're going," the doctor said.

A figure approached them, casting a still, ominous shadow on the tile in front of Gray.

"What the hell happened?" Detective Douglas Green crouched down, his brow furrowed with lines thick and deep for his age, thin lips pressed together and his face, much too close – close enough for Gray to smell tuna on his breath.

Gray had forgotten that he'd arranged to meet his junior detective.

Bracing against the couch enabled him to stand and feel the strength return to his body. He followed the doctor towards the emergency room. "Just a normal day in the life of a detective."

"You're bleeding, sir."

They entered the connecting hallway. Doug came up beside him, matching his strides, the young face more stern than concerned. Vivienne had once said Doug reminded her of a Chicago gangster from an old 1940's movie, something his square-shaped head, furtive eyes, and thug-like personality did nothing to dispel.

They passed mirrored walls, and Gray watched Doug in the reflection, shoulders straight, eyes hooded, the young man's mouth a horizontal slit, with only the requisite fedora and clutched machine gun missing.

Gray wasn't indulging in idle speculation. Someone had wired the Audi to blow, possibly a police officer with easy access to the crime scene, an officer with a certain kind of audacity. And now someone had shot at him. Come to think of it, Gray had seen Doug – a junior officer – interacting on multiple occasions with both Séverin and Cousineau, which was odd since both men conformed to a more formal hierarchy.

Pushing down his natural aversion to Doug, Gray filed the thought in a corner of his mind. He needed this detective's particular skills for this investigation, which would involve cutting through the impossible bureaucracy of a government hospital in Quebec. And he needed to keep his enemies close.

"Dr. Norman Everett was our victim," Gray said, breaking the silence. "We don't know yet for certain, but I have a hunch. He brought his stepson's Personalized Antibiotic System to the hospital. And I've read that PAS is worth a fortune."

Doug opened his mouth to speak, then closed it. They reached the emergency department, and the doctor led them to a procedure room filled with steel implements.

When Gray hesitated, the doctor gave him a stern look.

"All right." Gray climbed onto the medical bed. "I'll play the part of a pin cushion, but under protest."

To Doug, he said, "Go up to Norman Everett's office and look through his papers. I want documents relating to his stepson's startup, or their hospital trials. I'll meet you in the Infectious Disease Ward as soon as I'm finished here."

"What are we looking for?"

"No telling what's relevant. And who knows if anything is left to find."

The junior detective left, just as Gray registered the burning of the disinfectant on his ear. What a day.

A half hour later, stitched, bandaged, and having somewhat ungraciously thanked his doctor, he proceeded to the infectious disease floor. Gray hoped visiting the ID department would help him get an idea of how the startup's PAS system worked. The very sexy Nurse Adeline Dubois provided the explanation. She also informed Gray that Norman had changed the entire nursing staff on the ID ward a year ago.

Footsteps signaled Doug's approach. Thanking Adeline, Gray left the nurse's station.

"Get a court order to look at Everett's medical charts," Gray said to Doug while heading towards the elevators. "We need to know about everyone who received a PAS antibiotic in the last year."

"Man, that could be a huge list."

"Focus on any who died after receiving the startup's customized antibiotic."

Dismissing Doug, he rode the elevator down to the main floor and left by the back exit, not wanting to see the shattered glass or his blood all over the tiles. He paused outside the door and looked in either direction. No one.

Gray headed towards his replacement car. Snow had replaced freezing rain, and oversized flakes fell sideways across the air and over the nearby road and river. There had to be easier jobs than this, in other cities with departments less riddled with cynicism and corruption.

But what if Sita returned, and he wasn't here? Didn't he owe it to her to remain? Even as that question entered his mind, he wondered if he could be a family man again. Each morning, Gray looked pain straight in the eye and calmly moved past it to where nothing which occurred ultimately mattered: it was a deal with life lived in grays and, above all, lived in freedom.

He sincerely wondered if he could ever be with Sita again – if he wished to abdicate the solitary life tragedy had imposed – and wasn't that thought, in and of itself, the greatest betrayal of all?

Reaching for his car keys, he found a piece of paper shoved into his jacket pocket with Adeline's name and number on it. She must have slipped it in earlier. Hmmm.

As Gray drove away, he recalled the phantom bullet ripping through his ear, and a thought struck home – a memory of something Vivienne had once mentioned in passing: that Detective Doug Green always carried a concealed revolver. That he never left home without it.

CHAPTER 4

April 1, Noon

THE TERM SHEET GLARED back at her from the computer screen, but the person on the other end of the phone had to be placated first.

Holly Bradley, CEO of the tech startup HealSo, ran her blood-red fingernails over the white leather armrest of her desk chair. It scratched easily, leaving four parallel gouges.

"Of course, your investment in the startup will remain confidential. No one knows about you except Norman and me. Do you think I'm stupid enough to risk the company's sale by talking to the police?"

She dug her nails further into the leather. This was her third chair in the past year; she couldn't care less if she went through twenty. The pretentious startup owed everything to her. Including the genuine opportunity to sell their company for millions.

"I don't know where Norman is. Nothing's happened to him, I promise."

But the caller described the body by the beach, and Holly's heart slammed in her chest. Was this person responsible for that hanging body or merely informing her of the fact? Had Norman made a deal with the devil and dragged her into it?

"You're overreacting," she said. "Yes, I'll do what needs to be done on this end. Don't worry."

She ended the call. Engineers and other startup employees bustled outside her office door; their annoying feet shuffled and clicked on the lacquered cement floor, making it impossible to think.

Still, it was a step up from the modest family farm in Haiti where she'd grown up, with its severe erosion and steep slopes, poverty, and sluggishness; all that seemed a lifetime away – a childhood memory belonging to a stranger she scarcely recognized.

The intervening years of technology and startups had obliterated that young farm girl, and if colleagues derogatorily referred to her as having edge, they were purposefully understating; Holly aimed for an edge people frequently fell off.

Outside her expansive windows, sunlight glinted off a nearby silver-domed roof. Montreal sludged by below at its annoyingly slow pace. Nondescript figures walked on the road, people who experienced happiness they hadn't rightfully earned. Assholes. She had to get out of here, had to make it to the big time in the Valley or New York.

Holly re-examined Guilter Pharma's term sheet – outlining the conditions of sale for the company – on her computer, and slammed the top of her glass desk. Only forty million instead of the agreed two hundred. Why was it so damn hard to sell one bloody company?

Both Guilter and the startup's founder, Simon, would find out who they were dealing with – Super Bitch with a capital B.

The roar of anger and acid that ran through Holly's veins frightened even her, and if she could have breathed out fire and obliterate everyone in her way, she definitely would have. This world had given her few choices, all of them unsafe.

Everything hung on selling the company for a great deal of money. Then there would be peace; then there would be security.

The importunate burring of the phone yanked her from her reverie.

"You left early," the woman on the other end said. "I didn't see you this morning."

"You were sleeping, Mel." Holly cradled the phone with her chin while composing a well-crafted response to Guilter, one that would set them straight.

The silence stretched, save the tapping of keys.

"How are you?" Holly said.

"Alice cried most of the night. Didn't you hear her? What time did you get in?"

"I worked late, again. I'm sorry."

"We're supposed to be doing this together. I can't take care of her alone."

Holly stopped typing. A familiar pain crept up her chest, from too much coffee, too many arguments; she rubbed the sore spot. "You knew what this job meant when I took it. If it works, we'll have security for the rest of our lives. We agreed on this plan together. You agreed. The baby – I wanted to wait."

"I'm forty-two. I couldn't wait. I adopted her alone, remember."

"Oh, not that again." Holly got up and closed her door. She had no intention of showcasing her domestic troubles to the rest of the office. Reaching for her mug, she downed the cold coffee sitting on her desk; a hand twisted in her chest.

"You always do that," Melanie said. "You won't tell me why... it can't be the only reason. The adoption agency wouldn't have held that against you."

"Of course they would. What are we arguing about? We're together. We have a baby, just like you wanted. And it's only one baby, for God's sake. How hard can that be? I'm wrestling a pack of idiot programmers, a dozen lawyers, and a founder that wants me dead. I'm buried in problems, and I can't deal with this right now. You know I don't like it when you call me at work."

"You weren't like this before... it's since you met that doctor – Norman Everett – you've become obsessed with selling the company. You don't love us anymore."

"Of course I love you," Holly said.

"I miss Robert."

"I told you never to mention –"

"I know," Melanie said. "I have to move on. It's you and me and Alice – no one else. You were so different in Alabama. Maybe if you cut back on your pills–"

Melanie suddenly stopped talking, but the line had been crossed, the gauntlet thrown. Silence stretched between them – until the tapping of keys resumed.

If Guilter thought Holly would accept their offer of only forty million lying down, they were in for a big surprise. They didn't know who they were dealing with.

"Oh God, I'm sorry," Melanie was saying. "I can't seem to relax. It's like I don't know myself anymore. You're taking care of us. I'm just at home, and you're working. Forgive me?"

A cry echoed over the phone from Melanie's end. The familiar wail drowned out Holly's tapping.

"What's happened?" Holly said, gripping the phone.

The crying grew louder, accompanied by the rapid thudding of feet – Melanie probably rushing upstairs to the baby's room to pick her up, coddle her, help her get back to sleep.

The baby might have had another allergy attack. The last time, she'd needed an adrenaline shot at the hospital, and it had killed Holly to see the tiny ribs gasping to get in air, the large needle jabbing into the pale skin, the oozing of blood.

Breathe in, breathe out. Holly waited for the wailing to stop, but her heart jack-hammered. She'd wanted this baby as much as Melanie, even if she couldn't admit it.

Suddenly, a different scream sounded over the line, primitive and deep, and Holly nearly dropped the phone. This second scream momentarily silenced the child.

"Mel, was that you?" Holly asked. "Are you with Alice?"

Still nothing. Why didn't she answer?

A moment later, the phone was picked up, and Melanie spoke coolly and calmly in a stranger's voice.

"Yes. Everything's fine. I have to go."

"What happened? Tell me."

"It's nothing. Alice threw up, again. That's all. The room's coated in vomit."

Holly exhaled and hid her irritation. The baby was fine. Why did everything have to be portrayed as such a bloody catastrophe?

Though one didn't need to imagine the state of the crib, the blankets, the floor, not to mention the wet and sticky baby herself. Even the familiar stench lay fused in memory; thank goodness she wasn't the one to have to clean it up.

She refocused on her crucial email to Guilter's acquisitions team.

Muted sounds, tenuous at first, became clearer over the phone cradled between Holly's ear and shoulder. The sounds grew stronger, at first flat, then more jolting – two voices – Melanie's and the baby's. Mother and child were weeping together.

Then the line went dead.

For a solid minute, Holly didn't move. What her partner had said wasn't true. Late last night, Holly had tiptoed into Alice's room and stood over the baby's crib, watching the one-year-old sleep with a peace that she herself could scarcely contemplate.

She'd stood for a long time, absorbing the regular breathing, the pudgy Asian face puckering in a frown, then relaxing, the soft belly rising and falling. What could be more beautiful? And she'd softly sung, to the baby, the Haitian Creole lullaby her mother had always favored whenever Holly felt scared: 'dòmi, dòmi ti bebe – sleep, baby, sleep.'

If she didn't spend much time with Alice, didn't fuss over motherhood as Melanie wanted, it was because this distance helped put domesticity out of her mind. What was the alternative? Succumb to hormones and abandon the startup to the mercy of its infantile founder?

Holly shook herself out of it. Enough. She rose and moved to the window, her stiletto boots clicking against the lacquered cement floor of the formerly industrial space in Montreal's Griffintown, by the canal – now trendy and renovated using chrome, cement, and glass. The fifteen-foot ceilings of the startup echoed the clicking through the room and probably beyond.

Everything came together in her mind at once: the first caller who had unlimited power and might do anything – even to Melanie and the baby; Norman – who was probably dead if not hanging by the St. Lawrence River, and the shattering of an acquisition worth hundreds of millions of dollars... Oh God, what was she going to do?

A crash from the outside office made her swing around. Somebody shouted.

Holly ran to the door, wondering what would go wrong next.

***

HealSo's young Chief Software Architect Jimmy Cane, spoke in hushed tones while backing away from all the smashed glass. "What do you mean, Norman's missing?"

An overturned trolley with drinks glasses, beer bottles, and plates lay on the ground in the large open office.

Simon Everett, the founder of the health tech startup, answered him with his usual arrogant drawl. "You gotta do something about your shakes, man." He motioned for the office manager to begin the cleanup. The thirty or so engineers and programmers working at their desks had stopped to stare, including Holly who had jumped out of her office because of the commotion. After noticing the broken glasses, everyone got back to business.

"Just tell me," Jimmy said.

Simon pulled him into a private corner by the floor-to-ceiling windows of the trendy, industrial space. "Norman didn't come to our business meeting last night. I reported him missing to the police early this morning because I knew Mom wouldn't. In fact, I think she's relieved he's gone – and who the hell could blame her?"

"What could have happened to your dad?"

"Step-dad."

"But... but without him, HealSo may not sell."

The startup's revolutionary precision medicine technology allowed them to make custom antibiotics for each patient. It was the reason the fifty-person, not-yet-profitable company stood poised to sell for an estimated two hundred million.

Simon snorted. "Hope you're right. I got people looking up to me; they're my tribe. I'm not going to sell them out to a money-hungry big pharma."

Silence ensued, with only the thumping of Jimmy's heart sounding in his ears.

If the sale of the company got cancelled, there would be no due diligence process. And without due diligence, he'd be safe. Or else... or else someone had erased Norman permanently from the complex equation.

Simon leaned against the cold floor-to-ceiling glass and folded his arms. "I gave an interview to that sexy reporter, but our Halle Berry look-a-like barged in and cut it short. Apparently, the Board wants all interviews to go through her until the acquisition's done. Bitch. I invent the product, and she rides in as CEO and steals all the glory."

Jimmy could have pointed out that he alone had made Simon's "flash of brilliance" product actually work, but instead said: "Don't call her Halle Berry. Éric pointed out the resemblance, and now he's on the Quality Assurance team."

"No CEO, not even our delicious Holly Bradley, can demote someone for that, not in Canada anyway. You know, I think the reporter recognized her, but Holly claimed they'd never met."

"What do you mean?"

"Exactly what I said. Holly wouldn't let her get a word in edgewise and practically tossed this reporter, a delectable lady by the name of Ms. Chan, out on her bony yet sexy ass."

Simon switched to a conspiratorial tone. "Listen, this place won't be the same after we sell. You think a big corporation will let us play table tennis during working hours, or keep beer in the fridge? Some battle-axe from HR with a binder full of regulations will squash all that, and before you know it we'll be wearing suits."

"Suits?" Jimmy straightened the front of his Flash T-shirt, bought at his usual store on rue St. Laurent. He'd worn a Batman shirt to the office one day when Holly had teased him about the caption, "Hero of the all-nighters," and he hadn't worn it since.

He needed someone to latch onto – before life in a startup and life in the big city tore him to shreds, a life so different from the suburban ravine-side condo he'd shared with Mom in Laval before moving to Montreal – Mom who had warned him he was moving too fast, that despite his brilliance he had trouble reading people and needed things to be spelled out clearly.

He needed her now, yet couldn't ask. Not without risking his life and hers. He pulled his snug-fitting vest closer across his chest until the seams dug into his sides.

Simon returned to his glass-walled office in the center of the room, and Jimmy moved to the expansive adjacent kitchen to get a cola. The oversized drinks fridge held – on six removable shelves – an assortment of pop, juice, and multiple craft and factory brands of beer. He grabbed a drink and saw his girlfriend, Kate, in the main office.

Like a puppy, he sprang towards her.

"Hey, kiddo," she said, leaning a hand on one hip.

"You're here."

She'd served him cappuccino at Café Doigt across the street for two months without a second glance, until one day she'd passed him her number. It had been as simple as that. Before Kate, his hands had never caressed a woman's hair; his lips had never nibbled a pierced ear.

Kate's red tresses, cropped shorter on the left than the right, shifted with a toss of her head. That marked face; those sapphire eyes connected with his, glittering brighter than the stone in her belly button.

She raised her hand, and the small, braless breasts rose under a mesh tank top, making his heart thump and bringing a hard lump to his throat.

"I tried my new brioche recipe – you know, with four hundred and seventy-five grams of flour instead of four hundred."

"And?"

"It's better than the last experiment, just like I thought." She looked around the room. "Can't stay."

He hungrily sucked in her jasmine scent. "What? I thought you were taking the afternoon off? We could get a bite nearby?"

Now she had her hands on her hips. "Can't."

The silence tore at him. "Where are you going?"

His question came off more petulant than he'd intended, yet no more than he felt. Immediately the lines of affection on her face changed.

"Here's the stuff you left at my place." She handed him a bag. "I told you, I don't have room."

"Who are you meeting?"

"No one you know, Jimmy. No one you have to worry about."

He held his breath. Suppressing everything he wanted to ask, plead, or demand, Jimmy waited until the smile returned to her face. Slowly, it did, and she leaned in and gave him a kiss on the lips.

The sensation of her soft, cinnamon-flavored lips pressed against his made him lightheaded.

"Maybe I'll come over tomorrow night," she said. She moved, and her tiny waist swiveled towards him above low-cut jeans.

"I can make spaghetti, with chopped up hot dogs." It was one of the few things Jimmy knew how to make.

Kate smiled. There was affection there; he could tell. She liked him; although there were times when he wasn't so sure. Once, he'd seen her watching his reflection in the mirror, something wild in her eyes. But then her expression had relaxed.

Noise from across the room made him turn to where Simon was escorting a well-dressed man into the office. Simon was speaking while the other man listened.

The stranger moved with an easy stride, taking in the room, almost owning it. He came to a halt beside them, and Jimmy detected the faintest hint of smoke and rubber. Mom would have called him handsome, said he looked like some debonair movie star from an old black and white film.

Now, the stranger noticed Kate with obvious appreciation. She tilted her head to one side and returned his bold stare, lips pressed firmly together, jaw clenched: two grown-ups checking one another out. Something hungry jumped in Jimmy's chest.

"Meet Chief Inspector Gray James of the SPVM," Simon said, caressing his new hipster beard, which didn't suit him one bit and invariably carried bits of food lodged between coarse strands. "He's here to address the troops about Norman's disappearance."

The Inspector held out an awkward hand in an almost claw-like grip; the middle fingers didn't move, and a snake-like scar traveled up his wrist and into his cuff. That must have hurt a lot; maybe, it still did. Kate noticed the deformity, too, but almost clinically, like she'd seen this type of thing all the time. She shook hands but let go quickly, as though his hand were hot.

Kate made her excuses and left Jimmy to deal with the police alone. The Chief Inspector ignored her receding figure (unlike drooling Simon) and scanned the room with a serene, almost Zen-like presence.

A hand closed around Jimmy's throat.

"We need to talk," the Inspector said, his baritone voice calm and cool. "I have a feeling you can help me."

Simon led him and the others into the kitchen for the upcoming group meeting. To the right, Holly stood before her office with her legs apart and fists on her hips, glaring at Jimmy. That look said it all, and now the hand around his throat possessed thick, long-nailed fingers, painted blood red. Holly unclenched her fists and pointed one painted nail in his direction. And they both knew what that meant.

CHAPTER 5

April 1, 12:30 pm

GRAY RELAXED BEFORE the fifty or so HealSo employees gathered in the expansive kitchen, with Vivienne standing to his right. Most sat at the half dozen rows of tables, and the rest stood restlessly in the back against the kitchen counter and appliances, conveying their nervousness.

The pounding in Gray's head had subsided after a couple of pills, courtesy of Vivienne. He looked presentable enough to continue with the job, if only just, but the greater part of Gray's energy was being consumed by staying sharp.

"You feeling better?" Vivienne's half-smile brought normalcy to an abnormal day.

"It's been a jam-packed morning."

The room grew quiet. Startup employees sat in tightly packed rows and avoided Gray's eyes, none wanting to draw attention to themselves. Only the executives standing in the back of the room defiantly stared at the detectives. Simon leaned against a cupboard on the left, and CEO Holly Bradley

– tall and lithe, mouth set in a grim line – stood beside a glass-fronted drinks fridge to the right.

Her high stiletto boots, cropped hair, and exotic looks gave her the appearance of an actress rather than a business powerhouse. Steely gray eyes did more than hint at ruthlessness.

Simon crossed his arms, looking bored and annoyed, an interesting twist since he'd reported Norman missing in the first place. He made eyes at Vivienne and raised both eyebrows suggestively. She merely blinked.

Gray turned his attention to Jimmy, sitting by the wall at the end of a table. The young man of about twenty-eight stared down at his hands, the boyish face scrunched and pale. Straight, brown strands fell before his eyes. He knew something that frightened him.

"Cool looking group, more hipsters than tech geeks," Vivienne said, leaning towards him.

"This is Montreal," Gray said, by way of explanation. Style was a given here.

Gray and Vivienne planned to observe everyone's reactions while addressing the group. The initial meeting with the collected staff was crucial. In a group, reactions and explanations couldn't be contrived or controlled. Others were always willing to step in and correct half-truths. Gray noticed what got told as much as what was withheld during a group discussion. Facts held back for disclosure in private were immediately suspect.

All eyes focused on Gray. "Thank you for giving us a few minutes of your time. I'm Chief Inspector Gray James of the SPVM, and this is my colleague Detective Vivienne Caron. We'll be speaking to many of you alone, but it's helpful for us to address the entire company first. Some of you may be aware of the fact that your Medical Advisor, Dr. Norman Everett, has been reported missing."

There was a flurry of rustling and low voices.

"Even though twenty-four hours haven't elapsed yet," Gray continued, "Simon Everett has filed an official report, and we're taking it very seriously. Has anyone seen or heard from Norman since yesterday?"

Gray waited. No one spoke. He was about to continue when Holly said:

"Even if he's missing, which I very much doubt, why does this warrant a Chief Inspector from the SPVM Homicide Squad? Why not a couple of uniforms instead?" She met his eyes in a challenging gaze, daring him to explain. But did she know the reason for their presence? Her cocky stance implied she did; Gray couldn't be certain.

Holly's next words clarified the issue. "I only ask because you were on the morning news, weren't you? An Inspector's car got bombed beside the riverfront, and I'm certain I saw you in the footage."

Voices in the room rose, and bodies shuffled. Gray watched, registered their reactions, especially Simon's and Jimmy's. He'd wondered how to broach the issue of the faceless body without directly linking it to Norman. Without proof, that could blow up in his face. And he didn't wish to reveal to the startup what... or rather who had inadvertently brought him to their door; at least, not yet. Now, with Holly mentioning the television program, things became easier.

"You're correct," Gray said. "I was called early this morning to the beach park directly opposite Westborough Hospital to investigate a suspicious death."

More murmurs. All the blood left Jimmy's face, and if he weren't seated, he might have passed out. Funny how in tech startups, a naive kid – innocent and unworldly – could be one of the heads. The world had turned into a funny place Gray didn't always understand.

In the back of the room, Simon stood in a simian posture with his mouth hanging open, both arms flaccid in front of his body. Only Holly remained unaffected, although presumably if she'd seen the news report, she already knew of the faceless corpse found hanging by the beach; she might already suspect it belonged to her medical advisor, Norman.

Gray kept his expression neutral. The rest of the programmers and engineers shifted in their seats and fiddled with their hands, not all of them frightened, some intrigued by their vicarious brush with murder.

"Did something happen to Norman?" Simon said.

Vivienne took a step forward. "We're not sure. We have to wait for a formal identification. That's why it's important to know if anyone spoke to Norman in the last twenty-four hours and to ascertain his movements. No one at the hospital has heard from or seen him since six pm last night. And his family has made every effort to locate him this morning."

So far, people wanted information but gave back nothing in return. Two men carried in several large covered aluminum trays, presumably the team's lunch, and placed them on a side table. Wafts of marinated beef, chorizo, and lime filled the room. Gray recognized the restaurant label on the trays as coming from a small Chilean place he frequented himself.

"I heard from Norman." Holly's declaration produced instant silence. "He telephoned me at nine in the morning, to say he'd be away for a while and not to worry. He also said he'd forgotten about the Board meeting and to send his apologies, but other things currently occupied his time. Norman recommended I continue with the acquisition plans without him, and asked me to relate that to the Board. I've phoned them all in turn."

Someone in the room gasped. A couple of chairs screeched against the cement floor, but otherwise, they all sat in a pregnant hush. All eyes moved from Holly to Gray, assessing his reaction to this unexpected twist.

People must be relieved. If Norman contacted Holly this morning, then any violence by the river had nothing to do with their startup or their lives. The police would presumably go away and leave them alone.

"Where did Norman telephone from?" Gray asked.

Holly took her time. She punched a button on the adjacent automatic espresso machine and used a spoon to stir in some sugar. Wafts of dark roast blended with the tempting scents of beef, lime, and cilantro.

"The hospital. He said he'd arrived at work early, although he didn't plan to stay. You can check my cell. His caller ID came up, or I wouldn't have answered."

Gray moved forward and stopped before her. She held out the coffee, but he shook his head, his tone even, his face expressionless. "How long did he say he'd be away?"

"He didn't say." Holly sipped the coffee. "I got the impression that it was going to be a while, that maybe he was running away from something. At any rate, does this really involve HealSo? It's time for our team meeting, and everyone's anxious to get back to work."

So, that was her angle. Holly's implication that Norman wanted to escape his life, either temporarily or permanently, could paralyze Gray's investigation, especially as her ambivalence to Norman's disappearance mirrored Gabi's. The two women probably had allied objectives: to sell the startup and secure hundreds of millions for the founder, shareholders, and CEO – but would they collude to fabricate a ghost trail for a man who no longer walked the earth, a man lying faceless on Seymour's stainless steel table?

Vivienne stiffened beside Gray. He followed her line of sight. Jimmy. A rapid flush had flooded his face like a rash, and every muscle in his body looked fired up, ready to help him bolt out of the room. They would speak to him first. Before Holly or Simon got their hands on him.

Vivienne said, "Would Dr. Everett leave his patients at the hospital like that? Would he disappear from his practice without notice?"

Holly shrugged. "How do I know? He supervised our PAS system initially, though now it runs like a well-oiled machine and all the ID physicians use it. What he does with his patients isn't HealSo's problem. Besides, doctors have backup, don't they?" She looked from Gray to Vivienne. "I spoke to his wife, you know. Norman packed a suitcase. The man has a right to exit from his life if he wants to. We all do."

Simon's face, pinched and angry, carried blotches of red and purple. His eyes shifted from Gray to Holly, finally resting on a spot on the ground between them.

No other staff had anything to offer, and no one claimed to have seen Norman in at least a week. Holly was tapping her right foot on the floor, Jimmy got up and sat down a couple of times, and Simon kept stroking that ridiculous beard of his.

Gray and Vivienne took individual statements from all parties concerned.

***

Seated behind his glass desk, Simon mowed down his beef burrito. He chewed with his mouth open, revealing yellow and uneven teeth and a stomach-churning mix of saliva, tortilla, and meat, not to mention the added delight of a chunk of guacamole dangling from his beard.

The sight was enough to turn Gray off his tacos de carne, supplied on a plate courtesy of the administrative assistant who had handed it to him with a flirtatious wink, and an exiting swing of her ample hips. After only two bites, he pushed the plate aside – not because it wasn't good but because either he was still concussed, or else the messy sight of Simon eating was too much to bear.

His interview with Jimmy, a few minutes ago, had garnered annoyingly little: the young engineer was hiding something, and claimed to have been out with his girlfriend, Kate, and some other friends the previous night, a fact which Vivienne was tasked to confirm after she took Gabi Everett to the morgue to ID the faceless corpse.

Gray sat back. Instinctively, he understood the suspect before him.

And he had an important question to ask, but he'd lead in gradually and bury it with the others.

Simon had a sharp yet useless look about him, accentuated by a pudgy face which could not be successfully hidden under the Victorian beard, and a carrot-shaped body bubbling, in the midriff, out of his slim red pants and blue linen shirt.

Gray shifted in the hard plastic chair Simon had allotted for guests, taking pressure off a bruise on his right side.

"You spoke to my mom?" Simon said, in between bovine chews.

"Yes. She's the one who told me that Dr. Norman Everett is Medical Advisor to your company, and she mentioned you're planning on selling. Gabi was surprised you reported your stepfather missing so soon."

Simon mercifully put his burrito down and brought his fingertips together, in the manner of a professor addressing a particularly recalcitrant student. But he continued to lick at his teeth and gums for a while, making squishy, clicking sounds. "Norman missed a board meeting. He never misses one. The old guy lives for his work."

"I'm surprised the officer-in-charge filed a report before the customary twenty-four hours elapsed."

"Didn't want to. Our taxes pay for you guys, you know. I had to give him hell."

Gray bet he did.

Simon's long and dirty fingernails now tapped the desktop. The man clearly believed he controlled the interaction, which didn't bother Gray at all — at least, not for the moment. In a little while, his patience would boil down to nothing, and he'd need to resist slamming this jerk against a wall.

"Well, what are you going to do about it?" Simon said. "Norman's disappearance, I mean? So far, you're just sitting here staring at me, wasting valuable staff time. We have nothing to do with this."

"Your PAS system is revolutionary, I understand."

"PAS? Of course it is. That's not what I asked you."

"You're way ahead of your time."

This seemed to further bolster the other man's cooperation. Simon puffed out his chest as though he were some exotic bird and spoke, pacing the seven words: "I am a Messiah to the infected."

"I see. Your system makes custom antibiotics for each patient. Sounds profitable."

Simon waved a dismissive hand. "That's all Holly. Yes, she wants to sell the company. I'll tell you one thing: it's not going to happen; not on my watch. I didn't work this hard to sell out my public."

Discord amongst the ranks? That amounted to a major crisis at any company, but here, with hundreds of millions at stake, it spelled catastrophe. What buyer would invest in a team so divided? For that matter, what buyer would purchase a company tainted by the rumours of a possible violent murder?

Gray leaned forward. "Did Norman invest a lot of money in the company?"

"More than I wanted, I can tell you. He and Holly carved out his portion. God only knows where he got that kind of dough."

Gray kept his voice casual. "A silent investor?"

"Hah. Whoever he is, he won't tell me what to do."

"What happens if you don't or can't sell?"

"We grow the product ourselves, and I save millions of lives. Holly had brought an acquisition offer to the table, you know." The founder lifted his chin and stroked his beard, a wallop of drool hanging at the edge of his mouth; he slurped it back up. "I'm not allowed to divulge details, so let's just say it's not up to the standard Holly promised the Board. They're going to be very disappointed in her."

Gray doubted the Board would appreciate even this amount of candor.

"What was your name before you changed it to Everett?" Gray asked.

"Arnault," Simon said proudly. "Georges Simon Arnault. But Norman forced me to change it even though we don't do that in Quebec, change a kid or wife's name after marriage. Hell, we don't usually get married. But that was control-freak Norman for you. Typical English."

Gray's head throbbed; the painkillers were wearing off. Worse yet, the man before him picked up the half-mangled burrito and resumed eating, alternately dipping the bitten end into two sauce sections of the tripartite styrofoam container. The sound of his chewing bounced off the glass walls and lacquered cement floors and vibrated within Gray's skull.

"I've been invited to Davos." Simon paused for dramatic effect before continuing. "You know? In fuckin' Switzerland. They're asking if I have room in my schedule. Can you believe that?"

Gray understood more than the other man imagined. "And will your CEO allow you to go, as you put it, to fuckin' Switzerland?"

"Let's see her try and stop me. She'd rather settle for a few hundred million than risk us trying to grow the company." Simon licked his sticky fingers. "And I'll tell you something else: bloody Norman agrees with her."

The silence stretched.

Murder, the body on the beach, still hadn't entered the founder's mind, or else he was a consummate actor. Gray had met many of those in his time. No one could act forever.

Leaning in, he said, "Where were you all of last night?"

"What? Me? What's this got to do with me? You're here to find Norman."

"Didn't your mother speak to you after I called her?"

"Mom said you popped by the house and asked a few questions. That's all."

Gray pushed forward with his attack; he had Simon exactly where he wanted him. "We've found a faceless corpse by the river."

Simon spluttered. "What the hell?"

"It could belong to your step-father."

The founder shoved his chair back with a screech and jumped up. "Faceless? Holly mentioned seeing you on TV, that you're investigating some kind of murder, which has nothing to do with us. Right? Nothing."

"Your missing persons report brought me here. Your company is slated to sell for hundreds of millions, and people have killed for far less. I'll ask you again, where were you last night?"

Simon's mouth opened and closed like a guppy's. His eyes widened, probably recalling his indiscretions so far during this interview.

He spluttered. "Do you know what this kind of malicious rumor could do to my company?"

"Didn't do your Medical Advisor much good either."

"You don't know it's him," Simon snapped. "You're not looking for Norman. You want to pin this murder on someone – anyone. Well, it won't be me. I don't have to answer your questions."

Gray rose and spoke quietly. "Yes, you do. Either here or at the station. Legal representation is your right, of course. Although delaying my investigation may cause more negative publicity for HealSo. Especially, when the press links the corpse at the beach to this company."

"They... you wouldn't."

"Try me."

After a few labored breaths, Simon slumped back onto his chair. The air seemed to have gone out of him.

"I went out with some of the gang here for poutine and beer. I got home at nine, and my girlfriend and I watched a movie. We went to bed at midnight."

He was lying, Gray was sure of it. Everyone lied but not always for reasons that were important. "Are you certain? We can check with your girlfriend, and believe me, we will."

"Okay, okay. My girlfriend didn't come home. I don't expect you to understand since you're from a different generation that's stuck up and uptight —"

Different generation?

"— but Phoebe and I have an open relationship. You understand? She loves me and lets me sleep with whomever I want. I give her the same courtesy."

Gray, who couldn't care less if she slept with the entire Montreal Canadiens hockey team, told Simon to get to the point. Either he had an alibi, or he didn't.

"Technically, I spent the night alone. Phoebe didn't arrive home until morning. I got in at nine and watched TV until two."

A moment of silence stretched. A somewhat enjoyable moment.

"Don't just stand there judging," Simon shouted, rushing to the door and grabbing the handle.

"So, you have no alibi."

Simon stormed out, and Gray let him go. For now.

CHAPTER 6

April 1, 6 pm

GRAY SAT IN his office and rolled the bottle of Pradaxa in his hand.

Voices drifted from down the hall. The *Service de Police de la Ville de Montréal* offices never rested, and outside his window, the city traffic throbbed and moved like corpuscles through an artery. Pulling on his jacket, he awaited the expected knock and creaking of the door.

"Roll out the red carpet; that man is here." Forensic Pathologist, Dr. John Seymour entered unsmiling but exuding professionally suppressed excitement – like a man who truly enjoyed his work, but given its morbid nature had the good sense to hide it.

His unique scent followed him – a combination of oranges, cigar smoke, and the inevitable formaldehyde. No wonder Seymour arrived dateless to every departmental banquet or holiday event – much like Gray – but for entirely different reasons. They often ended up seated at a corner table, verbally sparring over single-malt scotch.

Seymour carried a blue folder, and without waiting for a response, plopped himself onto the leather chair opposite Gray and placed one long leg across the other.

"I could have come to your office for the preliminary report."

Seymour lifted and lowered his blond eyebrows. "I was in the building seeing Deputy Director Séverin anyway. No problem coming down a couple of flights. Shady man, your boss. The kind to beat your teeth out, and then kick you in the gut for mumbling."

"Philip Marlowe?"

"I only quote the best." A conspiratorial smile formed on his lips. "Find out who bombed your car, yet?"

The trundling of a passing truck sounded from the open window, growing louder and louder and bounding off the walls. Gray knew that anyone present at the crime scene this morning could have planted that bomb, but the dents in Seymour's Mercedes likely ruled the doctor out – since it was common knowledge he adored his vintage 450SL.

No one with hidden knowledge of the attack would have parked that close to Gray's ill-fated Audi. And no way did Gray believe that Seymour would want him dead – if only because the doctor loved ingratiating himself into Gray's more complicated investigations.

"A colleague is investigating and getting the debris analyzed," Gray said. "Thank you, for saving my life."

"All in a day's work."

"Except my day nearly came to an abrupt end. But enough about that. What's in the report?"

The other man clicked his tongue. "The victim died of a heart attack."

"What? With his face eaten off, he died of a coronary?"

Seymour smiled his annoying smile, and Gray knew how much he craved explaining his findings to an audience, preferably in scientific terms he thought no one could understand.

"It's all cause and effect. Torture a guy enough, and he could suffer a myocardial infarction, provided he's got the atherosclerotic propensity. Even the young have plaque formation in their arteries." Seymour uncrossed his legs and leaned forward. "First autopsy I ever saw – when I was a neon green first-year med student – involved this young twenty-year-old bicycle rider with unshaven legs –"

Gray suddenly heard nothing but a primal beat running through his ears, blocking out all else spewing out of Seymour's mouth. A heart attack?

"– not even the bikini line, can you believe it?" Seymour said. "Nor the underarms. And I thought to myself –"

This was it, Gray thought. A connection, and so remarkably early in the case. He reached for the handle of the top drawer on his desk, pulled out the small bottle Gabi Everett had given him only this morning (the bottle containing her husband's heart medicine), and rolled the small cylindrical object in his hand. The tiny pills rattled inside.

Norman and the faceless corpse shared two characteristics: a gap between the front teeth, problems with their heart. Or was Gray jumping the gun?

"– and it was pierced!" Seymour said, triumphantly. "I swear, I've never seen anything like it. And I've been to Thailand."

Awaiting an appropriate response to his tale, he threw an expectant look across the desk.

Gray shook himself to the present, now wishing he'd been listening all along. Instead he pursued the purposive line of inquiry.

"Let me get this straight, Doctor. John Doe died of a heart attack? What if he had a pre-existing heart condition?"

A sign escaped Seymour's lips. "I suppose if I had your success with women, I'd be similarly nonchalant with respect to female body piercings."

"Doctor."

"All right, all right. If the victim already had heart disease, he'd die faster. Wouldn't we all? Better for the murderer, I suppose."

Gray wasn't so certain he agreed.

"You found chips worn off on the facial bones."

"Yeah, that's what I said before." He waved dismissively. "Maybe the guy had a heart attack during the torture. I don't know. I'm not carrying around a crystal ball, you know, Gray. I report the facts. Just the facts."

Those facts currently caused Gray's thoughts to race. His mind whisked down to the street below: Rue St. Urbain, then down the tight road curving around the city's central park – past the cemetery and around Mt. Royal, and over to Gabi Everett's Westmount home – five kilometers away.

A corpse who died of a heart attack; a missing doctor with heart problems.

What else had Gabi said to him earlier that morning? *My husband packed a bag, Chief Inspector; it's gone, along with some of his things – he's run away, like my first husband.*

She had lied. Her husband was dead, and she knew it.

Across the desk, Seymour glared and arched one caterpillar-like eyebrow.

"You listening to anything I say? Honestly, Gray. How do you find your way home at night, let alone solve murders? Have you identified the dead man yet?"

Gray handed him the now-warmed bottle of pills. "I may be going senile, but I believe I have ID'd the unfortunate victim."

"Well, well. Who do these belong to?" Seymour read the pharmacy label and tossed the bottle in the air.

"A consultant at Westborough Hospital. The widow has yet to identify him. She says her husband had an irregular heartbeat."

"Yes.... yes." Seymour rolled the bottle in his palms as though he were caressing a breast. Gray pushed down the urge to grab the container.

"Tie a guy down and poke needles into his face," Seymour said, "especially if he suffered from atrial fibrillation – which this poor bastard likely did – and you've got yourself an effective method of murder, I'd say. Wouldn't you?"

"Yes." Gray rose and moved to the window. His organized his thoughts while Seymour's eyes burned into his back.

A cold breeze streamed in carrying the aroma of wood-oven-baked Montreal bagels, denser and chewier than the New York variety, from the bakery next door. Traffic hummed its familiar tune below. The shriek of one driver swearing at another in French drilled upward.

"Tsk, tsk, tsk," Seymour said. "The case is coming together way too quickly, isn't it, Chief Inspector? It's almost too easy."

Gray turned. "John –"

"Now for me, it's exciting." Seymour rubbed his palms together. "Not only do we have a faceless, hanging corpse with a heart problem, he's also a doctor unethically treating his own arrhythmia."

Gray frowned.

"Look at the fine print," Seymour said, tossing the bottle back.

Gray caught it, and lo and behold – the prescribing physician's name was identical to the patient's: Norman Everett. But Seymour wasn't done.

"And I'll bet my last dollar, which isn't much if you know what this department pays me, that this doctor has a space between his front two teeth."

Gray sat and brought his fingertips together. "Maybe you should be sitting here, and I should be carving people up in the lab."

"Add to that, the corpse and the consultant sharing the same coloring, build, et cetera, et cetera, and you have a very boring conclusion to what initially promised to be a thrilling case. Like I said, you must be disappointed. But stay strong, Gray. I'm certain some complication will present itself – something torrid and strange which gets the juices going and distracts from the futility of life and existential thoughts."

"You're a philosopher, Doctor."

"No chance. They get paid even worse than I do."

Gray chuckled. "Anything else?"

"Plenty." He leaned in and wafts of the orange-formaldehyde mix returned. "The body had two puncture marks – one on his upper right arm, and a larger one above his left femoral vein. Stomach contents reveal spicy food – maybe Indian – with coffee. And something strange – we found a laxative in his preliminary drug screen. I'll have the full results by tomorrow, tissue samples included. You know the routine."

Gray did. "The victim's tissues – frozen before or after death? And likely where?"

"Haven't a clue. I'll look into it after lunch."

Meanwhile, Gray slotted mental pieces of the puzzle together in his mind, trying to see what clicked. If the tissues were frozen before death, that led down one avenue. If they froze afterward, that led to another. He said to Seymour, "The vitriolage?"

"After death, thank God. I didn't find acid in his lungs, meaning he wasn't breathing when the stuff ate away his face." Seymour rubbed his jaw and yawned. Red veins, probably from lack of sleep, stood out in the whites of his eyes. "And before you ask me, time of death's between eleven and three in the morning. Broader window than I'm used to giving, I know. Your killer's lucky – or smart."

"Meaning?"

"All that damage to the eyes ruins my analysis. Can't measure the potassium – can't narrow time of death." He shrugged. "That's how it goes."

"Could the victim have died earlier, say ten pm?" Gray asked.

"Nope. It had to be after eleven, probably after midnight."

Gray slumped into his chair. The springs squeaked under his weight. "What if the killer intended the victim to be alive for the acid, but the heart attack got in the way?"

"You mean John Doe died too soon?" Seymour squirmed; his normally sardonic face took a serious turn. "Leaving the murderer unsatisfied – revenge incomplete? You're guessing, Gray."

"You don't take a man's face off for nothing. There's rage here, if nothing else. If the killer's motive was to conceal the victim's identity, faster to chop off the head."

"You have a point."

Gray was considering the very juicy motive of millions of startup dollars and a revolutionary technology for the taking. If Norman was the faceless corpse, then was the startup somehow involved?

Outside, another truck trundled by, and the sound echoed against the walls. Seymour took his leave, just as Gray's cell played "Voulez Vous" and Vivienne's sharp words rang out, slicing through Gray's sore head.

"Tell me you've finally changed my personalized ringtone. You know I hate that song."

Gray opened his mouth to reply, but she jumped ahead. "I'm at Seymour's lab, but he's stepped out. Gabi says it's not him."

The phone grazed his sore ear. "Wh–what? Is she certain?"

"Abso-fuckin-lutely," Vivienne replied with uncharacteristic color. "There's no face to identify, is there? Only the hair, body, and ... you know."

Should he take Gabi's identification as the definitive statement? The aggregate of evidence may not be overwhelming, but it pointed in one consistent direction.

Vivienne spoke candidly. "She claims all private parts in question definitely do not belong to her husband. She should know."

"You would suppose."

"I didn't like her manner, though, during the ID. She seemed distant, aloof."

"Meaning?" Gray asked.

"Most people aren't natural actors. I think she'd rehearsed her answer before I pulled back the sheet because her reaction came a split-second too fast."

His Lieutenant's instincts were always on the money. Gray had learned to trust them, even if she didn't herself. "Why should Gabi Everett want to misidentify her husband?"

"Mon Dieu, that's a leap. We don't know that for sure. But there is something else I should mention."

He held his breath.

"She has a bump on her head, the size of a plum. I'm betting she didn't when you saw her this morning."

Gray gripped the phone tighter. "You'd win that bet, Vivienne. How did she explain it?"

"Something about slipping by the side of the pool. Like I said, most people aren't natural actors, but I guess it could have happened that way. There's a covered solarium with an in-ground pool at the back of her house, and she says she slipped on the wet terracotta tiles."

"One should never swim alone." Gray thought fast, but his head hurt like hell. He pulled a couple of painkillers out of his pocket and popped them into his mouth. "Offer her protection. Maybe then, she'll confide in us."

"Okay, but we can't force it. And we can't go on assuming the body belongs to her husband."

"Sure we can."

"What? We contacted the phone company, and they confirm Holly received a call from Norman's cell early this morning. Telling her he was okay."

Where did that leave him? Vivienne's breath sounded heavy on the other end of the line. "We proceed along the same lines as before," he said, "and continue to assume Norman is our faceless victim."

"I don't like it—"

"Gabi's lying, probably to protect either Simon or the company. Or the killer has threatened her. It doesn't take a detective to figure out she didn't love her husband."

"You trying to convince yourself or me? With a negative ID from next of kin, protocol dictates we consider other leads. At least, until we can get a DNA match."

"Hang protocol, Vivienne."

"You think Séverin and Cousineau will let you pursue this course?"

"I'll try for as long as I can. What do you think? What does your gut tell you?"

She was silent, then said: "Gabi's hiding something. I kept noticing the dimple by her mouth when she pressed her lips together – really tight. Too tight."

"I too have a dimple. And in a far more interesting location. She's lying. I know it."

CHAPTER 7

April 1, 8:30 pm

RUE ST. VIATEUR, situated on "the Plateau," was one of Gray's favorite streets. While attending McGill University, he'd lived on the top floor of a brightly painted triplex. The bohemian area ranked as one of the hippest, most creative neighborhoods in North America, with its cafes, bistros, and independent designer shops. He'd descend the outdoor steel staircase on arctic mornings, always icy, always treacherous, and bike to the university in minus fifteen-degree weather. Now, green lanes tracked most of the city, separating bikes from other traffic.

The end of day meeting with the team stretched before him, where they'd discuss details uncovered thus far over wine and a good meal at one of Gray's favorite bistros, relax, and enjoy the elegance that life in Montreal had to offer. At least, they could discuss them in peace. With the startup tucked in for the night, the hospital wards dark and calm, time slowed down and the urgency of the day deflated.

Gray got out of the car feeling the ache in his battered muscles. No one walked the sidewalk on his side; no cars approached. Snow, falling in thick flakes, intermittently swirled down the road, creating the effect of a European village, frozen in time. Reminding him of a simpler time, but not one he was necessarily more content in.

A boulangerie that served the best kouign-amann in town, a pastry made of caramelized sweet croissant dough, stood to the left. A closed sign hung on the door, but he recalled the sweet aroma anyway. His wife had always eaten hers and demanded half of his.

He didn't linger outside, and entered Yannick's elegant bistro next door. Vivienne and Doug sat at a window table inside, with Vivienne looking anxious and annoyed at the company she was forced to keep in Gray's absence.

The room was decorated with green tablecloths, subdued lighting, and – despite being a French bistro – latin music. Relaxing into the familiar surroundings, he approached their table. On the way, Yannick, the owner, rushed over to deliver a hug, his body heat warmer than the heat radiating from the corner fireplace. The back of the other man's shirt felt damp against Gray's hand.

"Mon ami!"

"It's been too long."

Yannick leaned in. "Your Detective – he order a Beaujolais, for dinner, mon Dieu. I say to him, monsieur, this is not a picnic, but he insist."

"Make the second bottle a Côtes-du-Rhône," Gray said, before joining his team. The bistro owner smiled.

The Beaujolais was reluctantly poured into each of their glasses by Yannick. Looking at Vivienne, the old Quebecois winked. Vivienne winked back.

Gray took in the aroma of warm sliced baguettes and felt himself relax.

Each of them picked up a slice and added a wad of butter. Doug's choice of light and fruity red wine, made with Gamay Noir grapes, wasn't his favorite, but it warmed his insides.

He studied the menu in silence. Doug licked his lips and chose the filet mignon, adding a "since you're payin', boss," while Vivienne settled for the hors d'oeuvre, moules à la marinière, stating she planned to eat at home later. Gray chose the filet mignon.

The wood-burning fireplace crackled ten feet away. The clinking of cutlery and sounds of laughter overlaid a backdrop of Latin music, and rich reds and greens lent the space a festive atmosphere. Outside, the wind picked up, but inside, one could imagine it was Christmas time, and that the world was a safe and wonderful place.

Until the conversation turned to murder.

"Does Gabi stick by her identification of the corpse?" Gray asked Vivienne.

"She insists it's not Norman. I can't budge her."

Doug's nostrils flared. "Maybe she's right. If Norman's alive, we're barking up the wrong tree."

"What about the bump on her head?" Vivienne said.

"People slip by the pool," Doug replied. "Who knows if that faceless guy is Norman." His brusque tone implied Gray was off his rocker for believing otherwise.

Across the table, Vivienne shot daggers at the detective. No love lost there. They differed in culture, education, and sex. But mostly, they differed in how they saw the world and the people in it. Which was why Gray wanted both of their perspectives on his team.

Diversity in a team strengthened it, yet another factor came into play, one he wouldn't outwardly admit: it helped to have an officer around willing to walk the edge of professionalism and bend the rules. How far Doug would go had yet to be tested. Or had it?

Gray faced Vivienne. "Any trouble installing someone at the Institute to watch over Étienne?"

"I sent an officer, but Director Leblanc has him standing guard outside the front door. How's my man supposed to protect him from there? Plus, it's freezing outside." She wrung the cloth napkin between her hands. The small line between her brows always deepened in anger. "Legal assures me we'll get our way eventually since the boy's a murder witness, but it could take a while."

"Which means he's on his own tonight." Gray took another bite. This time, the delicate bread stuck in his throat, refusing to go down without a subsequent gulp of wine. He pictured Étienne alone at night within those depressing walls. Afraid and alone.

"What about Norman's dental records?"

"We found a dentist who knew him years ago," Vivienne replied. "No x-rays. Just some handwritten notes from the old days. Problem is, the corpse's teeth are nearly gone, making a definitive identification impossible. The gap between the front incisors is pretty common."

Gray said, "We'll continue the investigation on the same assumption as before – that John Doe is Norman Everett. Meanwhile, let's get DNA confirmation."

"Without a formal ID on the body?" Doug's tone bordered impertinence. He gulped the wine down as though it were soda.

"Is there a problem, Detective?"

"No, sir. Even if you're right, what's the motive? Who could have hated this guy enough to kill him like that? And where are we gonna get his DNA? We have no mouth swab."

"So we'll get a hair sample from his house," Vivienne spat out. "What's the problem?"

Doug emptied the remainder of the bottle, all into his glass. "The problem is the two-week backlog at the lab. We can't follow an unsubstantiated line of inquiry for that long. That's against all protocol. The DD would–"

"Deputy Director Séverin would what?" Vivienne demanded. "You in daily contact with him?"

Doug lifted his over-full glass to his lips, this time sipping cautiously instead of slurping. "Why would I be?"

"I'm just wondering if you expect to make Inspector cozying up to Séverin?"

"No. I expect to make Chief Inspector."

Vivienne nearly choked on her wine. "Do you? Not every officer has the merit and natural ability to make it that far."

Doug wiped his mouth with a napkin. "There are other ways to get promoted. Other ways to be useful."

"To whom?"

"To those in power."

Gray had let things go too far already. He waved Yannick to bring over the second bottle and some fresh glasses. He topped up all three glasses with the Côtes-du-Rhône. "What about the court orders to see medical charts on patients treated by PAS and Norman?"

Doug shook his head.

"Rodeau refused them?" Gray said. "On what grounds?"

"On the grounds that we have nothing. Judge Rodeau says he won't violate patient confidentiality on a hunch. The guy lectured me on Canada's strict privacy laws for twenty minutes."

Gray looked to his right. Outside the beaded glass, snow, white and glittering under the streetlights, slashed sideways onto the road. A few huddled figures help up their arms against the wet assault while scampering across the sidewalk.

The stem of the tulip-shaped glass felt firm and cool under his fingers. He swirled it to agitate the wine and draw in oxygen and sniffed the concentrated spicy aroma.

"You must have learned something, off the record," he said to Doug.

The Junior Detective donned a crooked smile. No one collected details faster, details they technically had no right to possess. To his right, Vivienne stiffened and looked out the window herself.

"Nine people died under Norman's care since he implemented PAS. Nothin' suspicious. The ones I found out about are Linda George from measles. An eight-year-old boy, Pierre LaPointe, and his dad." Doug accessed his phone. "A Jean-Marc Berger from TB, and a twelve-year-old girl," the tapping continued, "caught C. Difficile."

"And the adults who died?" Gray asked.

"I'm having a tougher time with that. Still working on it. Norman has a couple of pending complaints against him, too."

Gray put down his bread. "Find out about them and get more details on the dead children. Talk to the other families, and ask for consent to look at their charts, but proceed delicately."

Vivienne added, "No badgering them."

Doug's lips thinned, almost disappearing into his mouth; he gripped the delicate stem of his glass, so hard it looked like it would snap and cut his hand.

The food arrived. Gray's steak was prepared on a wood-fired grill, making it smoky, earthy, and tender enough to melt in his mouth. He cut a piece and turned towards Vivienne. "What have you found out about HealSo?"

"Simon's the type that talks to a woman's chest, not her face. Projects: many. Successes: nil – until recently. Even that he can't take credit for. He may have brainstormed PAS, but the Chief Architect Jimmy, made it work."

Gray cut another chunk of his beef and speared it with a bite of asparagus. "Customized antibiotics. They're way ahead of their time. Call me cynical, but it all sounds too good to be true."

"The antibiotic has undergone changes," Vivienne said. "An earlier variant had a bad side effect – something about a hell of a rash that doesn't resolve. The new ones don't do that."

"What about Jimmy?"

"Been with the company over a year. Moved out from his mom's and got a studio of his own on the Plateau, on rue St. Denis. He spends his time mooning over Kate, his older and somewhat cooler girlfriend. Mom apparently disapproves."

"Interesting."

"Oh, I have something more interesting than that." She stopped and looked at both men until she was confident of their undivided attention. The pause had the desired effect. Doug looked as transfixed as Gray felt.

"Holly, their CEO, swooped in to save the startup from Simon's over-spending. She's exacting and ruthless and responsible for HealSo partnering with Westborough Hospital. She and Norman brokered the deal together and got permission from the hospital board to test and implement PAS."

That much Gray had garnered from his own online research; so, why did Vivienne look like a cat who had just gotten the cream?

"Holly Bradley," she said, "doesn't exist."

Doug stopped chewing. "What?"

"That name goes back a few years; she doesn't have form. No police record at all. But no records of her before that exist."

Gray took another bite, tasted his meat slowly. "Good work, Vivienne. And go to HealSo first thing tomorrow," Gray said. "Get Holly's alibi for last night."

They finished their discussion, and Gray left the bistro.

Outside, the wind tore at his clothes, but it had warmed. The sweet smells of spring were pushing through the clutches of a relentless Montreal winter.

He crossed the road to his police loaner and glanced back at his team. Vivienne rushed out of the restaurant and caught up with Doug.

She spoke, gesturing with her hands, and Gray could guess what she was saying. That, perhaps, Doug should be more respectful to his seniors. Now the young detective spoke back, his stance aggressive, perhaps even pointing out that Gray's handling of the case could be construed as incompetence, deliberately ignoring the evidence.

But Vivienne had the last word before she crossed the street and came towards him.

"Who planted the bomb?" she said, now next to Gray. "You know, don't you?"

He unlocked his car with the remote and pulled open the creaky door. "No, I don't."

"You must have some idea."

Perhaps he should tell her about Séverin, but Gray wouldn't put her life in jeopardy.

Vivienne stepped closer. Hints of her citrus-scented shampoo wafted towards him.

She lowered her voice. "You and I both know a cop's behind this. Who else could get that close to your Audi in a secured crime scene?"

She stood silently, jaw clenched, and looked back at the Chevy Camaro shooting away. Doug Green had added a turbo booster to the engine, and it made an awful racket while shooting out a jet of smoke. "He's Séverin's protege," Vivienne said. "And no one resents you more than Séverin."

"You've heard about my indiscretions with Céline?" he said.

"Everyone has." Vivienne shook her head, the nonverbal message clear: that men were idiots; that Gray's rampant hormones would be the end of him. He could think of worse ways to go.

"What you do with your social life is your own business," she said. "But why keep Doug on your team, given his ties with Séverin?"

"I believe in keeping my enemies close."

"In your bed, you mean," Vivienne replied, pulling together the lapels of her cashmere coat. "Céline enjoys more than the Deputy Director's ear." She pinned him down with her eyes. "Is that why you've kept me close? After what I lost?"

"You're my second-in-command, Vivienne. Besides, you haven't lost everything. You have Saleem."

"I don't have Saleem, and you know it."

"Have you told him?"

"No, and I'm never going to. Why should he find out now? He keeps bothering me for a kid; it's like an obsession with him. I have no real husband and no best friend. Only you."

"Admittedly not much."

"What a sad pair we make." She smiled a wry smile and took a half step closer. "You're not up to this," she said.

"The investigation or the bombing?"

"The bombing, of course. I mean – I'm not sure." A pause. "Do you want to live, Gray?"

She never called him by his first name during a case.

"Why wouldn't I?"

"How does anyone survive what you've been through? And you haven't reacted to it in the normal way, have you? Part of you isn't even here with the rest of us. Maybe that's super spiritual of you, maybe it's bullshit – I don't know. If all you care about is the case – saving the next Étienne, catching the next killer – then you might become careless with your own safety."

He lifted his right hand and lightly touched her cheek with his index finger. She stared at the middle two fingers, lifeless, stiff. It encapsulated everything – this wound and all it represented.

"Get this fixed," she said.

He knew he wouldn't.

He would sculpt Craig's face nightly, and he would sculpt using both his good and claw hand: the frozen fingers and scar viscerally linked him to an event and a place – the place where he'd last been with his delicate son.

"You shouldn't worry about being left alone," he said to Vivienne, letting his hand drop. "I'll always be here for you."

"You don't know that... Chief Inspector."

He told her the only thing he knew for certain: "You've been trying so hard for so long, trying to make everything work perfectly. It may be time to let go; let everything that isn't yours fall away."

She didn't reply, merely raised an "isn't this the kettle calling the pot black" eyebrow before turning and crossing the road to her car. He watched her get into the silver VW and drive away.

He still held his car door open. Gray dusted the snow on the damp driver's seat and sat, noticing the passenger seat to his right – slashed in about a dozen places by a knife, the gray plastic separated with tufts of white filling visible in each cut. Someone had been inside the car, watching the bistro and their table as they ate. Someone who had dug an angry knife into the passenger seat. From where he sat, the inside of the restaurant was clearly visible, until the light switched off. Yannick was closing for the night.

Gray took a deep breath and contained the welling anger in his chest. He switched on the police loaner's sputtering engine and headed home.

It was late by the time he parked behind his house. Moving towards a drinks tray by the piano, he poured three fingers of scotch into a crystal tumbler and closed all the curtains. He downed the single malt and relished the smoky, slow burn. It seemed to course through his veins and relax his insides – the clenching in his gut, the aching of his tense shoulders.

He felt himself go limp and loose, the seeming vise around his head loosening.

Sudden fatigue assailed him – both sore and pleasurable. Maybe he could skip sculpting in the studio tonight, perhaps he could fall asleep without it. After having a drink of water, he went upstairs to his third-floor bedroom and undressed.

Peeking through the paned bedroom window, he scanned the street. Black slush coated the road. No shadows shifted in the dark cracks and crevices between trees and houses, and no cars drove by. The silence was absolute.

After sliding under the crisp cotton sheets, Gray closed his eyes and tried to get to sleep.

Something about the instructions he'd given Doug made him pause. He couldn't help thinking the answer already lay before them, as it sometimes did at this stage of an investigation, if only they could see it.

Gray reviewed the night's discussion, but his scotch-drugged mind refused to function. Still, he couldn't help feeling the elusive thread, if he could grab hold, would lead him to the killer. And sleep came.

He didn't know how long he was asleep, but suddenly he was awake, sitting up from bed. He threw the sweat-dampened sheets to one side and swung out his legs.

The room shifted; the walls closed in. Grief found its way back to him and flooded his insides with a juice which made his heart race, made him want to burst out of his skin – out of this existence.

Gray jumped up and raced down the steps naked.

Inside his studio, the moon's beams streamed in from the skylight under a backdrop of studded stars. The pinpoints glimmered like rhinestones suspended in the air – making time stand still.

Gathering some water and a chunk of clay, he moulded yet another bust of Craig's face, heedless of the cramp in his right hand, heedless of his aching forearm muscles. His heart began to slow down; his sweat-sheened naked body felt its first chill.

The sculpture began to take shape – a head, the outline of his son's ear... A half hour in the studio, and then he could sleep. Then, he could rest.

A man coped any way he could after killing his only son.

***

Vivienne parked her car across the street from her two-story house on rue Hotel de Ville. None of the rows of houses had a garage, so residents obtained permits to park on the street. Tonight, she was lucky enough to secure a spot close to her house, a few doors south of rue St. Joseph. Climbing the porch steps, she relaxed and let go the frustrations of the day, let go of worrying about Gray, her immense dislike of Doug, and the aching between her shoulder blades.

The house wore a hundred years of history in the manner of a grand Victorian lady in an embroidered, jeweled robe. After turning the oiled lock, she stepped inside.

The overhead crystal chandelier blinded her after the relative darkness outside. She held up her hand and dimmed it, wondering why Saleem had it on maximum.

Throwing her coat over the wooden banister and dropping her shoes to one side, she dug her toes into the southwestern rug her mom had knitted, and soaked in the atmosphere of home.

While it remained her home.

With the distraction of work temporarily laid aside, a sudden spasm hit her solar plexus, fueled by a reel of fatalistic thoughts projecting across her mind. Her insides felt eaten away. She'd probably be single again soon.

How would she face these upward curving steps alone night after night, knowing he wasn't here? How could she return to that solitary life?

The grandfather clock in the corner struck eleven o'clock. Wafts of egg, pastry, and fennel emanated from the kitchen, accompanied by footsteps coming towards her from the kitchen.

Saleem wore a crisp white shirt and an apron over his black slacks. His linen apron, captioned She's With Me For My Cooking, encircled his slim hips.

"How was your day?" he asked, giving her a firm kiss on the lips. Good, he wasn't mad after their most recent blow-up. She pasted a smile on her face and pretended, as much to herself as to him. His hips pressed into hers. There would be dessert after dinner.

Ten years had done little to calm her reaction to him. She had none of the sexual ambivalence shared by her thirty-something friends, and she wholeheartedly credited this to being childless. He was the most handsome man she'd ever met – six-foot-two with curly black hair that reached his shoulders in adorable disarray and smelled of musk, earth, and something primal. It felt of silk between her fingers.

"Another murder," she said. "Ever seen a body without a face?"

Saleem gave her an even look. Nothing surprised him. His stern mouth curved into that familiar crooked smile – always her undoing. Women frequently gasped when he entered a room. To think that this gorgeous man had eyes for only her – pretty, but somewhat ordinary Vivienne – defied comprehension.

"No," he replied. "Urologists don't notice faces."

Vivienne followed him into the kitchen, watching his slim hips move in supple, masculine strides. She retrieved a bottle of Chianti he'd brought back from a recent business trip to Italy and poured out two glasses. Out of the oven he brought out, as if by magic, a perfect soufflé. The golden egg and cheese dish began deflating, releasing an audible hiss, and making her mouth water.

Saleem believed in eating before it deflated, and he spooned them both a generous portion onto warmed plates. He'd prepared a side green salad with prosciutto and caramelized pears and walnuts. A fresh, warmed baguette sat beside the large bowl of greens – the aromas blended together, making her want to canonize the moment, keep it forever when she no longer had it, no longer had anything.

They sat together in strained camaraderie, and she sensed he was trying to make things right between them. Words stuck in her throat for fear she'd say the wrong thing and all hell would break loose.

If he discovered the truth, if he discovered what she'd done behind his back in the name of career and independence, she'd lose him. But she had to be able to make her own decisions or she'd suffocate, and the event only punctuated the central difference between them which no after-dinner dessert would fix. How long before he found out?

She wiped clammy palms on her pants. Maybe the stress of the case was getting to her. Outside, the neighbor's dog emitted his usual nighttime howl.

"So, who's the poor guy with no face?" Saleem asked, taking his first bite.

"A doctor. Maybe you've heard of him. Norman Everett? We haven't officially ID'd him yet."

Saleem gulped his wine down instead of sipping it, which was odd. Something unreadable passed across his face.

"Yes, I know him," he answered. "Infectious disease specialists get treated like royalty at the hospital."

"What do you know about the startup he's involved with, and their system, PAS?"

Vivienne took a bite of the soufflé. It tasted like a cloud melting in her mouth, smooth and creamy, the center moist.

Thank God Saleem could cook, or they'd be living on takeout, since her own expertise in the kitchen began and ended with boiling an egg.

"PAS is a big hit," Saleem said. "We're thinking of bringing it to the urology department if they can adapt it to our needs." he took another bite. "Norman is dead? How did he die?"

"His heart stopped. Something about an arrhythmia. The killer strung him up by the river, after removing his face with acid. Can you believe what the world is coming to?"

Saleem sat suspiciously quiet. He'd barely touched his food, while her plate was nearly empty. She must have been hungry. His silence continued to nag at her. More than once, she'd wished she could read his mind with the ease with which he read hers.

"An arrhythmia," he said, absently under his breath.

"Why? Do you know anything about his health?"

Saleem shrugged. "He popped his pills like clockwork. Didn't make his heart condition a secret. Everyone knew about it. Maybe the poor guy died naturally. Has Gray considered that?"

"And then strung himself up after burning off his face? Hardly." What could Saleem be thinking? Doctors made terrible detectives. Unless someone had found Norman dead; someone who wanted to make it look like murder? They might have mutilated the body... taken it to the beach...

Saleem put his cutlery down with a clang, sat back, and stretched out his arms. The fabric strained against his muscled chest. Fine hairs were visible under the thin, white fabric – not too many, just enough. Vivienne swallowed. Met his dark eyes.

"I see where this talk of dead bodies is leading us," he said. "You police are a little twisted."

"Oui," Vivienne replied. "Twisted, and complicated."

His Hand In the Storm

They completed their meal quickly.
A few minutes later, they were upstairs having dessert.

CHAPTER 8

April 1, Midnight

THE SECOND VICTIM was about to be chosen.

Jimmy got off the elevator and surreptitiously approached HealSo's double glass doors. A dimly-lit office, empty and teeming with night-time shadows, scared him to death. It reminded him of closet monsters imagined as a child, of Halloween nights spent huddled in the dark awaiting Mom's arrival home while trick or treaters banged on the apartment door.

He checked his watch – nearly midnight. Some part of him felt scared being out alone this late. Evil existed; Jimmy was sure of it. It might be beyond his comprehension, but flashes of it popped up in people's eyes, in the furtive touch of their hands, their dulcet tones.

If he hadn't scurried out of the office earlier after being interviewed by Gray, he wouldn't need to sneak back in tonight to retrieve his laptop. An important product deadline hung over his head, and he only needed a minute to run to his cubby hole, grab his computer, and jet out as fast as possible.

Placing his ID badge on the reader caused the door the click open, but the alarm didn't engage. Probably the last person out forgot to arm it. He felt annoyed before noticing a shaft of light streaming in from down the hall

His heart lurched. Someone was inside.

He slowly crept through the foyer, one eye on the light, his nails digging into his fists. The air became soupy and hot and impossible to breathe. A faint scent coming from the server room – sour and metallic – made him turn.

Only the black outlines of cupboards and computer servers stood delineated in the dark, but the server room shouldn't be unlocked at night. Julie, the admin, always locked it.

A woman's voice rang out. "Who's there?" Making him jump.

Damn. Not Holly of all people. Did she work day and night? Didn't she have a home and baby to go to? He should run out before she saw him. Facing her after Norman's unexplained disappearance made his hair stand on end, but leaden feet which refused to obey his commands kept him in place.

"I said, who's out there?" Holly's stiletto boots clicked across the lacquered cement, her long body stood backlit in the hall. Strong musk shoved the earlier metallic smell out of the way, causing his sensitive nostrils to flare.

He swallowed. "It's me."

"Jimmy?" *Click, click, click.* Holly strutted towards him, emerging from the shadows looking as thunderous and intimidating as ever. "What are you doing here?"

"I... I forgot my laptop, and we have a product deadline. You know I don't keep the security stuff from PAS on my home computer." Great. His babbling would only make her madder. She tapped her steel-toed boot against the floor, always judging, always impatient, and he reflected at what an awful mother she must be to that poor, defenceless baby she'd adopted. Nothing like Mom. No one was like Mom.

Holly switched the lights on without warning, blinding him momentarily. His hands flew to his face.

"What are you really doing here?" she snapped, standing backlit by the server room.

Pressure built inside him. Jimmy had something important to tell her, and it was best to simply blurt it out without fuss. He hoped rather than expected she wouldn't lash out.

"I've had a better offer from Flubber," he said. "I'm leaving HealSo."

She stiffened, a flush snaking up the tight cords of her neck. The throbbing muscle in her jaw appeared inhuman, almost obscene.

"I promoted you from the back end team," she said. "Catapulted you to Chief Software Architect, even though you weren't fully qualified."

"I know."

"If we'd advertised out of house, there would have been a dozen applicants. You'd be working at some other company doing menial tasks. Instead, you're Chief Architect at the hottest startup in the country, and I see no signs of gratitude or appreciation."

His feet moved with a mind of their own, shuffling back and forth; tumbled words, half-frightened, half-affronted, caught in his throat. Why should she assume he'd go nowhere with another company when he'd graduated first in his class at Waterloo, one of the most competitive Computer Science programs in North America, before Simon persuaded him to join the startup? Everyone had heard Bill Gates claimed Waterloo was one of the best universities from which to recruit talent.

"I... I didn't plan this. It's not about the money, and you know it."

"Then why?" she snapped.

"You're gonna sell. I don't want to be here when it all comes out."

Holly grabbed his arm and yanked, digging her long red claws into his skin. Her underlying scent always smelled strong and ripe, no matter how much perfume she used.

"Be quiet," she said. "Nothing's going to come out. You understand? There's nothing to come out." Her hot breath fanned his face – sour, stale, smelling of a sneaked cigarette and making his stomach lurch.

The world went in and out of focus which meant he must be hyperventilating again and must do what Mom told him: even out his breathing; calm down.

In.. .out... in... out.

Though a malevolent voice screeched in his head: Norman's gone, and someone might have killed him; maybe the very person you're looking at now, Jimmy.

"The acquisition will proceed as planned," Holly said. "You'll continue in your capacity as Chief Architect until we secure an offer, and after that, you'll deliver whatever the deal demands. That includes staying long enough to fulfill the terms specified in our agreement. Do you understand? Look at me."

And here, her voice grew soft, speaking those ominous, teeth-rattling words she'd said to him once before. That Norman had said to him prior to his disappearance.

"No one's going to hurt you, Jimmy."

A frog leaped in his chest. His eyes darted across the ground, searching for something else on which to focus, which they found at the center of the server room floor directly behind Holly.

A dark red blob lay over roughened, eroded tiles – a blob which absolutely hadn't been present a couple of days ago when Jimmy had come to the server rooms to check on one of the servers.

"What is it?" Holly asked. "You're turning green. You sick?"

He crept towards the puddle as though fearful it would pounce upon him at any moment, the sound of his raspy, asthmatic breathing abnormally loud within the confines of the small room.

Behind him, Holly pivoted, her boots scraping against the floor before clicking forward.

Dried splatters fanned out from the central spill as far as the opposite wall.

Was it blood? If so, whose blood, and how had it gotten there?

"What's that?" he blurted, pointing one shaky finger towards the offending, congealed glob.

She crouched beside him, lids hooded and lips pressed into a thin line – ever the inscrutable businesswoman. And an answer came fast – too fast.

"Oh, I spilled some red ink earlier. You know, the kind we keep in the cupboard. Don't worry; I'll clean it up."

Jimmy's voice cracked. "That's not ink."

The muscles in his thighs ached from being tightly clenched. Horrible possibilities flung across his mind like a boomerang – all returning to the same place – all returning to Norman declared missing... possibly dead.

The same Norman who only a few days ago had pushed Jimmy into a corner with one hairy hand gripping the edge of Jimmy's T-shirt, bullied him, and scared him half to death.

That last fateful meeting came to mind, with the older man's medicinal breath hovering far too close – and Jimmy threatening to tell Mom all that Norman wished hidden at all costs – and Norman's unnatural, almost scary calm response: telling Jimmy to go ahead, but to at least wait a couple of days before calling home.

What had Norman expected to happen in those couple of days? What could still happen?

Jimmy rose on quivering knees and finally found his voice. "Holly, that's blood. Maybe Norman's blood."

She yanked him back out to the hall. "No, it isn't."

"And there's something in the center. Something ate away at those tiles."

"Don't be crazy; it's ink, nothing more. The tiles have always been old and worn out; you just haven't noticed. Now, stop making a big deal out of this, get your laptop, and get out."

A rustling noise from outside the office glass doors made him turn. Coming, maybe, from near the elevators. He tried to swallow but couldn't. "What's that? Who's there?"

"No one," Holly snapped. Once again, her hot breath was on him. "I don't want you mentioning this to anyone – do you understand? No one! That isn't blood, especially not Norman's. Norman phoned me only this morning and said he's okay. We don't want to start any rumors, or cause a panic which might adversely affect the company."

"That policeman that came today. We have to call him."

"What?" She stepped back as though slapped. Both her cheeks flushed a deep mahogany brown. "I'm trying to sell this company, and you want to involve the police? Are you nuts?"

Spit sprayed from her mouth onto his face, which no amount of wiping seemed to remove.

A rustling sounded, again, from the corridor outside.

He had to get out; at all costs, he had to get out.

Her claws dug into his arm. "You can't mention this. The police will blow this place apart if you say anything, maybe shut it down."

"Someone's in the office," he squeaked.

"No. We're alone—"

Everything around him tilted. Every muscle in his legs tightened, ready to sprint.

Without a backward glance, he pushed through the glass doors and ran; Holly's voice called out from behind. No time for the elevator, Jimmy went against every instinct which told him otherwise and swung around the corner, yanked open the heavy door to the stairwell and bolted through it.

Blackness engulfed him. He scurried down the steps with his arms out, his runners pounding the cement, the sound echoing down to the black cavern below.

He breathed in thick, gritty dust as fuzzy images gradually took form: misshapen lumps which lined the corners and which might be moving, threatening to spring forward. He passed one, then another on the level below with his breath coming heavy; his chest whistling with each exhalation.

Down one level, then the next. Until the lumpy bags clarified and his eyes adjusted, and he saw they were bags of cement, tools, and fixtures, sitting amidst the torn stairwell renovation.

At which point, a sound fell from above — and he froze... and heard it again.

Cre-e-eak.

Was that Holly, or someone else? The walls closed in; the ceiling looked ready to crack and plummet onto his head, burying him alive.

Cre-e-eak.

Oh God, Mama, I need you.

He covered the six flights in record time, tasting the salty snot dripping into his mouth, his heart lodged in his throat

No security guard watched the lobby at night; there was no one to call for help, and he flew through the front doors like a bat out of hell.

Outside, a gust of wind nearly threw him sideways. He covered two blocks without looking back.

The familiar metro sign came into view, and he bounded down the station steps two at a time – towards the double-sided platform where bodies huddled together, some drunk and swaying, some speaking to themselves about nonsense he didn't understand. A few bumped into him, making him jump back.

Seconds felt interminable as he waited for his train, but unwelcome thoughts kept flinging back to what must lurk at the office. In the shadows. Near Holly.

Crouching on the ground, he buried his face in his hands. Montreal had a rubber-wheel metro system. The train wheels rumbled and whined to a halt before him, the piercing shriek of metal seemingly inches from his head.

He heard the doors whine open but didn't look up, his face still deeply buried within his dampened palms, until the doors closed, and the scent from the train's rubber tires drifted upward. Only then, did he peek from between trembling fingers at the blur of cars whisking by – blue with a horizontal white stripe – the clanging from the traction motors now vibrating his insides.

It took concerted effort to stand on legs which wanted desperately to run.

He pictured Holly cleaning up the blood to prevent its discovery, her long-nailed hands squeezing the pink-tinged water from the sponge again and again; a dark figure coming up from behind, looming over her with a weapon –

Chief Inspector Gray, who Jimmy suddenly saw as some sort of hero, would never leave a woman in danger, and Jimmy, too, must act. God, he had to go back.

He wiped his clammy hands on his pants and climbed the metro steps; each step heavy, his thighs burning. The two blocks back to HealSo passed in a blur with strangers faces staring at him open-mouthed, accusing. The cold wind whipped through his thin jacket and rattled his bones. And finally he reached the ominous, looming structure.

The heavy door opened with difficulty and slammed behind him in the wind. Precariously placing one foot before the other, he crossed the mirrored lobby, sweat beading on his forehead, his heart hammering in his chest.

What was that? Frantic clicking reached him from afar. From inside the stairwell?

A woman's single scream bled through the air.

He ran forward. "Holly! Holly!" And unseeing rushed through the stairwell door – not knowing what lay beyond: a killer with a gun, with a knife? And he was beside the shadowed metal handrail.

Only an exit sign illumined the rank, still space. Footsteps scurried away in the blackness before a distant door slammed. Whoever was there had likely fled.

Jimmy edged his way noiselessly forward and stumbled, his arms both flailing until he clutched the nearby handrail. An object lay spread out at the bottom of the stairs – maybe a cement bag, or something else.

Cracking open the door slowly, he let in a moving beam of oblong light, moving over brown and dusty cement until finally settling on black stiletto boots. Holly's.

He opened the door fully and lighted the rest of her, including muscled thighs and hips lying spread-eagled on the ground. Her faux-fur coat lay sprawled under her, unbuttoned.

The pale stream highlighted Holly's hollowed face in a way he'd never previously seen, just as her eyes flickered shut – giving her a vulnerability in unconsciousness he wouldn't have thought possible. Glistening blood oozed onto an enlarging pool beneath her head. She released one last moan, and then nothing.

The room split into a double image – two images of Holly, fusing in and out into one; two stairwells.

He gripped the rail again, and bile rose in his throat. Crouching on his knees, he lowered his head until the dizziness passed. Disorder and chaos crashed down on him, ripping his ordered world, tearing out his insides.

Kate would know what to do; she'd help him. He had to get out of here. But Jimmy couldn't leave Holly like this, on the brink of death. He had to call someone – the police, an ambulance – before she died. Before the killer came back to finish the job. Before the killer returned to finish him.

CHAPTER 9

April 2, 2:20 am

A MUSICAL SHRILL penetrated his sleep from a distance, refusing to stop. He ran from it, legs pumping, but it grew louder and louder until it seemed to vibrate the bones inside his skull and pierce his eardrums. Then he jolted awake, groggy and confused, exiting a disturbing dream which gradually floated into the clouds of oblivion.

Gray blinked, eyes grainy, trying to focus. The still and darkened room looked momentarily foreign, unfamiliar until he realized where he was.

Moonlight streamed in from the window. Outside, the street slept under a sheet of snow, and the onyx surface of the distant river bubbled. It clearly wasn't morning yet. The shrill continued, now identifiable, and the song, "Voulez-Vous," continued to bounce off the old plaster walls of the large attic bedroom.

"You may not need your beauty sleep, Vivienne, but I do."

"Someone bludgeoned Holly Bradley during the night. Jimmy found her in the ground floor stairwell. He called it in and disappeared, so I haven't been able to talk to him – and Holly's on her way to the hospital. She hasn't regained consciousness, and who knows if she'll remember anything if or when she does."

Gray cleared his throat and pulled back the sheets. A draft from the inch-open window hit his naked body. "But she's alive?"

"Just. The killer didn't get a chance to finish her off and maybe remove her face, thanks to Jimmy. We don't know why either of them returned to the office at that time of night."

"I can picture Holly burning the midnight oil, but he seems the type to stay away from empty buildings after dark."

"We have to find him. He might well have seen the assailant and fled – or worse, maybe the killer got him, too."

Gray clutched the crisp cotton sheet. He'd only questioned Jimmy briefly, but the thought of the naive young engineer lying bludgeoned in an alley somewhere made him see red.

"Get an officer to check every floor of that building, including the stairwells and underground parking, and the surrounding area."

"Already done," Vivienne said. "So far, no luck."

"Send someone to his apartment as well."

"D'accord."

Another victim, and so soon – only twenty-four hours into the case.

Vivienne read his mind. "It's only day two of the investigation. The killer isn't giving us time to breathe, let alone catch him."

"I'm going to need lots of caffeine to get through today – possibly, to live through today."

"Don't joke."

"I rarely joke about death. Particularly my own."

He stood, put on his robe, and trudged down the hall carrying his phone. The cold of the floor, broken only by the soft woven runner in mauve and gold covering the hall, was reassuring, as was the intermittent creaking under his bare feet.

A tired and hollow-faced man greeted him in the bathroom mirror.

"Secure the office and stairwell," he told Vivienne. "Get SOCO to go through both with a fine-tooth comb in case the attacker chased Holly from HealSo down to the ground floor. Call Simon to get a verbal okay on the search and demand he come in. I'm sure he can tear himself away from his open relationship. I'll be right over."

Five minutes later, a latte gripped awkwardly in one hand, he raced the car over ice and snow. The starry sky spread out over the empty roads, reminiscent of a Van Gogh, almost unsubstantial and unreal, while the rest of Montreal continued to sleep.

Gray pulled into the office lot, got out of the car, and breathed in the mulchy scents of city and spring. Mt. Royal loomed in the distance, a shadowed protuberance watching over the center of the city, silent and unperturbed by murder.

The peak held the hundred-foot tall, LED-lit, steel Mt. Royal Cross – reminding him of the ceremony by the cross he'd attended in 1992 with his first girlfriend. Sarah, who had smelled of a sweet, inexpensive scent mixed with young sweat. She'd clung to him in between kisses, opening her lips, and he'd plunged his tongue inside her – his sense of triumph unrivaled by anything he could hope to experience now.

Sarah's pointy, somewhat average features now took on a remembered glamor only possible due to the canonization of time. No lips could ever taste so sweet again. No aroma would ever be more arousing.

Gray dug his cold fists into his coat pockets and strode towards the eight-storey building entrance.

Two police officers met him at the ground floor stairwell behind the elevators next to the open fire door, and a SOCO worked on hands and knees collecting samples from the blood-stained cement within.

Dust laced the air, making his nose itch, and supplies from a construction project lay in one corner. Two broad beams from the team's portable lights contrasted with the dark bleakness beyond and above.

"It's like being buried in a mine," he said.

"Watch out for the light fixtures and cement bags lining the sides, Sir."

Gray ascended the steps, answering: "Thank you, Gerard. I'll do my best not to break my neck."

Upstairs, Vivienne stood speaking to another SOCO inside the startup's glass doors. Her eyes bright, she pressed a button to allow entry and bypass the keycard lock.

He said, "Do we know why Holly came in last night?"

"No. I've tried Jimmy half a dozen times. He's not answering. Holly must have used her entry badge to get into the building, which registers an exact time. I'll get that from the super, as well as any surveillance tapes."

"Check if Norman used his ID card to gain access over the last few days. If he's been here, I want to know about it."

"D'accord. There's something else you should see."

Vivienne led him to a compact room off the hall, light on her feet. His pulse immediately quickened with the certain knowledge that she had found something.

Two SOCOs presently collected samples from the wall and floor of the small room containing a couple of cupboards and a series of computers.

"I saw this almost at once," she said, eyes beaming. "Look at those eroded tiles and the color in the cracks. Maybe remnants of blood and acid. Someone's done a bad job of cleaning it up."

Gray whistled. "Vivienne, I could kiss you. Perhaps that someone was interrupted during the cleanup. But who's most likely to clean up blood and acid found at the startup? Clearly, Holly. This could be where our faceless corpse met his maker. And it could also explain Holly's presence at the office last night. I can see her tampering with evidence, but what about Jimmy? I can't believe he'd help her."

"If she tried to clean up a crime scene, she'll deny it."

"Let's not give her the chance. Send someone to the emergency department to get her nail clippings. I want them analyzed for blood, and cross-reference with the body at the beach."

"No problem," Vivienne said. "She might have scratched the killer."

"Tell Seymour to check her nails against what's on these tiles, and against John Doe. If the victim died here and Holly cleaned up the blood, all three will match."

"That still doesn't confirm Norman as the faceless corpse, Chief Inspector. We'll have to wait for DNA confirmation, provided the lab doesn't put our sample on the bottom of their pile."

Gray heard what she said, knew they were groping in the dark. "I want a complete list of employees, investors, advisors ... everyone connected to the company, or to Norman. We need all of their alibis for the last two nights."

"Got it. But you said something about Norman being the front-man for a silent investor. Who could that be?"

He didn't know. They walked out into the hall together. "What about Kate Grant's alibi for Norman's disappearance?" Gray said. "And Jimmy's. Do we have confirmation?"

"I finally got in touch with their friends late last night. They were at a club from eleven pm to two in the morning. The friends confirm that neither Kate or Jimmy left their sight for more than five minutes the entire time."

"Reliable?"

"Afraid so."

"That clears them of Norman's murder but not of Holly's attack. Go thorough Holly's office and see what you can find. Where does Kate work?"

"Café Doigt, across the street."

"Let's interview the other key staff as they come in to work, and I'll talk to her later."

The hours it took to sort out the crime scene at HealSo passed at a snail's pace.

Outside the window, the city looked dark and sheeted in a blue-tinted glass. Only two huddled figured scampered across the road beneath him, buried in their coats. The remainder of the morning crowd had yet to rise and hustle to work.

Rubbing his scratchy eyes, Gray arched his back and put on his coat, deciding he needed some air.

His interview this morning with Simon, when he'd finally arrived, had yielded nothing. Simon claimed to be home with his girlfriend. The alibi didn't amount to much, but he couldn't break it either. Simon denied any knowledge of why Holly should clean a potential crime scene – except the obvious – to protect HealSo.

At the office entrance, Gray slammed into someone rushing inside. Jimmy fell onto his backside, and, flailing all four limbs, scrambled up. Gray helped him, the delicate bones under the young man's ski jacket feeling thin and fragile.

"Where have you been, Mr. Cane? You ran away after contacting the police. Didn't you think we'd have questions about what happened here last night?"

"I know; I'm sorry." He stared at his shoes. "I have to talk to you. The server room –"

"Has blood on it. Yes, we saw. Let's go somewhere private and have a talk."

Gray led him towards the corner office, but Jimmy strayed into the kitchen.

Punching commands into the automated machine – a large, pricey contraption which delivered a multitude of caffeine choices – he brewed himself a hot chocolate. The delicate hand shook when he lifted the mug from under the dispenser. He carried it gingerly to a table in the far corner, presumably to get away from curious eyes or ears. He needn't have bothered, as most of the startup staff hadn't been allowed back into the offices.

The overly full mug of chocolate threatened to spill onto his pale hand.

Sensing the engineer's fear, Gray took a seat opposite and didn't immediately jump into an interrogation; he allowed the engineer to get his bearings for a short while. Overhead, a TV silently played a medical program.

"You and Holly found the spilled blood in the server room?" Gray asked.

Jimmy nodded, the hot chocolate cupped between his hands but left untasted. Its dark and rich scent drifted forward.

After looking into Gray's eyes, he silently pushed the chocolate before Gray and got up to make himself another.

After he'd returned, he said, "I came here last night to pick up my laptop, and Holly was already here." His Adam's apple bobbed up and down as he swallowed, his cherub-like face bunched up, the pinky cheeks coloring.

"She's scary, you know? I just stood there, shaking, and noticed the red spill on the floor nearby. I'm in the server room a lot, and it was clean a couple of days ago, I'll swear. When I showed Holly, her expression changed."

Blood pounded in Gray's ears and the world swung into sharper focus. His pulse trilled under his skin, that same glorious trill he always got when he was on the right track. "How did it change?"

"She covered up her surprise... I think. I don't know for sure because I don't read people all that well. Holly told me to keep the spilled blood a secret, and she wouldn't let me leave. When I heard someone prowling around outside the office, I ran – made it as far as the metro before turning back. That's when I found her on the floor, bleeding."

"Why did you come back?"

"I told you. I heard someone. I couldn't leave her here alone, with the blood, with a stranger lurking." His voice cracked. "Someone died in our server room, didn't they – the victim you found on the beach? Was it Norman?"

"Why would anyone kill a Medical Advisor?"

Jimmy's face went blank, his eyes widened.

The answer came out in a tremulous whisper. "Holly, Norman..."

A sense of urgency rose in Gray; the tick of an imaginary clock matched the blood pumping through his ears. He was close. He could taste it. "Yes? What about Holly and Norman?"

Jimmy wrapped his arms around his chest. The hands looked soft and delicate, like a child's, and when his wide brown eyes met Gray's, they immediately skirted away and up towards the TV, where closed-captioned images of post-C-section scars now flashed across the screen.

"I can't tell you more; I really can't." He still averted Gray's gaze, continued watching the TV. His brow furrowed; the delicate mouth fell open.

"What can't you tell me?" Gray demanded. "That Holly's somehow involved in this case, but how?"

The young engineer's words sounded distant and hollow. Distracted. "Someone killed Norman, took off his face, and hanged him by the river? Oh God."

"We haven't confirmed for certain it was Norman."

The engineer's eyes glazed over; his pink skin went deathly pale. Gray had pushed too hard, been too impatient.

"Oh God," Jimmy repeated.

"Are you all right?"

Jumping to his feet, the engineer gripped the edge of the table. Something had gone terribly wrong during their conversion, and urgency hit Gray like a shovel. More was now at stake than simply solving this case, much more. He could sense it and taste the acid coming up into his mouth.

"Calm down," Gray said.

But Jimmy leapt off the stool and scampered out of the kitchen.

Gray caught up to him at the front door. "Where the hell are you going? I need your help. Please, before someone else gets killed."

"I... I can't."

"What happened in the last few minutes? What scared you?" Gray held out his palms. "What did you remember?"

"That documentary – I have to talk to Mom or someone else, but not you – never to you."

"Why not me? I'm here to help."

"No. You're the police. Don't you see?"

Gray saw nothing except the desperate need to act. His heart raced, and a sheen of sweat coated his back. If he let Jimmy go, something terrible was going to happen – he felt it in his bones. "If you leave, I won't be able to protect you, and a dangerous killer's loose. Do you understand?"

"I... I can't."

"This interview isn't over. Come back inside."

A few employees came into the hall to investigate the commotion. Vivienne reached their side, but Gray indicated she should step back.

"Come with me," he said to Jimmy. "We need to speak further. After that, you're free to leave, I promise." This was his last chance; he had to make the boy understand.

Jimmy yelled, "I'm not saying anything," and ran out of the office before jumping into a waiting elevator.

What made him change his mind about speaking to Gray? What had happened in those last few minutes? Gray pursued him, but the doors shut in his face.

But by the time he'd reached the ground floor, the engineer was gone. And so were any forthcoming answers and hopes.

Gray stood on rue William for a solid minute, slowing his breath and racing heart and pushing down the instinctive knowledge that they hadn't yet seen the last death at the fashionable startup.

***

Ahead, the sun peeked up over the city's central mountain, and shot out red and orange rays, lighting the treetops of Mt. Royal on fire.

Gray couldn't yet speak to Holly, and he needed to interview Jimmy's girlfriend – but not yet, not until he'd cooled down, or else that interview might go as badly as the one he'd just messed up.

Picking up his pace, he headed towards the canal, initially dug to make this part of the St. Lawrence more accessible to trade. The canal merged into the river eastward, and the cobalt water glittered in the distance under a burgeoning blue and purple sky.

The planked boardwalk under his feet jostled slightly with each step; bikers passed him, fit and seemingly warm in their thin tight jackets; an occasional jogger bolted by, panting and wearing.

To his left, condos sprouted out like mushrooms, and soon, he found himself in historic Old Montréal, once the old port on the St. Lawrence River, now home to boutique hotels, tourist restaurants, and quaint cobblestone streets, resembling a movie set in the early dawn light.

His heart drummed, and he looked up and down the cobblestone street. Most of the tourist shops hadn't yet opened. A horse-drawn carriage trotted by; the animal's unbrushed mane and tired face gave him pause.

The soulful brown eyes connected with his, sad, resigned, hitting Gray in the gut before the caleche driver looked his way expectantly, hoping to snare his first customer of the day. How could a man make his income by hurting another creature all day long? How could tourists finance him to do it?

Gray waved him away and wished the city hadn't retracted its ban on the tourist-driven attraction. The horse trotted past with a melancholy click.

He watched the animal move further and further away.

And what he feared, what came upon him suddenly during his unguarded moments, morphed his lens of the world. The dark shroud, imagined but also real, shaded the river, the city, and the sky before him in a layer of gray. His head felt burning hot.

Dissociation grabbed him, morphing the surroundings into a foreign land in which he couldn't live without pain, agony, and each passing second punctuated that agony while his heart drilled a hole into his chest.

How could he go on with the case? So much remained to be done; so many people relied on him.

Without thinking, he grabbed the only remedy he knew and sprinted back towards the startup – towards the cafe, his suspects, Kate... away from what churned inside him.

Every action, every choice remained his to make. No harness encircled his neck; no one would rein him in, not Séverin, not anyone.

Sweat soaked his back despite the frigid cold as he flew past the old Five Roses flour company sign across the canal, up and across rue de l'Inspecteur, again to rue William – back to where he'd begun his early morning walk. Back to work –

Where the chokehold loosened its grip; where his breath began to even, and the breeze finally cooled his cheeks.

Café Doigt stood directly across from the startup, on the ground floor of a restored nineteenth-century brick factory. The street still carried the faint scent left behind from a long-gone candy factory, yet what Gray needed most right now lay within the cafe itself. A dark, strong espresso to help him refocus.

He lifted his collar against the early morning chill. Yesterday's freezing rain had left a treacherous sheet of ice under soft snow on the pavement. The street looked deserted and bathed in the last vestiges of the blue early morning light.

Inside, the aromas of soup, baked goods, and bodies clamoring to get their morning coffee filled the air. The sudden warmth burned his frozen face, and the bright crystal and gold chandelier hanging from the textured aluminum ceiling made him squint.

"Oui, Monsieur?"

Gray focused on the twenty-year-old man with quarter-inch long hair and a tattoo of a scorpion on his left cheek. "A double espresso and a pain au chocolat, s'il vous plaît."

He scanned the food on display: Peruvian beef with ahi and coriander, salmon tartare and oyster sandwiches; two dozen flavors of coffee beans – almond, butterscotch, chocolate-cherry, coconut butter, chocolate liqueur, to name a few.

The swinging door leading to the back kitchen lay wedged open with a knee-high metal trolley. Beyond, he could see the glittering surface of a large counter space, a gas stovetop and oven, and a door to an industrial-sized fridge.

The server nodded silently and indicated Gray should sit. He chose a place by the window.

Old sheet metal secured by rivets decorated the sides of the long counter. Original paintings lined the walls. One acrylic caught his eye.

An African woman stood barefoot on a dirt road wearing rags and a patterned turban-like scarf wrapped around her head. The sunlight couldn't outshine her eyes or her smile. This woman clearly had nothing, and she was still exuberant, triumphant. A feminine voice whispered from behind.

"Why should she be so happy with so little?"

The slim wrist weighed down by rings and heavy bracelets placed his espresso and pastry on the table. His eyes traveled up her bare outstretched arm, trim and muscular, to that bejeweled and bare midriff that impelled the eyes downward. Apparently, he felt better.

"A simpler life?" he suggested.

"What's the struggle for, if not to win the fight for happiness?" Kate straddled a chair opposite. "What's with your ear?"

"I cut myself shaving." He took a bite of the pastry. The tastes of nuts, butter, and flour swirled in his mouth, washed down with the beautifully sharp espresso.

Caffeine coursed through his system; he breathed in and out, feeling more like his usual self again.

A long swath of red hair curtained her right cheek; the rest was cropped short. Something churned behind those eyes, something he couldn't quite grasp. Guilt? Suspicion? Or cloistered knowledge of the crime? He hoped Kate Grant wasn't destined to be the killer's next victim.

"Where were you last night after ten pm?" Gray asked.

Her head whipped back. The long strand moved and exposed her cheek, and she pushed it back down, but not before Gray noticed a scar – a two-inch diagonal slash of puckered flesh, as red as the ruby on her nose.

Welcome to the club, he thought. He knew they had something in common. Something beyond the bejeweled belly button which twinkled in what seemed like Morse Code – sending him a message he had no business receiving.

"I have something vital to tell you," she said. "Don't know if I should say."

"I'm listening."

But she merely stared, her stunning sapphire irises framed by almond-shaped eyes.

He blinked first and looked from the eyes to her hair. Black roots. She had mixed heritage which wasn't evident at first glance. A blend of Caucasian and South Asian?

Kate was sidestepping his request for an alibi. If she thought she could distract him, she was in for a surprise.

He tilted his head to one side and waited.

"It's about last night," she said. A momentary hesitation. She bit the side of her lower lip.

The internal fight played in her eyes, and then she finally said, "Jimmy came to my apartment."

"After he found Holly? What did he say?"

"He came to see me all crazy and confused. It took forever to calm him down and at first I figured he was just making it up. You know? Then, when I'd given him some brandy, and he'd choked it down, he explained."

Was she presenting Jimmy on a platter as a suspect? Kate gripped the back of the chair tighter, causing two chunky rings to clink against the metal. Reggae played loudly overhead, the primal beat drumming through his insides, punctuating his impatience.

"Take your time," he said.

"Jimmy told me you're investigating a murder and that one of the executives at the startup is missing. Then, he kept going on and on about Holly and some blood they found together at the startup. He thought she'd hurt him if he told anyone. He also figured she planned to clean it up – to cover up whatever happened at HealSo."

"Holly Bradley was attacked last night."

"Yeah, he said as much. He found her lying in her own blood, but what I want to know is: if she's so innocent, why threaten Jimmy? Why cover up evidence?"

"Has he contacted you this morning?"

"Course not. But I'm still askin' myself: why she wanted to wash away the evidence."

Kate leaned back, arching out her chest. Despite himself, he looked down before meeting her half smile. "Unless she had an accomplice to the first murder," Kate added, "and that accomplice got 'er in the end."

"Who might that be?"

"No idea, man. Your job, not mine."

"How do you know Jimmy didn't attack Holly?"

She chuckled. "No chance. I know the boy intimately, remember? Besides, ask yourself this: why did Holly survive when the first victim didn't?"

"Your boyfriend chased the attacker away?"

"He ain't scaring nobody."

Gray took a moment to churn her words in his sleep-deprived mind. The muscles in his back ached for a heating pad or a massage – but no such reprieve lay in his foreseeable future. Outside, the keen wind buffeted pedestrians trying desperately not to slip on the wintery sheet beneath their feet.

"Were you alone at home last night?" he asked.

"Yeah. All night until Jimmy showed up." She clicked her tongue. "I don't have a ready alibi for you, and Jimmy ran off before I woke."

Gray left feeling a foreboding of danger, but was it for himself or for the woman in the café? She knew something more, he was sure of it; perhaps, something else her boyfriend had told her.

This theory – of Holly having an accomplice – might not have come out of Kate's imagination. In which case, she was in danger.

Now, more than ever, he had to find Jimmy Cane.

CHAPTER 10

April 2, 1 pm

THE SMELL OF ANTISEPTIC assailed his nose. This floor of the hospital smelled worse, far worse than the lobby or the elevators on his way up.

Gray stopped short of entering Holly's room when he detected Simon's voice booming from inside.

"You can't speak to me that way. I'm the founder of this company."

"Listen to me." Holly sounded hoarse. She lay in bed, eyes swollen, forehead bruised. "Forget about Guilter's offer. Juva Pharma jumped into the game last night. They want to talk about buying us. And not for a mere forty million either – we'll receive the full two hundred."

"What–"

"I'm continuing as CEO, even in hospital. These negotiations will go on through me, and me alone. Nothing can be allowed to mess them up."

"You're going to work after that blow to the head?" Simon said. "What are you, a woman or a machine?"

Holly's breath came heavy and ragged, and she was turning alarmingly greener by the second. Yet her voice remained strong.

"If I find out you had anything to do with my attack—"

"Don't threaten me," Simon said. "Have you forgotten how you got to be CEO in the first place? Should I call your loving partner and tell her about our affair? Melanie adopted the baby, right? Not you. You think she'd leave and take the brat with her if she knew?"

Holly's jaw clenched, and her lids lowered. "That secret had better stay in your pants, or else —"

Suddenly noticing Gray by the door, she stopped. Her eyes flashed before fixating on a person behind him.

A familiar-looking doctor came into the room, said a few predictable niceties, and began shining a penlight into her patient's eyes.

Simon merely stood and watched, seething. Finally, he stormed out of the room, and his departing footsteps echoed down the hall while Holly, now looking even more unwell, began to retch into a stainless steel basin.

Any other smell Gray could endure, but vomit made him literally sick. The doctor completed the exam with Gray waiting outside. When she came out to join him, and he presented his ID.

"Dr. Jenna Peters," she said, holding out her hand. Her wild ringlets framed an angular face. He guessed from her crumpled greens and the glasses perched over her unadorned face that she'd been on call the previous night.

"How is Ms. Bradley?"

"Not up to an interrogation. You don't recognize me, do you? I've seen you around the neighborhood. You're on Leeson, right?"

Of course. Dr. Peters lived in that large corner Victorian, one street over from his.

"Yes, nice to see you again, Doctor."

Her long lashes nearly brushed the insides of the purple, square-rimmed spectacles. She had a lazy way of talking. "Now, Chief Inspector. You know I can't discuss the patient's condition without her consent."

"This wasn't a random attack. We're investigating a brutal murder, and the two crimes are related. I don't have confirmation, but the first victim may have been Dr. Norman Everett. He's missing."

The silence stretched. Jenna Peters didn't harass him with all the usual questions; the long lashes rose and fell, her features inscrutable and her hands firmly planted inside the pockets of her white coat.

Gray followed his instincts. "Is there something I should know about Holly? Something you want to tell me?"

"I can't break the rules."

"Doctor, she's not just a victim, but also a suspect who tampered with vital evidence."

"Then she's unlikely to confide in you."

Gray rubbed the growing stubble on his chin. It had started to itch. "No. Murder suspects rarely confide in the police – which makes help from other professionals all the more important. I know you want to preserve patient confidentiality."

"I wish to preserve my job, Chief Inspector." She examined her nails. "But I do know Dr. Everett. He runs, or perhaps, ran, the infectious disease consult service for the entire hospital."

Gray ran a hand through his hair. "Consult service? Above and beyond the ID department?" She nodded. "You mean, every bloody ward in this hospital? How many patients is that in the last year?"

"A great many." She offered him a conciliatory half-smile and left.

Gray's cell sounded. Vivienne's voice rang out.

"According to Seymour, the blood matches," she said. "That's his quick and dirty preliminary analysis, anyway."

Gray walked to the nearest stairwell and made his way to the lobby. "Holly's nail clippings?"

"—match John Doe's blood, and the remnants from the server room floor. All three came from the same victim, just like you thought. That means our faceless corpse, whoever he is, was killed at the startup, but why should the CEO tamper with evidence?"

"Either to protect her company's sale or to protect the killer. She can't deny cleaning up the murder scene now. Anything else?"

"You also asked me to check if Norman's identification card was used to enter the startup. Their system records him entering the building at ten pm the night he disappeared, and again last night at eleven-twenty."

"Again last night? The killer's using his ID badge to gain access. Why haven't they revoked it?"

"I told them to, but they didn't," Vivienne replied in a clipped tone.

Gray let it go, knowing Vivienne would remedy that situation and that the person responsible would soon be missing a piece of their hide.

"We have a bigger problem," Gray said, judging now to be as good a time as ever to drop the bomb on his second-in-command. "Norman ran the hospital's consult service, which means countless patients and countless charts to examine."

"What? We don't have the manpower."

"Get Doug on it. Perhaps one of the other sergeants at HQ can help." He delivered the pertinent details and ended the call.

The team had one additional confirmation: the same killer responsible for the hanging corpse had returned to the startup last night, in possession of Norman's entry card. Though hadn't that been obvious from the start? Each piece of evidence continued to link Norman to the faceless victim, despite his wife's statement to the contrary. Without intending it, had Gabi pulled herself and her callow son to the top of Gray's list of suspects.

Or was everyone around him right, and was he about to make a fatal assumption – one that would inexorably lead to another death?

CHAPTER 11

April 2, 2:30 pm

CARS HEADING TO and from downtown whizzed past him on le Chemin Bord Ouest; pedestrians hustled on the boardwalk tightly ensconced in coats, gloves, and hats. Only the river across the road looked asleep, the still surface resembling molten silver, sluggishly gurgling eastward, unaffected by the day's dramatic events. Thirteen years earlier, he'd proposed to Sita on this very beach: her hair blowing in the wind, a faint musky scent from her breasts drifting down to him as he bent before her on one knee, the gentle surf soaking through his linen pants. It had all occurred a lifetime ago, to a different person.

The uniformed officer outside the Westborough Psychiatric Institute, where Étienne remained, nodded somberly to Gray, all the while ardently rubbing together his leather-encased hands.

"Sir."

"You must be freezing," Gray said, checking his smartwatch.

"Nothing I can't handle, sir. I'm used to guarding construction sites, and they're mighty cold as well."

"Anything grab your attention?"

"Nothing at all. It's just that I feel wasted out here. Even if someone attacked the kid in his room or the halls, I wouldn't hear him. What use am I?"

Gray scanned the lot and surrounding garden. The day and night promised to be bitterly cold. "You're right. Go home when your shift is complete. You can't stay out here indefinitely."

Five minutes later, Gray found his witness in the cafeteria. Fluorescent lights hung from the high ceilings, encasing the room in a blue hue. Rows of institutional tables and chairs filled the space. Étienne sat in a corner by himself, slouching, pushing frozen peas across a steel plate. He looked the same: hair greasy, a small and skinny frame, and a pimply face. Seeing Gray, he gave a toothy grin.

"Inspector?"

"Hello, Étienne."

Étienne's warmth and enthusiasm felt at once welcoming and disconcerting. Was he so deprived of affection and acceptance that he'd trust a relative stranger? Looking around, Gray could understand the reason. The other occupants of the room must seem frightening to a child. Two older boys arm-wrestled at a nearby table, their faces scrunched in concentration. The larger one swiftly won and slammed the other boy's hand on the laminate surface. The resulting thud made Étienne jump.

"You come to see me?" The puppy dog eyes, wet and apologetic, looked at Gray who, straddling a chair, asked: "Étienne, how are you?"

"Okay. No killer come to get me. But I have no guard."

"Director Leblanc won't allow my men inside the Institute. I'm working on it. Give me time."

The boy's eyes fell to his plate. Gravy congealed on the sliced turkey. At least it looked like turkey, the edges of the meat ominously gray.

"I won't ever get out of here," Étienne said. "Claire want me to join her, with her foster parents, but no one help."

"Claire?"

"My little sister. She live with her new mama et papa who will shortly adopt her, and they like me. Once, they come to visit, but the other boys yell at them. They only bring Claire sometimes now."

"Where are your birth parents?" Gray asked

"There are none."

"We all have parents, Étienne. Even someone as old as me."

The small lips pressed together. "Once."

Gray lowered his voice. He wanted to know what made the boy tick, what path had led him here to this desolate place. "How old were you when they left?"

"Me, I'm three. But Claire, she was a baby."

"What happened to them?"

Étienne jumped up and shouted. "I don't know what happen to them. I don't care."

The inmates looked their way; a guard made eye contact, and after Gray's reassuring nod, turned away. Leaning his head on one hand, Gray waited. After sheepishly looking around, Étienne took his seat.

Always extenuating circumstances, Leblanc had chided. You bet there were. The silence stretched, but he needed the whole truth. "What did you do to land in this prison? Why are you here?"

Clumps of the gravy now coated the frozen peas, and Étienne pushed them across the steel tray with his fork. "I want to forget."

"That's up to you. But I can't help if I don't know the reason you're here. Leblanc told me you killed another boy."

"He hit my sister," Étienne said. Leaning in, he spoke in hushed, urgent sounds. "He grab her hair and hit her. We are in the playground. She cry, but she can't get away. And boy was too big for me, so I run and pick up a rock."

"When was this?"

"I was ten."

"You defended your younger sister, and they convicted you of murder?"

"But I not stop. I keep hitting and hitting. Like a father hits. I see my father's face, and I am him, but I don't know his face or remember it." His mouth opened and closed. "It is the face of a stranger. Claire yell at me to stop, but I don't stop, and my hand has blood all over." He lifted his right palm; his voice shook. "I am a bad boy, a killer."

Gray swallowed. The rasping of his breath, in and out, sounded inordinately loud in the nearly empty room.

A loud clang made both him and the boy jump. An inmate had dropped a metal tray onto the floor nearby. The spell broke.

Étienne examined his feet. "Director Leblanc tell me, I have delusion."

"I bet he does."

"You have a son, Inspector?"

Gray blinked. "I used to."

"What happen?"

The high-pitched voice made it hard not to answer, and Gray found himself wanting to talk for the first time, but he couldn't burden a child with the brick wedged in his heart. "I didn't take good enough care of him. And he died."

Étienne touched the scar on Gray's wrist, a feather-light touch which tickled. He smiled. "He was lucky to have a dad like you who cares and misses him. More lucky than me." Now, the boy squeezed his hand. "It is not your fault, Inspector."

Gray blinked and swallowed.

A guard approached their table. "Sorry, Chief Inspector. Visiting time's over."

Gray walked Étienne to the staircase. He put a hand on the bony shoulder. "I'll try and visit tomorrow. If I can't make it, Detective Caron will come in my place."

Étienne nodded and went up the stairs. Instead of possessing the bounce of youth, he had the lethargy of an aging man.

Once outside, Gray pulled his lapels together against the bone-chilling air. The full moon hung low in the azure sky, enormous, expectant.

But he found it more ominous than beautiful.

His cell burred, and he answered it, realizing his day wasn't yet over.

Gray rode up the elevator of the Service de Police de la Ville de Montréal headquarters, each successive number on the panel lighting, each floor upward inexorably leading towards the enemy. Towards the inevitable confrontation with his boss. Séverin had called demanding an update, and Gray was expected to deliver now.

Watching the cold steel elevator doors, Gray evened his breath, firmed his resolve. His fists clenched and unclenched, but they wouldn't have the satisfaction of meeting with Séverin's jaw. Not today.

The elevator opened to a hot draft, stuffy and claustrophobic. The after-work office looked deserted. His boots sank into the beige wall to wall carpeting, and stale cigarette smoke gripped his throat. Institutional furniture and the overall impression of blue, gray, and red hit him. Nothing like being transported back to 1984.

He reached Céline's desk. She swiveled side to side in her squeaky leather chair and looked up. Her tight silk dress matched the overly fruity perfume, which must have put Séverin back a few hundred.

Gray felt nothing of the temporary desire he'd indulged the other night and got down to business. "He called me; I don't have much time."

"I'll go in with you."

"No."

Her mascaraed lashes lowered. The coolness of their earlier exchange hung in the air. Both she and her boss wanted to use him; he wouldn't be used.

Céline buzzed Gray in. He turned the handle and stepped into the lion's den, entering the usual miasma of sweat, old takeout, and damp socks.

The fat man stood backlit, both arms planted on his desk like wooden logs. His face lay in shadows, the large, wobbly jowls outlined in gray and black.

On the right wall, a dozen misaligned frames held photographs of Séverin shaking hands – with the Provincial Premier, the Governor General, and various politicians on both sides of the French and English standoff. In each, he looked at the camera wearing the same toothy smile.

Gray felt dirty just being in the room.

"I call, and the puppy comes running." The Deputy Director's thick Quebecois accent, more suited to a truck driver than a Deputy Director, slammed across the room.

"Séverin —"

A tall, thickset man with heavy bags under his eyes and a perpetual half-smile moved up from a corner. Gray hadn't expected to see Cousineau, and if the two directors had called him in for a discussion, it could only be about one thing.

He braced himself for the inevitable, choosing the strategy that would buy him and the team the most time. Every Canadian boy grew up knowing hockey, and here, a good offence was the best defence.

Cousineau motioned for him to sit. "Thank you for coming, Chief Inspector. I believe you know police procedures exist for good reason. You have not kept us apprised of your progress."

Gray bet he knew how they'd found out. Having Doug on the team had both advantages and disadvantages.

Séverin lit a cigarette, but no fire alarm sounded. He dropped into a creaky chair and put his feet up, foot odor drifting across the room. "You have no identification of the body. The victim is not Norman Everett."

"Those feet could be biological weapons."

"Mon Dieu." Cousineau sat to his left. "Perhaps you should not lead this investigation. I will assign you to another case."

"And I won't stop investigating, even if I have to do it unofficially. Not until the bastard who bombed my car and shot at me is behind bars." He looked at Severin.

"How dare you?" the fat man said.

"Deputy Director —" Cousineau waved a calming hand. "We are all friends here. Now who would risk killing a Chief Inspector of the SPVM? Only a fool, certainement?"

"I agree. A big fool. I can guess who planted that bomb. And I know who ordered it."

Séverin sprung forward from his chair. "I hope you aren't accusing me." His breath smelled sour from coffee and bagels, and poppy seeds dotted bared teeth. "You work here because of Director Cousineau. Not because I want you on my force. No matter how many cases you solve."

"You're quick enough to take credit for my successes." Gray's gaze didn't waver. The back of the wooden chair dug into his aching back. "No more violence."

"Or what? You will ride up on your white horse and fix the rest of us? Except, it isn't white, is it? It's jet black. You're no hero; you're a villain. As that voice inside you whispers at night. Killer, it says. Murderer."

Severin puffed out his chest. "Outside, the thousand-dollar suit. Inside, the storm. That is you, Chief Inspector."

Cousineau moved between them. "I could order you off this investigation."

"I've never left a case unsolved," Gray said. "And I never will."

Gray strode out of the office, passing Céline. She followed him to the elevator and squeezed through the doors just before they closed, her breath heavy, the silk dress stretching over high, pointed breasts.

"When will I see you?" she said.

"You won't. I'm sorry. From the bottom of my heart, I'm sorry."

"It took me two years to get you into bed, and you're dumping me after one time? You enjoyed it. So why?"

How could he tell her that she was merely a temporary if ineffective respite? How could he say anything that cruel to anyone? "I'm sorry. Impulse got the better of us. We both agreed to a one-night stand. And we both had too much to drink."

She waved her hand. "Men always say that. They don't mean it."

"Perhaps I'm not enough of a man then. But other things need my attention. I have to get on with the case."

"Other things? Other people?"

"A child's life may be at stake—"

She hit him on the chest, hard; it knocked the breath out of his lungs. "I don't care," she said. "You and I belong together. You'll be Director one day —"

"I won't be Director, Céline. I'll never accept that position." He stopped himself from saying the rest. That he wouldn't, couldn't get serious about anyone. Let alone her.

Céline's face paled. Her chest rose high and rigid. Her stilettos clicked on the elevator tile as she stepped closer. "Séverin will believe what I tell him. And I'll say we love each other, that we're going away together – unless you come to your senses. There's no telling what he'll do if he thinks he's lost me to you. He's a jealous man, Gray."

The elevator jerked at the ground floor. The doors slid open, letting in fresh air.

She got out and turned back. "Compris?"

No one understood you better than your enemy.

***

The house lay quiet, save the crackling of a fire, and the gentle clang of ice in his scotch-filled tumbler. Red and gold embers danced in the fire; the wood shifted and crackled, moisture sending off sparks against the surrounding red bricks. Outside his window, dusk gently settled over the tree-lined street.

It was too early to sleep. On impulse, he grabbed his coat and sprinted the two blocks to Dr. Jenna Peters's house on Pearson Avenue. With a little luck, she'd be home from the hospital, and be willing to discuss her tenebrous patient, Holly.

The Victorian structure stood in darkness, except for a gentle glow emanating from the main ground floor window. He passed a mature lavender tree which dominated the front yard, its trunk corrugated and patched below the dominant branches, each sprouting new shoots lined with opening leaves and puckered buds. The ripe, rich scent teased his nostrils, and he sucked it in hungrily.

Jenna opened the door carrying a drink. A backlight darted through the glass of red wine forming a mahogany kaleidoscope. Chopin's Etude No. 9 drifted in from behind.

"I'm sorry to bother you," Gray said.

Jenna still had her work clothes on. "It's all right."

After wiping his feet, he stepped inside. A fire crackled in the living room and sent soft, buoyant arms of light onto the foyer wall, the shadows of the flames like people dancing. It was the kind of room that you curled up in to nurse a burgundy and contemplate existence, or disappear into a leather-bound volume.

"You held something back about your patient today, didn't you? I have to know."

"Why don't you come inside, Chief Inspector?"

She poured his red with a steady, slender hand. A linked chain of varying shades of pink and yellow gold slid from her wrist down her angled hand, sounding a gentle tinkle as the metal hit the side of the bottle. Setting the bottle on the sideboard, she passed him the glass. The long stem was hard to grasp, and her eyes fell to his hand. He could see her physician's mind processing and diagnosing: *median nerve problem, some atrophy, probably operable?*

"Go ahead and ask," Gray said. "I wouldn't want to deprive a physician of an opportunity to satisfy her medical curiosity."

Jemma's eyes flicked up to his; she smiled, turned, and sat on the sofa, inviting him to take the matching red and white chintz armchair opposite. "That won't be necessary."

"Is Holly well enough to be interviewed?" he asked.

"Soon."

"As I said earlier, she isn't merely a victim," Gray said. "She's also a suspect, one willing to shield a murderer."

"Are you sure?"

"Yes."

Jemma crossed and uncrossed her legs, slowly. But the movement wasn't deliberately provocative. She was buying time, plain and simple. "If someone were hiding something about their past," she said, "it could impact your investigation?"

"Possibly. I couldn't say without knowing what was concealed."

She stared past him and sipped her wine. Two candles flicked on a small piano against the far wall, the flames seemingly swaying to Chopin. Gray sat back and relaxed, not wanting to pressure her. A full minute passed before she spoke.

"Did you know," she said, "that medical charts contain a list of the medications the patient was taking prior to admission?"

"You're referring to Holly's admission after her attack?"

"I'm speaking generally."

"What I could use are specifics, but I suppose beggars can't be choosers." Gray was quick on the uptake. "The information I need is in her chart? In the list of medications?"

"I have no idea what you need. And as long as you access it legally, I've told you nothing confidential."

"Understood." He gulped the rest of his wine and thanked her for her time.

Sadly, she didn't seem sorry to see him go.

Getting access to Holly's private medical information would be no problem since she'd made herself as a suspect by cleaning the spilled blood at HealSo.

He flew down the porch steps on renewed legs and made his way along Pearson Avenue, around the corner to Martin, and then onto Leeson.

The night lay still, his steps sounding hollow and distant to his ears. Gray called Doug on his cell to make the necessary arrangements. He wanted to see that file tonight. If anyone could manage that, the junior detective could.

Fifty-year-old maples towered overhead, shrouding the houses and keeping them safe from the city's rapidly changing terrain. Patches of clear sky peeked through the clouds, but the calm wouldn't last. A storm was brewing. He could smell it, feel it in his bones.

Within the hour, Gray sat at the nurse's station at Westborough with Holly's chart before him. He considered getting Seymour to look at it but decided to read it himself first.

Much of the terminology seemed straightforward. Holly had visited the hospital with a urinary tract infection two years previously and visited the hospital several times for tension migraines that required opioid therapy. He paid particular attention to the list of medications. It wasn't until he got to the night of Holly's attack that he saw it: instructions stating the patient's Esovin had to be continued, despite the risks.

Gray didn't understand. He needed Dr. Seymour's expertise after all. He dialed his cell, and it turned out the pathologist was already home but didn't mind having company – especially when that involved discussing a murder case.

Printing out the relevant pages and placing the file under his arm, Gray drove towards the doctor's home for an impromptu consult.

Seymour met him at the door and led him into his overcrowded and musty study, eager to help Gray as always.

Was the medication necessary? Gray asked.

Yes, they were... but...

They? Multiple pills?

Yes. Three, in fact, the pathologist said. The other two were called Finasteride and Spironolactone.

Meaning? Was Holly Bradley sick or something?

Seymour took his time explaining.

CHAPTER 12

April 2, 6 pm

JIMMY TREMBLED, scrunched in the fetal position on his white sofa. If he could sink further into the familiar gold weaved cushions, he would. Inside, the apartment was hot, stifling. Outside, the wind whistled, and dusk fell on the quad of triplexes just off rue Saint Denis, where the pedestrian crush of professionals, hipsters, and tourists never stopped.

Usually, he liked the city's smog and croissant-scented hustle and bustle. The area retained enough grunge to temper the tide of gentrification, so that trendy boulangeries lay side by side with decrepit coin laundromats. But today, he felt safer behind his locked door.

A loud pounding shattered the quiet. He leaped up with his feet together and his fists clenched, waiting for the knocking to stop; when it didn't, he glanced through the peephole and exhaled, then opened the door an inch.

The visitor forced it the rest of the way and let in a cold draft that chilled Jimmy's bare feet. He dug his toes into the small shag rug, and avoided the blazing eyes, instead focusing on the central fountain, hedges, and cherry blossoms of the quad outside, behind his visitor.

The unwelcome guest entered the living room. "We need to talk."

"About what?"

"The wisdom of keeping your mouth shut."

Eyes followed Jimmy across the room before taking the worn cushioned chair. Jimmy returned to his spot on the sofa, knees pressed together, shoulders hunched. He looked down at the white fabric with its delicate woven gold pattern. Mom had given him this old sofa from home when he'd moved out a year ago. It brought back memories of running home for lunch every day and eating baloney sandwiches while she cooked in the kitchen.

The guest leaned back, unsmiling. "You're leaving HealSo?"

"Y—yes."

The reproachful eyes watched him, making his face burn. "Bad idea, Jimmy."

Wanting to get distance, he sprang up and scurried behind the kitchen counter, craving something hot. He'd make himself a cappuccino, even though the caffeine would probably keep him up. He compacted the grounds with the tamper. It took five seconds for the first drops to dribble into a ramekin underneath and scent the air with hazelnut and cardamom – all done with precision and neatness. Still, he wiped down the machine and counter several times, never convinced it was clean enough.

"I've seen something," the guest said.

"What?"

The guest told him.

Jimmy's shoulders tightened. The container of milk shook in his hand. He suspected the same thing, but he wasn't going to admit it out loud. "I don't believe you."

"I don't care what you believe. If you know what's good for you, you'll remain at HealSo. And stay under the radar."

His knees shook while he frothed the milk, and he thought of shared mornings with Mom: sitting at the breakfast table in their modest condo, listening to the chirping of the sparrows, and the melodic rush of the nearby river. He'd begun making coffee for her at the age of eight; if only he were sitting across from her now. Why hadn't he taken a bus home instead of coming back here?

The coffee tasted bitter and sour. Jimmy gulped down the rest as though it were chocolate milk. The guest approached him and planted two fists on the counter and spoke, the flushed face inches away from his. "You'd better keep your mouth shut."

"And be blamed? Everything I programmed has my initials stamped all over it. I said at the time, we can't do this." Jimmy's voice cracked; a frog lodged in his throat. "No one listened."

"You're not thinking straight."

"If I get blamed, I'm taking everyone down with me."

"What do you mean?" The guest's voice was soft, too soft. Jimmy blinked. His breath caught in his lungs, and his fingertips felt numb.

"I... I mean, I've set things in motion, that's all. If they blame me, everyone'll know the truth."

Hard eyes bored into his. Jimmy's heart hammered in his chest, pounding against his ribs. Words spluttered out. "I won't tell you! You think I'm stupid. I have to take care of myself. And... and I'm not going to prison for any of you."

"What have you done?"

Jimmy leaned forward. "Wouldn't you kill to know?"

***

An hour later, Jimmy sat alone at the two-person dining room table, contemplating his next move. Contrary to what he'd said, he hadn't done anything yet. But the manila envelope crackled in his hand – sealed, the address written, the appropriate postage affixed. All that remained was to mail it. He couldn't bring himself to tell Mom in person, hated telling her at all.

Envelope in hand, he left the apartment and sprinted to the corner mailbox. Rue St. Denis was better in the morning when the street was still and empty. Now, it felt wild: the sidewalks crowded under Victorian street lamps, the lit-up bistros, shops, and brasseries cluttered together as far as the eye could see.

He slipped the letter into the slot, unsure of his decision, but desperately needing to do something, anything. Then a thought came to mind: what about his Mom's safety? Always his savior, who would protect her?

Hurrying back to the apartment, he locked the door behind him, sat down at the table, and pulled up two trembling knees to his chest. Chief Inspector James might be able to help. He'd know what to do and how to protect both Mom and himself.

He dialed the SPVM police station on rue Saint Urbain and left a message for Gray with the officer at the precinct. It would be a relief to unload all he knew onto the police.

Yet a nagging restlessness remained. He needed to keep himself occupied while he waited for the call, but a pain in his stomach made him dismiss most of the activities that came to mind, including eating or playing Cosmo Kill, the video game Kate rolled her eyes at. He straightened a few books on the shelf before returning to the table, when suddenly the tug in his belly morphed into a knife-like stab.

Without warning, he retched. Coffee-laden vomit poured out of his mouth onto the dining table, the clumpy liquid puddling and snaking its way over the edge until it spilled onto the pine floor.

Two more excruciating knife stabs followed. The retching assailed him in spasms even though there was nothing left to come out, until something red and scary did. Blood spluttered out like bursts from an old tap. The blood mixed with the vomit, the red and the brown now flowing freely together.

He watched in horror as the viscous blood coalesced with the thinner coffee on the table top. Some long-forgotten memory of a childhood science experiment was ignited, involving two immiscible liquids being mixed...

The retching stopped, but the stabbing pain in his stomach continued – and Jimmy knew that he was in terrible trouble.

He had to reach the phone by the side table. He stood up quickly, too quickly, and his vision blurred. Arms forward, legs like lead, he moved gingerly towards the object – but his foot caught, causing him to trip.

Jimmy fell face forward onto the sofa. Tears rolled down his cheeks; his nose ran.

He was alone. She wasn't there to help him. It had never happened before – this time, she wasn't there. He clawed his way to the cordless phone and dialed 911.

After several rings, the dispatcher answered, and when she did, she spoke frustratingly slowly, wanted him to repeat what he'd said, which was impossible because the retching came back.

"S'il vous plaît. Again, monsieur. Are you all right?"

"I'm... ah... ahh." He gasped and fought to form words over the weeping. Where was it coming from? Was there a child crying outside? Then he realized that the noise was his.

"Monsieur. Tell me what's wrong? Is there anyone with you?"

"I'm throwing up blood. Send help." The few words sucked up his strength.

"We're sending an ambulance to your house now. Is there anyone there with you?"

"No. Alone... ah.. ahhh!" Jimmy screamed in pain. Something inside him ripped. More blood poured out of his mouth, no longer needing any retching, and the crimson fluid stained, somewhat artistically, the gold threaded pattern of his mother's white sofa. He watched, dissociated, as the fluid scuttled along the embroidered valleys before soaking into the fabric.

"Mom," he mouthed, but only a whisper came out between the gurgles. The ambulance was on its way. They would take him to the hospital, and he would see her. Everything would be okay when he saw her.

But what if he didn't? What if he never saw her again? The envelope. He had to tell her to destroy it. He had to undo what he'd done.

The dispatcher on the other end continued, asking him questions he heard from a distance, from the far end of a tunnel. The ambulance was on its way, she said. He should unlock the door. If only he could make it there without passing out.

He hung up. A cloudy blackness closed in, encircling, making his lids heavy. He fought to stay awake, but his head kept slumping back onto the sofa, a dead weight.

He had to call her. More than anything, he needed to hear her voice, needed to hear he'd be okay, that she'd nurse him and take him home where he belonged.

Flashes of that fateful day returned when he'd announced his decision to move out. That as a grown man, he needed independence. He remembered the pensive look on her face, the silent reserve as she'd said little, not wanting to discourage him. She'd been kind and gentle, not reminding him of his Asperger's – it was so mild, after all – all the doctors had said so. He could take care of himself as long as things didn't get too complicated. But they had, and Jimmy had met people ready to exploit his gifts and his innate vulnerability.

He wanted Mama, just like when at age seven one of his schoolmates beat him with a stick in the schoolyard. The class was learning how to carry when adding two-digit numbers, and he'd been at his desk solving complex algebraic equations. The other kid resented that and attacked Jimmy during recess. Through a screen of trees, the teachers hadn't heard his wailing for the older boy to stop. His right wrist had been cracked from fending off the blows, and the bridge of his nose remained crooked to this day.

His mother had stepped in forcefully, admonishing the teachers, the child, the child's parents, and ultimately taking her complaint to the school board.

Mom had been there countless times for him, the two of them alone in the world. If he was clueless about relationships, she supplied all the emotional ingredients needed to make theirs complete.

Gripping the phone in sticky red hands, Jimmy dialed her number, praying she was home.

She answered immediately. "Hello?" The calm, familiar voice carried across the line.

"Mom?" Jimmy choked. The word came out hoarse and barely above a whisper.

"Jimmy?" his Mom exclaimed. She keyed into his distress instantaneously, always on the alert to protect him. "Jimmy! Where are you? I can barely hear you. Are you sick? Are you at home?"

He choked out a yes. Then he felt wetness suffuse from below, a steady stream of diarrhea soaked his pants, both brown and red dripping down his leg and into his shoes. The pungent smell enveloped the room.

"Oh God, Mom!"

"I'm calling an ambulance right now, Jimmy. Do you hear me? They'll be right over."

"Already... called."

"What's happened?" She was shouting on the other end. "What can I do? I'm coming right now."

He managed to choke out a few words and, struggling, began saying what he needed to say, to warn her against what he'd done, against the people who might hurt her.

Then the retching returned. He retched and retched again, in a blind panic that there was no time left to explain the long, complicated situation to her... before she hung up the phone and hurried over to his apartment... before it might be too late... he fought to get out a few words.

"I love you, Mama. I need you, Mama."

"Jimmy... Jimmy!" his mother was screaming now. About her boy, her darling boy who had never quite grown up...

"I sent... letter... don't open it. Don't do it... mistake... danger... for you."

"Jimmy... Jimmy! I'm coming over now. Hang on. I'm calling the ambulance again. God! Why aren't they there?"

"Someone died... may kill you, like me..."

"Who died? Who's trying to kill you?" his mother asked frantically. "Save your strength. I'm coming, baby. I'm going to hang up the phone, and I'm coming."

He stared at the door before him. He could hear his mother's voice, but now, no words came out when he tried to speak. All control over his mouth seemed lost.

There was a hiatus of all thought, of movement, of control. His gaze fixed on the door across the room, his ears registering the loud thumping, the calling of his name.

The phone fell out of his hand and landed on the sofa. He heard his mother's voice yelling out his name over and over, so loudly that it traveled across the room. She was suffering like an animal in agony, because of him. And for once, he thought first of her, not himself. How hard it would be for her. How he had endangered her by sending her that letter. How she would have to clean up the mess he'd left behind.

A black outline surrounded the image he saw of the door, the blackness widening, the image narrowing – as the wood gave way and uniformed strangers hurried to the sofa that was now more red than white, the gold threaded pattern of flowers and bees covered in congealing blood.

The black perimeter widened further, the central image of the broken door narrowed until finally all was black, sound was obscured, and there was a deafening nothingness. And the last thought Jimmy had was not of the startup, not of his girlfriend Kate, not of being murdered – it was of his Mom and how he would miss her, and how she would forever miss him.

CHAPTER 13

April 2, 7 pm

NOW BACK AT THE INSTITUTE, Étienne left the musty bathroom after his shower wearing his robe and slippers. He didn't dare waste time drying properly, and as a result, water dripped freely down his legs and onto his ankles. Already, a new sheen of sweat was forming on his back; already, he was breathing heavily. He hated being back. If only that doctor from last year had gotten him out. If only the Inspector would get him out now.

He glanced right and left and hurried back to the safety of his room. Several of the boys frequently teased him about leaving the Institute at night. They hated the fact that a twelve-year-old had found a way out, while they remained locked away. He was clear-minded enough to understand their grievance but had pointed out that they were criminals, after all. So how could they resent being treated like ones?

His frankness only made matters worse, and the atmosphere had become thick with tension. Being younger and smaller than the other inmates had obvious disadvantages, and there were other differences – they were rough, scary. Some even saw and heard things that weren't there.

Probably, Leblanc could include him with the crazies, but Étienne had never regretted the action which landed him at the Institute. Looking back, terror had made him keep hitting that boy. The doctors didn't understand. He'd never intended to kill, only to save his sister from being attacked. At ten and a half, he'd made the best decision he could.

Neither of them remembered their parents. The aid worker told him his mom and dad had walked out of the house one day and never came back – that a neighbor called the police because of the abandoned animals in the backyard, never suspecting that three-year-old Étienne wandered around inside, unable to get out. And that his baby sister, after endless hours of wailing and whimpering, lay listless in the soiled crib.

Images flashed in his mind, whispers of memories of him leaning over a baby, of his grabbing the cold, pale fingers, filling his cupped hands with water and bringing it to Claire's mouth, and her lapping it up and licking her lips.

Who knew what really happened, and what his imagination might have filled in over the years? But those two days bonded them together like nothing else could. And Étienne would take care of his sister, no matter what.

His room was now in sight. Keeping low, water dripping and leaving a trail on the splintered floor, he made his way down the hall. Any time now, one of the bigger boys might pounce out of the woodwork. Once, three inmates had surrounded the hall, pinned him against the wall, and held a needle next to his eye. The guard had broken it up, but he couldn't count on being that lucky again.

He reached his room and scurried inside, wishing the room had a lock.

One of the older boys, Carl, appeared outside his doorway, fists resting on his hips, a snarl on his face. Étienne's eyes flew to the crawl space. If only he'd had time to hide. He called out, but no one came. The guard was probably making his rounds on the other side of the building, or worse, letting the boys settle their disputes by themselves.

"You think you're smarter than us?" Carl snarled.

"Non."

"Non!" Carl mimicked Étienne's higher voice.

"S'il vous plait. Go away. I do nothing to you." He backed further into the room. Carl moved towards him. Étienne called out, louder this time, but still no one came. His room was two floors up from the Director's, and one of the other boys had closed the door to the stairs, effectively sealing them off.

"You think you can steal that access card, go out at night, and then come back anytime you want? You think you're smarter than us?" Carl's eyes blazed with something strange. He wasn't right. The snake tattoo on his arm rippled as he flexed. "It makes fools out of us. I've been here two years."

"I sneak out for myself," Étienne said. "Next time, I will give you card. I get it for you."

"I don't need your help." Carl threw a wooden chair across the room. "I can get out anytime I want."

He had an even chance with Carl, despite the other boy's larger size, but fighting wasn't an option. He'd promised Claire the last time she came to visit that he'd never fight again. There was every chance he could live with her foster family, provided he behaved, provided the doctors weren't worried about him killing someone else. After he convinced them, he could finally get out of this hell-hole and be with Claire.

His high voice cracked. "I don't want to fight."

The other boy paid no attention. The first blow hurt, the second, a little less. And in the ones following, Étienne held up his arms in front of his face, his stomach, his chest to try and ward off the fists. He curled up in a ball on the floor and screamed, but still the punches came.

With each one, he begged for a different life, a different place to live. He heard the other boy's insults from a distance and shut his eyes tight against the monsters. Behind his lids, there were flashes of light, blurry images of parents he never knew, unreal and invented in his imagination, and Claire's worried face looking down at him. The images began to fade and thin before receding into nothingness.

And so it was that two patients arrived at Westborough Hospital Emergency with serious bleeds simultaneously – one treated by the staff surgeon and the other by his senior resident. Jimmy Cane had been brought in after vomiting up blood.

But only one would live.

CHAPTER 14

April 2, 8:20 pm

HOW COULD THIS happen?

Gray had only just returned home after seeing Seymour. Gripping his cel, he resisted the impulse to smash it onto the tessellated floor. The metal dug into his skin. His teeth hurt from clenching.

He dialed Vivienne's number, the urge to punch a hole in the wall staying with him, but he controlled it – just.

She sounded subdued. "Bonjour, Chief Inspector."

"Meet me at Westborough emerg, now. Jimmy Cane was found bleeding in his apartment an hour ago."

"What?"

"I know. We're losing our grip on this fast." He ran a hand over his eyes. "Jimmy is an innocent. No telling who will be next." He didn't have to say more. She knew how worried he was about Étienne.

"After we're done at the hospital," she said, "I can plant myself outside Étienne's room at the Institute. Leblanc will have to drag me out himself." Her words came out of frustration, not practicality, and they both knew it.

Grabbing his keys, he stomped towards his car. His kitchen door slammed behind him, and the cold bit into his cheeks. "It might come to that. But I'll be the one they carry out, not you. First, we have to help our innocent engineer."

Vivienne's voice became distant and staticky. She must be on the hands-free in her car now. "How did you hear so quickly?"

"Jimmy left a message an hour ago saying he wanted to speak to me. The front desk delivered it five minutes ago. When I called his apartment, a uniform answered."

He didn't repeat what the officer had told him, that the sofa and rug were soaked in blood. That the ambulance discovered the young man slumped over it, deathly pale and unconscious. All this must be as hard for her as it was for him, and Gray needed her unemotional. "I'll meet you there."

"Oui."

He ended the call. The short drive towards Westborough passed in a red haze, the emergency department as chaotic as any he'd visited in the past. He crossed the sliding doors, answered some screening questions, and flashed his ID.

Dozens of people occupied the main waiting area, some shuffling in their seats, others leaning against walls, but no one sat behind reception. The antiseptic smell hit him, this time laden with more basal odors: vomit and sweat.

He momentarily held his breath, opened the inner doors, and stormed into the treatment area, where patients lay on stretchers in the hallways for lack of rooms, and an orderly brushed past pushing a wheelchair.

A nurse directed him to a back room on the right, where a new stench emanated from several feet away.

Inside, two doctors and two nurses worked around a man, his shirt and pants soaked in blood. Brown stains went down the insides of his legs.

Jimmy lay unconscious, maybe dead. While one doctor inserted a needle into the engineer's neck – a central line to reach the heart – another intubated. Two IVs pumping saline into the limp arms stood erect on either side of the boy like sentinels.

Gray stood watching and breathed evenly, his heart feeling firmly wedged in his throat. The ministrations on the supine body went on and on. A few minutes later, Vivienne arrived. She must have raced the entire way from her house, and seeing the prone figure on the stretcher hastily wiped her eyes. She felt too much for a police officer, always had.

"You think this is attempted murder?" she asked.

"Don't you? We have three people attacked within twenty-four hours – all members of the same startup. It's crazy to interpret this as anything other than a deliberate attack. Question is, how was it done?"

A commotion from behind caught his attention where across the hall, a uniformed officer came and stood by the door, his arms crossed and his feet wide apart.

Instinct kicked in. Gray grabbed Vivienne's arm and pulled her with him, a foreboding propelling him forward, one he couldn't analyze or explain.

He smelled peanut butter. It had to be a play of his mind, an olfactory association.

Inside, a young doctor worked over a small boy. Blood caked the child's head, the face lay swollen, and bruises covered his bare, bony chest.

Few moments in life feel so disconnected, so unreal that you imagine seeing them as though hovering from above. How many times could one man face the same demon? How many times could one man fail?

He grabbed the side of the door. A steel grip twisted in his belly. The uniformed officer, whose face seemed vaguely familiar, called him by name.

For a full minute, Gray couldn't speak. He stood watching. And the body that gently jostled up and down from the doctor's probing exam could have been Craig's: that little limp hand, the out-turned feet, the vulnerable pale neck.

Except no doctor ever worked to save Craig. Gray hadn't given them that chance. He'd left home with his son and come back alone. His wife's eyes, uncomprehending, searching for a way out of the tunnel collapsing around her, haunted him still. The feel of her fist clutching the fabric of his shirt still tugged on his chest. The violence in her voice still rang in his ears. How could you let it happen? How could you?

Vivienne said, "Why weren't we notified? The police guard wasn't outside the Institute?"

"I told him to go home."

He could predict her next words. "It isn't your fault. It wouldn't have made a difference."

Gray didn't welcome absolution. He turned to the police officer, every muscle in his face tight, his voice guttural. "What happened to that child?"

"Just a nutcase from the looney bin next door. Got into a fight with one of the older boys – probably over drugs, or cigarettes, or whatever. You know how they are." The officer shook his head and gave a lopsided grin.

Gray counted to five. The man was young, inexperienced. He hissed through clenched teeth. "Tell me exactly what happened."

"I—I don't know anything else, sir." The officer moved perceptively back. "I've been instructed to keep him under tabs; that's all. He's a dangerous criminal."

"He doesn't strike me as being dangerous right now. I want hourly updates. This boy is an important witness in a murder inquiry. Don't let anyone near him without checking with me. And don't leave him unguarded for a second. Do you understand, constable? I'm going to hold you personally responsible for his safety."

"Yes, sir."

Overhead, the intercom spat out a garbled announcement no one could understand. Gray looked all around him, seeking a distraction – anything to get away from himself.

In one corner of the hall, a fourteen-year-old girl sat on a stretcher, a bandage wrapped around her head and another around her left wrist. A thin elderly man in a wheelchair stared at Gray, his eyes blank, resigned. A reminder that all dramas eventually end.

A brittle wail traveled down the hall, coming from a woman seated on a bench. Her chest rose and fell in gasps. She jerked forward, and her long black hair tumbled in front of her face, the long silk strands reaching the tips of her cowboy boots. She pushed them back and buried her face in her palms. Tears seeped between her fingers, and the droplets rolled down her hands.

This must be Jimmy's mother.

She lowered her arms and noticed him now, revealing a beautiful face, entirely unlike her son's, both exotic and worldly. Without conscious thought, Gray walked towards her.

"Mrs. Cane?"

She spoke in a cultured, smooth voice. "Do you have news about Jimmy? Can I see him?"

"I'm Chief Inspector Gray James. The doctors are with Jimmy now. Is there somewhere we can talk?"

"I'm not leaving." She straightened. "They told me to go to the waiting room. I won't. I won't leave my baby."

"Do you know what happened to him?"

"No. He called me. Bleeding and screaming–" She let out an involuntary choke. "He'd already dialed 911, and then I called them too... but, by the time they got there... Jimmy was..." She looked up at Gray. "My baby! Tell me what happened to my baby!"

Her head slumped between her legs. Her body shook in spasms. Gray sat on the bench and waited. He put a hand on her shoulder, knowing he couldn't help, knowing the gesture was empty, meaningless, and that nothing could ever help.

"I'm sorry. It's important we move quickly and find out what happened. Is there anything you can tell me?"

"Jimmy said someone might kill him." She gasped in a breath. "A person died, and he knew about it."

Gray kept the urgency out of his voice. "Who might kill him, Mrs. Cane? Who died?"

She shook her head. Her long earrings jangled and bounced against her cheeks. "He mailed me a letter, said I shouldn't open it, or they'd kill me too."

"When did he mail it? What did it say?" Gray kept his voice even.

"I don't know. I don't know. Why did he leave me to live so far away? My little boy." She clutched Gray's arm. "He has Asperger's. I take care of him. Why did she take him away?"

"Who?"

"That bitch, Kate Grant. Oh God, will my Jimmy be okay? Will my Jimmy live, Inspector?"

"I don't know, Mrs. Cane. I'm sorry, I just don't know."

She stared, her eyes desolate. "I have no one else."

Gray held her hand and stayed with her awhile. He left her sitting on the bench and returned to Vivienne.

"What did his mom say?" Vivienne asked.

"She doesn't like Kate much, I can tell you that. Jimmy mailed her a letter and later warned her against opening it. Someone died because of the startup. We need to track that letter down. Norman was a clinician, and Jimmy supplied the technology. Both of them knew something; both of them paid the price."

"Does the killer want to expose the startup, or protect it?"

"That's the million-dollar question, isn't it? All this violence only draws attention to HealSo, so my money's on the former." Gray's thoughts spun in all directions. He brought them into focus. "I'll wait here. You try and trace that letter. It's the biggest lead we have. After that, check on Étienne and try and reach Leblanc. He owes me a damn good explanation for what happened at his allegedly secure facility, or I might just wring his wrinkly neck."

"If Jimmy regains consciousness, he'll be able to tell us everything."

Gray exhaled. "If."

But it wasn't to be. Gray and Vivienne watched the doctor leave the trauma room and approach Jimmy's mom. During his short steps, her eyes grew wide, and her jaw fell. The doctor sat beside her.

She listened as the he spoke, staring straight ahead with a look Gray knew too well. So familiar. So well understood. How many times had he been an interloper in these moments because his job demanded it? How many more Jimmy's would there be?

She asked no questions, didn't ask the doctor if her son had suffered. They all knew she'd heard Jimmy's screams over the phone and would hear them every day for the rest of her life.

She stood and walked into the trauma room where her son lay on the stretcher. Said nothing, made no sound, and lifted one limp hand into hers. Tears leaped out of her eyes, entirely missing her cheeks.

Evelyn Cane lowered Jimmy's hand to his side and placed them under the sheet, as though she were tucking him into bed. Then her eyes rolled back into her head, and she fell onto the hospital floor.

***

He needed to see Jimmy's apartment himself before the SOCOs completed their analysis. Collecting the anemic vehicle, the pedal mushy under his feet, Gray headed out of the hospital lot and joined the freeway.

The 720 was crowded and polluted. Restless drivers honked and cut in front of one another, trying to hack seconds off their commute. Heading north on rue Saint Denis, he turned left into Jimmy's street with its neat quad defining the quaint French neighborhood.

A grassed area surrounded a central fountain, and all along the road squaring the quad, tightly packed Victorian triplexes stood neck to neck: beige, blue, silver. Faint scents from nearby bakeries and bistros lingered in the air. Old-fashioned lanterns dotted the pavements, casting a glow on the ornately carved entrances.

Gray parked in front of the ground-floor apartment with the bright red door. Taking the large stone steps, he nodded at the uniformed officer standing outside and entered the high-ceilinged foyer.

The SOCO's in the living room collected evidence, including a retro-style phone covered in blood. One of them waved to Gray as he entered. Here, too, the stench of feces and blood permeated the air, along with Jimmy's imagined lingering presence.

Gray had expected to see blood but not the play of contrasts before him. Immaculate white walls, books arranged on shelves in order of ascending height, and a bare and pristine kitchen gave the unit the sterility of a surgical suite. And in the center, blood and brown liquid soaked the rug and sofa, crimson on white. Only a hanging picture of Jimmy and his mom, placed next to a standing houseplant, brought any warmth to the room. In it, Evelyn smiled broadly, standing before a clear, blue beach and holding a possessive arm around a tight-lipped but grinning Jimmy. They looked to be on vacation since in the backdrop there was a clear, blue beach. Neither would ever go there again.

"Hardly a speck of dust in the place," a SOCO said to Gray. "Makes our job easier."

"Get any prints you can. Check them with Jimmy's and the ones we collected at the startup."

The SOCO nodded and returned to work.

A pulse throbbed in Gray's temple, and he consciously faced his failure. Evelyn Cane had lost her son. Jimmy had lost his life. Gray let it pass through him like a ghost. Failure tasted like acid. He'd played by the book so far, respecting Gabi's privacy, respecting the privacy of Holly's medical records, and look where it had gotten him. He should have forced Holly to speak sooner.

All that was about to change.

His Hand In the Storm

The startup sat at the center of things, and one woman ran the startup.

Gray held open his claw hand and clenched his fist.

He would make her talk. No matter how rotten she felt.

CHAPTER 15

April 3, 9 am

GRAY CLIMBED UP the stairs leading to HealSo's office.

He'd just left Étienne at the hospital, relieved the boy was doing so well. Aside from some bruises and cuts, he was fine. Better than fine. Étienne looked more relaxed in the regular hospital than at the Institute. He even smiled upon learning that Director Leblanc was considering transferring him out of the Institute and into the regular psychiatric ward. Étienne hadn't fought back during Carl's attack, and Gray had made certain Leblanc knew it. He'd spent an hour on the phone with the man this morning. Hopefully, it would do the boy some good, but just in case, Gray had left Étienne with an alarm. A way to make contact in the event of an emergency.

Gray reached the fifth floor. He couldn't believe it. Holly had already returned to work at the startup. Was the woman made of steel?

She had checked out of the hospital against medical advice early this morning. Apparently, the impending financial deal took precedence over her health.

The administrative assistant buzzed Gray in through the startup's front door and into the foyer. Diagonal slashes of police tape sealed off the server room to the right of the long and narrow corridor until further notice, despite Simon's ongoing protestations. In fact, the more the founder whined, the longer Gray planned on keeping him out of that room.

At the end of the corridor, the space opened up to the hustle and bustle of the startup, the open industrial space so typical of trendy startups – all glass, chrome, and cement. Five people stood together to the right for their morning stand-up meeting. Others hunched over their workstations wearing headphones. Wafts of coffee and buttery croissants called out from the distant kitchen.

Holly's office sat in the corner straight ahead. Despite the rustling behind the door, she didn't respond to his knocking. Turning the knob, he peered inside.

Her fruity perfume hit him at the threshold. She wore far too much, as though it were a talisman. Through the glass windows covering the opposite wall, a plane could be seen slicing across the sky.

Holly's head was cradled in her hands over the desk. She looked up. "Oh God, what do you want?"

"May I come in?"

"No. I'm not feeling well."

Stepping inside, he closed the door and crossed his arms across his chest. "I want to know who attacked you."

Shutting her eyes tight, Holly exhaled. Her bruises still looked fresh and blue. "I told you; it was too dark. Why won't you leave me alone?"

"You're lying."

She pounded the desk. An empty coffee cup fell to the floor and broke in pieces. "I am not lying. Now get out before I file a formal complaint."

Gray took a chair opposite her. Leaning back, he crossed one leg over the other.

"Did you hear me?" she said. "Unless you're here to arrest me, I want you to leave. I know my rights. You can't stay here and interrogate me against my will or without my attorney." Cursing, she stood, picked up her phone, and began dialing.

"Jimmy's dead," Gray said.

Holly froze with one finger poised over the numbers. Her lids lowered, the shutters came down. "I heard."

"Jimmy sent a letter to his mom, outlining a cover-up at HealSo which he claimed you knew about. Someone died because of HealSo's faulty code, didn't they? And Norman covered it up."

Holly stiffened; a vein on her temple pulsed. Slowly, she lowered herself back into her chair and hung up the phone with a gentle click. Her quiet, almost disembodied voice resounded in the sparsely furnished room. "Where is this alleged letter?"

He didn't reply; the moment stretched.

"I see. Evelyn hasn't given it to you and isn't planning to when it arrives; I think you know that, and that's why you're here harassing me. She won't want her son's name blackened." A plucked eyebrow arched. The hard, jutting angles of her face seemed sharper alongside the bruises, even menacing if he used his imagination. "You have nothing, Chief Inspector. Nothing."

Gray held her eyes. In a few days, all traces of the attack would vanish from her face. Her expression hovered dangerously close to smugness, a reaction which would evaporate the second he told her what he knew – the two secrets she'd chosen to keep hidden from the outside world. But knowledge of one inexorably led to knowledge of the other. Both facts were married together; he knew it, and so did she.

Her red nails grazed the lump on her forehead, and she winced, making something inside him waver. Compassion? Understanding? These were luxuries he couldn't afford with a ferocious killer loose, bent on stripping faces and hanging victims from trees.

Holly linked her hands behind her head. She raised her false lashes. "Jimmy's death is regrettable. We took him on after graduation, gave him a coveted position, and look how he thanked us. By accusing HealSo of wrongdoing."

He opened his mouth and closed it. Of all the things she could have said....

Jimmy's pale and limp body sprang to mind. The agonizing cries heard by his mom, her limp body falling to the floor at his bedside.

Any reticence within Gray died a quick death. It was Holly's company, her people – yet she chose to aid the killer and protect her bloody acquisition.

She watched him expectantly, no doubt measuring his strength, always the ruthless negotiator reading the opponent's weakness. Each second he hesitated, she grew stronger, so he dived in.

"Does anyone at HealSo know about the charges of fraud filed against you?"

Silence.

Whatever she'd expected, it wasn't this.

Cat-like eyes bored into his. "Are you blackmailing me?" She rose, a clenched fist coming up into the air. He half expected it to make contact with his face. "Do you want money?" she said.

"Please sit down."

She repeated the question.

"I have enough money. I'm interested in the truth. In catching a murderer and saving your staff."

"By using coercion? Nice. I could have your badge for this."

Gray kept his voice even. "Coercion? I'm an investigating officer interrogating a suspect. I have reason to believe your startup acted unethically, and now I find out the CEO has an outstanding charge of fraud she never faced. How is that coercion? Don't paint me with your tainted brush. Nothing you say is off the record, and I recommend you choose your words carefully."

Holly fell back into her chair; the air seemed to go out of her. "You can't get away with this."

"We both know you have a legal obligation to your investors. You lied to them. Will anyone buy HealSo if your secret gets out?"

"But–"

"This fraud charge," Gray said. "will expose your real identity."

"You want to expose me?"

"I want an honest account of PAS, past problems, and reasons why someone should kill your medical advisor. That's all. I need that information to catch a murderer."

He waited a full minute for her to reply. She leaned her face in her hands, but she wouldn't want pity. Her eyes asked for something else.

"The other thing stays out of your official report?"

"You know I can't promise that, as much as I want to."

Holly licked her lips, and breathed heavily. She moved to the window, her back to him, feet planted widely apart, giving him space from her strong scent. Another jet silently streamed through the sky ahead.

"Who attacked you?" Gray asked.

"I didn't see. It was too dark."

"Tell me about PAS, Norman, and Jimmy."

No answer. He didn't want to push too hard, for fear she might clam up.

"So many years of pain, of suffering." She turned to face him, her expression soft. "I can't let them be for nothing. I can't let Melanie down after all we've been through." A single tear slid down her cheek. He resisted the urge to wipe it from her face. Sometimes Gray hated his job. He hated the things he must do.

"You win, Chief Inspector."

Holly moved forward and slumped into her chair. All the blood drained from her face, so that the mottled bruises made her look inhuman. "Jimmy warned us. We didn't listen. Then later he feared getting caught."

"Getting caught for what?"

"The early version of PAS had a flaw. No big deal; programs often have flaws. We expect them."

"I want specifics."

"Do you? Of course, you do. Your type always does."

"Ms. Bradley —"

"Everything comes easy to men like you. Life falls at your feet, and you think you rule the rest of us, but you don't."

"This isn't about me."

"It is. It's about all of you."

"Tell me what Jimmy feared, or all bets are off."

She slammed the table. "Simon! Simon ruined the code in one of his fucking flashes of genius, like the one he had when he first came up with PAS, which led to nothing because so many of his flashes lead to nothing."

She breathed heavily. He worried she might pass out.

"Simon altered Jimmy's program? And that led to what?"

"What do you think?" Holly leaned in close. He could smell the coffee on her breath. "Jimmy wanted to fix it before the clinical trials, but Norman wouldn't risk the Hospital Board changing their mind about allowing us to do trials in the ID ward. We went ahead, but... but..."

"Someone died. Who?"

She looked away. "I don't know. I didn't ask."

"You didn't ask?" She turned away. "How could you not ask?"

Any sympathy he felt for her was immediately squashed.

"It haunted Jimmy," she said. "He bounced between guilt and terror, and no matter what I tried, he grew more and more frantic, like some stupid child. Someone had to be the adult." Her eyes whiplashed back to his as if reading his mind; her voice rose. "Only one person died, for God's sake. Out of hundreds. You think nobody died when they developed the measles vaccine? When they eradicated smallpox? How many lives will PAS save in the future?"

"PAS might kill again."

"No, Jimmy fixed it. The system underwent multiple trials afterward. There's no danger to anyone now. Precision medicine has revolutionized health care by tailoring treatments to the genetics of every individual. How can you jeopardize that for one mistake?"

"Which you covered up." But Gray felt uncertainty yank at his gut. Was he endangering countless future lives, maligning a life-saving technology to solve one case because he himself couldn't face failure?

How many killers did he need to lock behind bars before he'd done enough? And did the execution of professional duty exonerate him from all consequences? Nothing could bring his former life back. Nothing could make him whole again.

Taking a deep breath, he counted to four. Holly's eyes narrowed a fraction. She made deals for a living, deals worth hundreds of millions of dollars, and she was wheeling and dealing at this very minute.

"The code," he said. "Did you destroy the evidence?"

Her eyes widened. A pause. "Jimmy destroyed it."

"No, he didn't, did he? Why destroy his only proof of Simon's meddling? And I bet neither you nor Norman had the technical expertise to do it."

"Can't you let all this go?" she said. "I don't... I don't want to suffer, any more."

Holly turned her head and looked out the window. "Norman forgot his phone in my office the day before. When I saw the report of the faceless body on the beach... and Simon told me Norman was missing... I tried to buy some time by dialing my number from Norman's phone."

"To save your startup from scandal, to preserve the deal."

Her eyes flared. "To protect the acquisition. That's my fiduciary responsibility."

"Your fiduciary responsibility doesn't involve illegal acts – such as cleaning up blood from the server room or sabotaging a murder investigation."

With proof of thefaulty code, Judge Rodeau would finally give permission to examine the hospital charts of patients treated by PAS. Gray could finally get what he'd wanted all along – what his instincts had screamed would solve the case.

He stood; his voice was firm. "I want the faulty version of that program in my hands today. You're going to give it to me."

Holly searched his eyes. "I wonder if your department understands you. I do, even if they don't."

"You understand wealth and success, Ms. Bradley. I'm going to protect your team, even if you won't. I'm going to make damn sure there isn't another Jimmy. And you'll give me what I need – whether you like it or not."

CHAPTER 16

April 3, 10 am

HE COULDN'T WAIT to get his hands on those hospital records. The answer lay somewhere in the patient files, charts, trials... Gray could feel it in his gut, in his bones. And after Holly's guilty confession, getting access to the charts was a given.

Snow blew across the road on the route back to his office. The car's upper vents sent short, rapid bursts of hot air onto his face, and the lower ones didn't work. His body effectively inhabited two different climate zones, leaving his cheeks burning and his toes numb.

A navy Chevy currently followed him on the freeway, keeping its distance two cars back while swerving and sliding with stealth and skill. He recognized the maneuver from his training days as an undercover officer.

Gray managed to lose the tail, pulled off route 720, and turned north on rue Saint Urbain. He pulled into the SPVM lot and parked, scanning the area around him, but nothing moved as he stepped out of the car. No one drove past.

At his office, he saw the green folder on his desk

Jimmy's autopsy results.

Gray stared at it, hesitant to open the plastic cover.

Sliding the file under one arm, he headed towards the pathology department, preferring to discuss the findings with Seymour in person.

The lab smelled like a butcher's shop and evoked half-forgotten memories of high school dissection classes. Shelves, filled with multi-colored jars containing lumpy tissues soaked in formaldehyde, lined one wall. He purposely didn't look at them too closely. A computer sat on a high bench in the corner.

One small window provided the only natural light, accompanying the depressing gloom of the overhead fluorescent bulbs. Everything possessed a faint blue hue, including Seymour's animated face. He looked like the walking dead, cutting up the other dead.

Gray clutched the green file to his chest, still unable to open it, and his hesitation wasn't lost on the doctor who looked up, narrowed his eyes, and continued to wipe an examination table with a wet sponge. Pink liquid streamed down the stainless steel table before circling into a drain. Going where, Gray wondered? He couldn't get his eyes off that tell-tale pink; shallow breaths couldn't keep out that metallic smell.

"That report makes you want to punch someone in the face, doesn't it?" Seymour said. His caterpillar eyebrows went up and down. "Or maybe hook them up to a Madras curry IV for fun."

"Please, just tell me what's in the report."

"I personally would choose someone who hates Indian food and only eats butter chicken."

"Doctor –"

"No, on second thought, I'd choose the imbecile who translated the sign over the emergency stop lever on the metro train from French to English: 'Use forbidden without valid reason.' I mean, for God's sake."

Gray felt another headache coming on. Seymour's next move –running a gloved hand through his hair – didn't improve matters. "I suppose one must have that sense of humor to spend all day in this place. If only to live through that disgusting smell."

After taking a few steadying breaths, he noticed the other man's crooked smile. The doctor had something hidden up his sleeve.

"You may as well just spit it out," Gray said.

"Arsenic."

"I've heard of the stuff. What about it?"

"Arsenic poisoning, Chief Inspector. Not acid, but arsenic. Wake up and smell the coffee."

What? In the background, Seymour continued to speak. Moving towards the window, Gray could just make out the gesticulating gloved hands in his peripheral vision, looking like severed, rubber appendages floating in the air. He finally keyed into the jumbled words. "What did you say?"

"I said, poor kid was ripped open from the inside, which only makes your job harder. Two victims, dead from two separate modus operandi." Seymour put down the sponge and snapped off his gloves. Gray half expected them to whip through the air and slap him in the face. "We analyzed the discarded coffee grounds in Jimmy's apartment. And the vomit and stomach contents. They contained a very concentrated form of arsenic."

His heart beat fast. He knew he couldn't keep the smug expression off his face. "How concentrated?"

"Pharmacologically engineered. Not the usual stuff in rat poison. Couldn't have been easy to get, and with all the regulations controlling poisons in the mass market, your killer had special connections to procure the stuff."

The smell of bodies and flesh was thick and wet in the air. No wonder the doctor always stank. Gray moved to the small window.

Outside, a blue and gray hue blanketed the street, and snow swirled around the road coating cars and people. He could see their breaths in the freezing cold. The breaths of living people, not corpses sliced and jarred up as decoration.

"So –" Seymour jumped onto the stool and faced his computer. "– one killer or two? What do you think?"

Gabi's police records came to mind. "How long would the arsenic take to work?"

"An hour or so. Not right away like with acid. The murderer couldn't predict the victim would exsanguinate either, since acute arsenic poisoning normally takes hours or days to act. Normally, the patient dies of cardiovascular insufficiency."

Gray felt annoyed. "Why the hell do these things always have to be so medically complicated? Are you saying Jimmy could have suffered a heart attack, like Norman?"

Seymour shook his head while punching the computer keys and cross-referencing what he found in a file.

"Doctor, will you spare me a minute more of your precious time?"

Seymour swirled around. "Don't get your knickers in a knot. Such a large amount of arsenic is unpredictable. I'll say one thing – no amount of resuscitation could have saved the poor kid." He removed his glasses, bringing one of the tips to his mouth. The nose pads left indents in his skin. "Not an easy way to go either, Gray. Your killer likes an agonizing, grotesque end. I don't want to think what the next victim will suffer."

"There won't be a next victim."

Neither man spoke until Gray said, "Who'd have access to this type of arsenic? Someone with a knowledge of biochemistry?" Simon had a degree in biochemistry. Pretty well everyone at the startup had enough education to be the culprit.

"Some knowledge, for sure. The hard part is getting the stuff so concentrated. And you know, the coffee grounds could have been laced at any time. Your alibis are useless."

"Thank you. I'm beginning to realize that for myself."

"We've checked prints on the coffee packet," the doctor continued. "Only Jimmy and one other person's. They don't match anyone we've printed at the startup. He bought it from somewhere. They probably belong to whoever sold him the coffee."

"I have an idea about that. Vivienne will get you several more prints to compare." If the coffee was bought at Café Doigt, and that was easy to check, the prints would be Kate's. If instead an unknown person had given Jimmy that packet of poisoned coffee – well, Gray had some thoughts brewing in that direction as well. "Someone may have visited Jimmy at his apartment," he added. "Perhaps that very day."

"Who?"

"That has yet to be determined."

"But you know, don't you –" Seymour continued to speak, but Gray's mind was a long way away until the doctor said something about the faceless corpse –

"What?" Gray asked.

"His tissues were frozen before death."

The resulting explanation about renal cell dysfunction and decreased levels of vasopressin which lead to the production of a large volume of dilute urine... diuresis plus fluid leakage into the interstitial tissues causing hypovolemia made Gray want to slam Seymour over the head. But what was the use? Best to let the doctor have his moment. It boiled down to one thing: Norman was exposed to the cold before he died. The tissues hadn't simply frozen afterward.

Returning to his office, he sat behind his desk and watched the red and yellow hues of sky bleeding into one another like watercolors in a child's painting.

His finger stabbed the numbers on his phone. Vivienne answered after one ring.

"I can't find anything on Holly from over a year ago," she said. "She joined the startup, but before that, zilch. I'm looking deeper into records."

Gray already had the answer, but he'd wait to discuss it with Vivienne. Best to keep her out of it for now. His second-in-command had her own problems to deal with.

"I want Gabi's prints," he said, rising. "Go by her house and process those large hands of hers. They're stronger and more capable of murder than either yours or mine. Match them against what SOCO's found in all the crime scenes." Pulling on his jacket, he cradled the phone on his ear. "Seymour also needs prints from everyone in the café, including Kate. Two prints were found on the coffee packet – Jimmy's and another person's."

"You think Gabi's prints are on that packet? You think she poisoned the coffee?"

"I think it's dangerous to speculate," Gray said, all the while believing he knew whose prints they'd find.

CHAPTER 17

April 3, 10 am

THEY WOULD BOTH be late for work this morning. She ran from the pain caused by their relationship. This frantic coupling only bought her a detached hour hinting at intimacies of the past. Nothing more.

Saleem's arms pressed around and into Vivienne's ribs as he climaxed over her. She lay motionless, still and wet but breathing heavily. The surrounding world was a blur, secondary to this primal need to be with him, almost to merge into one and keep what she could close to her heart before it slipped away. Which she couldn't. No matter how hard she tried. But that frantic grip could be felt as a vice within her chest. The thought of being alone again was abhorrent to her, but she'd been happy as a singleton before and could reproduce that now.

Loneliness didn't scare her. She was terrified by something far worse: seeing Saleem with other women; kissing them;

being happy without her. Just thinking about it turned her blood blue, her vision red. No matter what feminism said, what Vivienne's need for fairness and independence said, she'd be the one left alone. It was still very much a man's world. An unfair world.

That they could come together physically, while they mentally occupied opposite sides of the room, amazed her. At least it was some sort of connection other than mutually-inflicted pain. Sex made her forget; she needed to forget.

"God, you're great," she murmured, squirming under him. Their bed felt like a cocoon.

He stiffened over her and rolled onto his back. The air thickened with unresolved grievances, promises which couldn't be kept without injury to one party or the other. Why the hell did marriage have to be this way, anyway? Why couldn't it be simple?

He looked stern, unreachable. The mood evaporated before he spoke. He was usually the one to bring things up. "Any developments in the case?"

"Huh?" It took Vivienne a minute to understand the question. Her heart still beat fast; the sheen on her skin suddenly cooled, making her circle her arms around her naked breasts.

"Norman's murder," Saleem said. "Who's the main suspect?"

At least, he wasn't bringing up the other thing. The case, she could safely discuss. Vivienne turned to her side and licked her lips. She let out a gentle sigh before speaking.

"So far, three of our suspects have managed to get themselves either hit on the head or killed. There won't be anyone left to charge soon." An embarrassing squeak escaped from her — the result of arduous lovemaking "Sorry," she said.

"Gray always has a favorite by now," he persisted. "You're days into the investigation."

"He thinks he has identified the victim – I told you about Norman and the hospital – but the killer remains a mystery."

"No witnesses?"

Vivienne sat up, leaning her back against the headboard and pulled the gold satin sheet over her body.

"There was this boy, at the psychiatric unit next to your hospital," she said. "He saw the murderer strung up the body."

"And?"

"And nothing. The killer wore a sack over his head, and the boy's delusional. Not to mention incarcerated for murder himself." She felt pensive now, the sexual high evaporating by the second. Saleem's face didn't soften.

"Étienne's such a small thing." she continued. "Only twelve. Killed a fifteen-year-old."

"Why did he do it?"

"I don't know. He probably couldn't defend his actions, so they drugged him. The more confused he got, the more the psychiatrists upped the medication until he finally snapped. You know how those places are. You can guess the rest."

Saleem slumped back on the bed but said nothing.

Vivienne turned on her side to face him. "I feel sorry for the kid. So does Gray. He's always had a soft spot for children, even troubled ones. He's worried the killer might come back if the boy remembers something."

"The boy's at the Institute?" Saleem asked.

"No. One of the other inmates attacked him. He's at Westborough recovering, poor thing. He shouldn't be at the Psychiatric Institute in the first place. He's too young. That's our garbage health care system for you."

Saleem went quiet. She couldn't hear his breath. The grandfather clock chimed six am on the floor below.

"Étienne," he repeated.

The topic of children was a sore spot between them. She wanted to say what was on her mind. It always amazed her how close a married couple could be, and still remain worlds apart. The abyss only grew wider with each passing year since more was invested, more was at stake. Topics that were hard to discuss with a boyfriend were impossible to discuss with a husband.

"Did you see your doctor?" he asked.

Vivienne stiffened. Her nostrils flared. So, it was the same old thing after all. The same old attack. Interest in her work had merely been a preliminary for this more uncomfortable topic.

"I went in to get my birth control pills, and I got them," she replied. "Is that what you're asking?"

"Vivienne—"

"Don't start. Not again."

"Pills have complications."

"So does pregnancy. Honestly, this is an obsession with you." Her voice rose and bounced against the walls. "Why do you want to have a kid so desperately? We agreed when we met – you agreed – that we never would. Our sex lives, my career, how we feel about each other – you know it would all change. And I can't live with that."

"You're not going to lose me, or the child," Saleem said. "The world isn't as dangerous a place as you think. You see violence everywhere, it's a side effect of your job. Marriage with a family is not a dangerous battleground. Each new murder, each investigation brings a stench into this house." He inhaled deeply, held her eyes. "We've been together a decade. I want a kid. I need to have one."

"Why?" she demanded. "What's changed?"

Saleem jumped out of bed. The muscles in his back rippled in turn. He pulled on his boxers and yanked up his pants.

"A lot of women would gladly have a family with me, but not you, Vivienne. Not you. What makes you so damn special?"

They exchanged a look. Too much honesty was dangerous. Even before he spoke, she knew the words would be strong, the ultimatum unfair.

"I want to know if you're in or out," he said.

"What? You're threatening me?"

"I'm not threatening you."

"That's exactly what you're doing," she said. She kicked her feet against the sheets, trying to untangle herself, but the silk twisted and turned, tying her legs. "Who's going to take care of a baby? Huh?"

"Both of us, together, and we'll hire help. Lots of women doctors around me have nannies."

"I'm not a bloody doctor, okay? I'm a cop. You're at the hospital sixty hours a week. My hours are often worse. Someone has to be home with a child. What do you think, that you married some nutritionist or some glorified hospital secretary that calls herself an administrator while spewing out regulations to medical students from a manual? I'm also not one of those drooling nurses you pass in the hallways."

"Vivienne–"

"I have a real career. And I'm not going to throw it away. There's no job sharing among detectives unless I want to settle for a desk job, which you know I could never do."

He yanked on his shirt, hands fumbling and trembling trying to do up the buttons. "Other women do it. They manage. It's what women were created for after all – to have children – not to chase down murderers and avenge faceless corpses."

Vivienne finally tore the bedding from her legs and stood beside the bed. "I'm not other women."

"You bet you aren't." He sighed, seemingly regretting his choice of words. "We could try. How do we know if a baby is possible? I just need to try."

Her face burned, her breath caught in her chest. Half-digested food from late last night came up into her mouth. Jumping across the room, she reached for her pantyhose, tearing them as she pulled them over one leg. The rip reached her thigh.

Vivienne teetered between hell and panic. He'd brought this topic up too many times, and each time she'd suffered through it, tried to reason with him. Too much had been pushed down. Too much hidden and endured alone. The burning spread from her face to her eyes. Tears rolled down her cheeks. She threw the torn hose to the ground.

"Oh, it's possible! Believe me, I know!" Vivienne screamed. "Does that fact ever leave my mind, do you think?"

Saleem grabbed her by the shoulders. "What are you talking about?"

"Do you know the self-hatred I've suffered these last two years? It's hard, painful. And physically painful too – not like they said. You expect the bleeding. They give you this form to fill out, and then you wait in an impersonal line full of women in hospital gowns, wait for your turn like you're cattle getting branded and marked forever. They don't talk about the emptiness you feel afterward. Nobody tells you about that. You expect relief, but instead, you get a one-way ticket to a desert. A barren, horrible desert. And you walk it alone."

"What are you talking about? You –"

Saleem fell onto the edge of the bed. His Adam's apple bobbed up and down.

She kneeled before him on the hardwood floor and looked into his eyes, a sledgehammer pounding inside her chest. This was it. It all came down to this.

The gold flecks in his eyes filled.

"Without discussing it with me?" he whispered.

Her answer was gentler, more hesitant.

"Yes."

"A boy or a girl?"

"A girl."

Disbelief flooded his face. A tear streamed down his cheek. Then, his eyes hardened.

How was he ever going to forgive her? But maybe forgiveness wasn't the only issue. How could he ever trust her again, or live with what she'd done?

They were mere inches apart, and she could feel his warm breath on her cheeks. Vivienne looked at him until he reluctantly met her eyes, searching for something she wasn't sure he could give.

"Am I going to walk the desert alone forever, Saleem?

CHAPTER 18

April 3, 1 pm

LIFE MADE MONSTERS of us all.

Gabi's background check had uncovered something surprising. It might not directly tie into the investigation, but it gave Gray insight into her character, and understanding his suspects helped him to predict their actions and reactions.

As he approached her street, the weight of the knowledge he carried felt like a brick in his stomach. Sometime during the morning, his ear bandage had fallen off, and the wound felt cold and unprotected, with its five nylon sutures tugging and pulling painfully whenever he spoke or smiled or moved his head.

Would he use what he knew against her? Could he? And if not, what did that say about him as a policeman? That he would allow another attack to occur on the heels of the last, that he'd let another unsuspecting startup employee to be bludgeoned, hung, burned with acid?

Gray ran a hand over his face. He may thrive on the challenge of a case, but what sort of man could make her face this? Did righting the greatest wrong of all – murder – justify his every action?

Gabi's street was gloomier than the last time he'd visited. He parked a block away and walked to her house. The brisk wind stung his eyes, inciting wetness and blurring the moving images of a boy and girl playing Cowboys and Indians on the sidewalk as he passed. The little girl gave Gray a cold look; he smiled back.

No one answered his ring or his knock, and Gray resigned himself to waiting, seated on the top cement step before the wooden door. Fallen petals from the cherry tree covered the ground. A wind picked up and twirled them with leaves and small stems across the short, damp lawn. He breathed in, able to detect the reassuring scents of spring, which would soon be contaminated by the dregs of his words and her resentment at hearing them.

Ten minutes later, she turned the corner carrying two shopping bags, noticed him, and picked up her pace. She didn't nod or acknowledge his presence, silently pushing past him and unlocking the front door.

Inside, she dropped the bags on the now clean Persian. They took the same seats as last time.

"How are you feeling?" he asked.

Her eyes blazed with a glare designed to intimidate lesser men, but he didn't flinch.

"Why have you come?"

"You identified the body as not belonging to your husband."

"That man was not Norman. You think I don't know what my husband looks like? Do you honestly claim to have a better conjugal knowledge of his body than I do?"

Her life experiences were rooted in hardship, like his, but their approaches could not be more different. "You're lying," he said. "And protecting a killer."

Her eyes bored into his. "I will not be pushed around by anyone, anymore."

"No one's trying... "

"Not even you," she said. "Not even you."

Gray moved to the window, his back to Gabi. The children still played across the street, the boy firing an imaginary pistol with one eye closed and a face focused in concentration, and his sister keeling over while clutching her blotchy red pullover. Even after she fell, the brother continued to shoot.

"We both know you're lying about your husband's body."

"Prove it, mon cheri."

A difficult decision had to be made, and he made it. But was there any doubt he would? Even as he hated to do it, he turned towards her and spoke.

"After your identification, I looked into police records, which in your case go back a long way. In the bowels of the SPVM, a two-page report documents the mysterious death of your neighbor in St-Henri, John Burrows. He was the father of your childhood friend. The police interviewed you at the age of ten, alongside his daughter."

"So what?" Her lower lip quivered. A bad taste came up into his mouth. He didn't want to continue, but she'd left him no choice. Murder tainted everyone in its wake. Including him.

"The daughter claimed her father abused her. She also said you spent a great deal of time at her house... with her father."

Gabi began to shake, first her hands, then her entire body. His instincts hadn't been off. She'd been involved, either directly or indirectly, in the incident. And here finally was the bombshell. "John Burrows died the day after your younger sister passed away," Gray said.

Electricity charged between them. Her eyes flashed a bottomless pit of rage, but instead of speaking, she sprung up with the suppleness of a schoolgirl and fled the room.

***

Gabi took her time in the kitchen. She didn't rush.

She ground the fresh French beans, frothed the milk, choose her favorite cups – again, the ones with small lavender flowers over a sturdy white porcelain – and placed it all on a gleaming silver tray. Beside each cup, she laid a small biscotti on the saucer. That was a nice touch, she decided. Yes, a nice touch.

Carrying the tray, her leaden feet seemed to stick to the hardwood with each step. Each click of her heels sounded abnormally loud, as if broadcast over a loudspeaker or sounding through a tiled tunnel.

He didn't know, couldn't know the truth. It was all a bluff, and anyway, she'd been a child at the time. What could he possibly do about it now?

But the weight of the past lay heavy upon her heart. Forty years hadn't lessened its vile grip. It only made her yearn to confide, to share untold horrors and seek absolution, not for John Burrows' death, but for the inexorable chain of events that had preceded it. And it was a child's yearning for comfort she felt, not a woman's.

In her living room ahead sat a magnetic man with an irresistible pull. She'd never met anyone so self-contained, so calm. At least that's how she'd seen him before today, before he'd ruthlessly decided to bring up the horrid past.

Even that fact didn't lessen her need to confide, to give in to those meditative green eyes, looking so much like polished emeralds. Something had left him transcendent of ordinary human turmoil and uncertainties, but what? Something had made him what he was.

She entered the salon, the aroma of the coffee intoxicating, soothing. Gray accepted his cup gracefully, almost enthusiastically.

"I'm sorry," he said.

Sorry? Even if Gabi could no longer be charged formally for murder, she couldn't escape her past. Everything she'd built – her home, reputation, status in society – would dissolve with one spoken slur. She'd become a pariah to the neighbors. The local country club would ask her to resign her membership. A messy past was about as pardonable in her circles as poverty – or weakness.

The Inspector sat stock still. How old was he, maybe forty? Such focused concentration must come in handy in his job, and absurdly, she found herself imagining him as a lover, imagining that scarred hand with the long fingers caressing her stomach, in between her thighs.

Gabi shook her head and pulled herself out of it. "All of this," she gestured around the room, "is very different from my roots in St-Henri." She described the old apartment, reeking of fried food, dirty laundry, and mildew... her mother weeping after her dad died... how they'd been left penniless. Then, she talked about Chloe, only seven at the time, and Chloe's asthma attacks. Gabi had never spoken of her sister to anyone, not even to her two husbands.

"Chloe's breathing echoed through the place," Gabi said, describing that last day. Her sister's blue lips and translucent skin flashed through her mind. "She sat in the living room wheezing – a delicate doll who couldn't breathe.

He–lp... Gabi..

Where is it? Where is that damn puffer?

Not in the stack of old magazines. Maybe in Mom's purse... tampons... two worn down lipsticks, a travel-sized vodka bottle, several cards with telephone numbers on the backs, a dusty old hair-covered comb...

Ga–bi...

Found it. In the left-hand pocket of Mom's coat.

Open your mouth, Chloe. Yes, one spray, two.

Now hold your breath. Yes, just like that. It should work soon. You'll be okay soon, I promise. And I never lie to you. Mom lies, and Dad used to; I never do.

But the sprays aren't working, and I don't understand why. Can't call 911 because the phone's disconnected. What do I do? God – what do I do?

"I tried to take her to get help," Gabi said to Gray. "I helped her with her coat, wrapped her scarf around her neck and took her hand. I had two bus tokens to get us to the nearest hospital. We stepped out of our apartment."

"What happened?" Gray asked.

Her friend's father had come out of the neighboring apartment.

I can't. We have to go. My sister can't breathe. Don't you understand? We have to go.

Chloe, wait for me inside. He won't let us go. You wait inside, and I'll be back really really soon, as soon as I can.... As soon as I can...

I'm back.

Chloe. Open your eyes. Why won't you open your eyes?
Chloe?
Baby?

"My mother was drunk and unconscious on the couch, and Chloe lay on the cracked parquet floor, huddled into a ball."

Gabi fell silent and stared ahead. Her mom was now rotting in a home for the aged. Gabi never went to see her.

The Inspector lowered his eyes and put down his cup. "I'm sorry."

And here lay the temptation, the need to share after so many hollow years of torment – years no amount of wealth could salve. She yearned to reveal that she kept her sister's red satin scarf tucked inside her bedside drawer. That she placed it over her face and breathed in and out on nights when she couldn't sleep.

Gray's kind intelligence threatened to seduce her into talking. Maybe, stripped of the power of secrecy, the daily remembrances would go away. Maybe, she and her sister could finally rest in peace.

Gabi lifted her cup; some of the coffee spilled on her hand. "There were other things."

"Your neighbor, John Burrows?"

"Yes." She took a sip. "He threatened to turn to Chloe if I didn't cooperate."

At once, she felt transported to that room, the smell and stink, ghost images of the moldy room with that shadeless single bulb at the center of the ceiling, always making her squint and leaving dark halos in her vision.

Gray's voice sounded far away, so gentle and reassuring. "Then your sister died. And you had nothing left to lose."

The bubble burst. He must be psychic to use those exact words. Someone with nothing left to lose – that's what she'd thought of the figure stalking her house. And look where that had led – to a plum-sized bruise on her forehead.

Gabi looked at Gray more closely: the chiseled good looks, the emerald eyes, not to mention that silky-smooth voice. Tall, dark, handsome – and lethal.

What the hell was she doing? A policeman sat before her. Nothing more. How stupid to have forgotten.

Gabi pressed her lips together, all discussion about her childhood neighbor at an end.

She didn't tell Gray about that last night all those years ago when she'd made her neighbor's tea afterward as she always did. The walls of the microwave, caked with burnt food, had smelled of the TV dinner on his mouth.

She didn't mention the box of rat poison by the garbage in his kitchen.

Didn't describe how she'd heated the water, milk, and tea bag in the microwave, taking care to add extra sugar, lots of it... to mask the taste.

She hadn't stayed to watch. Afterward, when the police had finished, her friend left with a social worker. Their eyes connected in the hallway – and Gabi knew she'd gotten away with it. After all, who would ever suspect a ten-year-old?

Most of all, Gabi didn't tell Gray the thing he most wanted to know.

Gray sliced through her reverie. "Your neighbor died of arsenic poisoning."

"So?" Gabi shrugged. "I was a kid. I don't remember the interview, and I never saw my friend again."

Gray stood up and paced the room. His head lowered, he stood by the window but didn't look out. After a minute, he turned and sat back down. "I'm not going to push you, or dig up old crimes."

"It feels like you're pushing me."

He ran a hand through his hair, leaving the perfect dark tresses disheveled. The urge to reach out and smooth the defiant strands coursed through her, and she forcibly kept her hands pinned to her sides.

"I can't let these killings go on, Gabi. Someone else could die. In my gut, I know someone will die. And Jimmy died of arsenic poisoning."

"You suspect my son of murder. I know you do. I have nothing more to say."

He didn't answer. He looked so worried, so harassed. Many a woman must have fallen for that immeasurable charm. Women without her wisdom and experience. Gabi had lost everything in her life, once. No way would that happen again.

She rested her chin on her hand and waited. He sighed and looked down at his feet. He'd dredged it all up for nothing, and it would cost him. As far as she was concerned, tall, dark, and handsome was on his own.

CHAPTER 19

April 4, 1 am

ÉTIENNE HOVERED AT the edge of sleep, hearing the Inspector's kind words from a distance. Call me, and I will come.

It must be the middle of the night. Noise in the room roused him, but he didn't want to open his eyes, the sounds becoming more distinct.

First, a squeak, maybe his door, and then a shuffle. Heavy drawn curtains to his left muffled the low howling of the wind.

He lay still, and even turning his head to look at the bedside clock felt dangerous, as though it would tempt imaginary ghosts to show their faces, open their mouth wide, and swallow him whole. Half-weighted by the dregs of slumber and painkillers, he stayed frozen, dreading the inevitable.

The Inspector's alarm sat in the drawer by the bed. The nurse had made Étienne take it off during his bath, and he'd forgotten to put it back on. He swallowed, careful no sound escaped his throat and cracked open his eyes.

A timid light shined from under the door to his right leading to the corridor. The rest of the room lay shrouded in darkness. Then a shadow traveled across the path, so fast it could be a phantom.

He stiffened under the cotton sheets. An ambulance siren sounded from outside, and he nearly swung around. Mon Dieu. Not again.

But was this his imagination? A nightmare fueled by his night at the river, or by Carl's attack? Or was it a delusion after all?

He whined and quickly clamped his lips tight. Mustn't let the ghost know he was awake. He must reach the Inspector's alarm – jump up, open the side drawer and press the button – if only he could get his muscles to work, if only he could get his heart to stop hammering.

A shadow to the left pounced on him and blocked the light. Dead hands with no nails, white and domed in plastic, shoved down his shoulders – not gray claws like before but smooth and alien.

The sack-covered head breathed down heavily. Étienne plunged towards the drawer, but the plastic hands grabbed him and pinned his arms. And the sack lowered, now inches from his face and smelling like damp cloth and rotting potatoes.

Étienne was breathing hard, and all his bruises hurt, especially his belly where Carl had kicked and kicked. And now the ghost would kick him. Why did this keep happening?

His whimpers gave way to soft moans and weeping. One of the plastic hands covered his mouth. His tummy was covered in bruises, and the gasping and shaking hurt so much, but he couldn't stop himself from sobbing into the cold rubber until it felt damp and hot. The ghost grip loosened a fraction before clamping down again.

Seconds ticked by, which turned into a minute. The eyes weren't visible in the dark, but he could imagine them – red, scary globes that watched, assessed, and Étienne prayed, mumbling and mimicking half-remembered words of the priest who sometimes came to the Institute.

'Je crois en Dieu, le Père tout-puissant, créateur du ciel et de la terre.... Donne-nous aujourd'hui notre pain quotidien... Pardonne-nous nos offenses comme nous pardonnons aussi r ceux qui nous ont offensés.'

The grip loosened. The ghost spoke. The interrogation began.

CHAPTER 20

April 4, 10 am

GABI STEPPED OUT of HealSo's board room. She had taken Norman's place on the Board for the two-hour discussion about the company's sale to Juva Pharma. The three investors came out wearing mixed expressions, not knowing what had hit them: Holly.

Holly had told the Board of the death caused by PAS and offered a life raft: an asset sale where Juva would buy the valuable intellectual property behind PAS from HealSo, and leave the empty shell of the company behind. No shares would change hands; no options would be vested. Gabi and the others would continue as the directors and owners of HealSo, without it being operational.

"Forever," Simon said, storming out of the room, glaring at Holly's departing back and turned to Gabi. "We'll be carrying its liabilities for the rest of our lives."

"But we're still selling the company. With hundreds of millions at stake, we'd be idiots to pass it up. The alternative is nothing. Nothing!"

Simon stood, feet wide apart, stroking that ridiculous beard. Always her troublesome little boy. "Remember," Gabi said, "the VPs at Juva have been selling this deal to their CEO nonstop for months. They have a lot invested in making it happen and won't want to walk."

He shook his head and strode to his office. Gabi followed.

Voices suddenly rose outside. Through the glass wall, Gabi saw the administrative assistant arguing with a woman who pushed her way through towards them. Gabi's heart lurched in her chest. A second later, Kate stormed in and faced Simon. "You killed him."

"What?" Simon said. "You can't just barge in here."

"Unless you want the whole office to hear what I've got to say, I suggest you shut the door."

Simon reassured his assistant. "It's okay. I'll speak to Miss Grant alone." The door closed, leaving the three of them in the room.

Fists planted on his desk, Kate leaned in to Simon. "Why did you do it?"

"How dare you?"

Gabi fought to speak, but the words caught in her throat. Whatever she said could make the situation worse. Whichever way she turned, a minefield awaited. If they knew what she'd done, all hell would break loose. But it wasn't her fault, was it? Some people asked for violence through their self-absorption and immaturity. Jimmy was one of those people.

"He told me," Kate said to Simon. "About everything that happened at HealSo, a secret you all forced him to keep. He said someone died. Is that why you killed him? So you could protect your stupid company? Jimmy was worth a hundred of you. A fucking thousand."

Simon shook his head. "No... no."

"Jimmy also told me about the blood in the server room. How your bloody CEO planned to clean it up, but you two killed him before he had the chance."

Simon yelled and slammed the desk. "I don't know what you're talking about."

"Don't lie to me. Jimmy told me."

"Told you what? Shut up."

"Simon," Gabi said.

"Stay out of this, mother."

Kate said, "You're a murderer. And a stupid one at that. Holly couldn't have done it from the hospital. And the police think Norman's dead, so who else is there?" The cords in her neck flexed. Gabi noticed the sharp edges of her teeth.

Gabi's heart lurched, slamming inside her chest. What was Simon going to say? God, please don't let him say anything stupid.

"My stepfather is not dead."

Kate said, "He's a faceless corpse on a slab. Deal with it."

"Get out of here before I call the police," Simon shouted. All eyes in the central office glared in their direction.

Gabi had to do something. Her son's future was at stake. She pushed between them. "Stop now, both of you."

"Maybe you poisoned Jimmy," Simon said to Kate. "Isn't it usually the partner in these cases? The police are going to come after you, not me."

"I'm onto you," Kate replied. She turned and left as precipitously as she'd arrived. Gabi watched her run out and let go the twisting in her gut long enough to see Simon slumped in his chair.

"Someone died because of HealSo?" He buried his head in his hands.

Hopefully, he wouldn't confront Holly. The trouble with knowledge was, you then had to figure out what to do with it. But fortunately Holly had left the office earlier without a word.

His computer beeped, and he pounded on the keys hard enough to make Gabi jump.

"There's another email from that reporter I told you about," he said. "The one who recognized Holly."

They read it together. It said the reporter had discovered something controversial about HealSo's CEO, and that Simon had one chance to tell his side of the story before it all went online.

Simon pushed his chair back. "What the hell is she talking about? If I had dirt on Holly, you think I wouldn't use it?" He looked accusingly at Gabi. "Do you know what she's talking about, Mom?"

"No, no. How could I?" What could this reporter know about Holly? Another cover-up? How many goddamned secrets did HealSo have anyway?

Simon burst out of the room towards Holly's office and returned a minute later saying she'd already left. Gabi didn't know what to say, or what to tell him.

The delay in responding to the reporter cost them any chance they had of tempering her exposé regarding Holly.

At four pm Eastern Time, the story hit the technology industry. Gabi and Simon read the headline together:

"CEO OF TECH STARTUP, HealSo – IS ALLEGED EMBEZZLER ROBERT BLACK, USING NEW IDENTITY"

Simon read the article out loud and slumped into his seat. Gabi's mouth hung open, and she couldn't believe her eyes. The citations were all there, the testimonials, the proof.

"This reporter has discovered from several sources that Holly Bradley, the Chief Executive Officer at HealSo – the hot Montréal based health-tech startup – is really Robert Black, indicted for two counts of fraud six years ago. He was accused of embezzling twelve million dollars from his then West Coast based company, Levguard, and because he vanished, was never tried for these charges. In the intervening years, Mr. Black underwent gender reassignment surgery and lives under a new name, Holly Bradley. The outstanding fraud charges against Ms. Bradley make any upcoming acquisition of her startup unlikely. Simon Everett, the company's founder, refused to comment...."

Gabi felt nauseous. The pounding in her head wouldn't stop. She'd done it all for nothing. Juva wouldn't acquire them now, not with an outstanding charge of embezzlement and evidence of a death under PAS.

Simon leaned his head in his hands. "I remember this reporter looking at Holly funny the other day. She asked if they'd met before, but Holly denied it. Mom! I hired a CEO who stole twelve million from her last company... and –"

Simon suddenly froze, his eyes distant, vacant. He went white as a sheet. Gabi flew to his side. "It's fine, darling. Everything will be okay." Her vulnerable little boy. Always a mess when things got rough.

"I... I." Now, he was whimpering. A grown man, whimpering. Still, she put her arms around him.

"You don't understand, Mom. I—I can't tell you." He brought his fist into his mouth and bit down hard.

"Simon!" Gabi grabbed his hand and smoothed out the tooth marks. "What's come over you?"

"Nothing," he said, straightening. "It's private. Very private." He shot out the door without looking back and then left the office.

***

Gray sat in Café Doigt at a window table and watched the people drift in and out while he sipped his aromatic latte. Hammering and drilling sounded from a few feet outside. In a sudden shift of weather typical of Montreal, the temperature had soared upwards by fifteen degrees.

The second the warm weather had arrived, everyone wanted to be outside – every second of tolerable weather in the city as precious as gold.

In the tradition of all Montreal establishments, Café Doigt was embracing spring. He watched the three workmen assembling an elaborate outdoor wooden patio, positioned directly in front of the café on the road. Most bistros and eateries in Montreal did the same. This particular wooden seating area contained room for a dozen tables, flower pots bordering all sides, and several abstract sculptures which resembled entwined bodies. Two other men unloaded large light fixtures and heating elements which would reside outdoors for the next few months.

Kate was going all out, but she had to compete with two similar patios being constructed just down the block. His wait was over when she finally entered the café, and he took a deep breath. He planned to get more out of this interrogation than his last with Kate.

Not noticing him, she headed through the open kitchen doors to the left, donned a pink apron and pulled out some baking trays from the oven.

He could observe her working from this angle, and the warm scent of chocolate chip muffins and scones drifted towards him across the café. Unexpectedly, she downed a muffin in three large bites and followed it with large swigs from a milk jug. White streaks ran down her mouth and were wiped away roughly by the back of her hand.

When she turned and saw him, her eyes hooded over; her features went blank. She threw off the apron and marched to his table, today smelling of flour, cinnamon, and something more primal. Not a speck of makeup marred her freshly scrubbed face.

"Why are you here? You think I killed Jimmy?" Her brittle voice rose enough to make several customers turn. The hammering outside seemed to match the throbbing vein in her temple. "His mom does. She called and yelled at me. I didn't have anything to do with Jimmy's death."

Instead of asking her to sit, he rose. Gray took off the metaphorical gloves. "You could have poisoned him. The special order coffee came from this café, and I'm sure your prints are on it."

"Of course they are. I sold him the coffee. Jimmy got a special order of cardamom-hazelnut flavored coffee no one else drank. When it came in, I gave it to him."

"You could have tampered with it, leaving Jimmy to die alone at home without a soul around to help. Leaving him to bleed."

"I didn't."

"Did you kill Norman as well? Strip off his face and hang him from that tree?"

"Shut up. Shut up." She put her palms to her ears. The cool woman of a few days ago had disintegrated, but he mustn't let up.

"Jimmy vomited blood. Did you know that?"

"No."

"Did he have any medical problems? Did he eat anything from here?"

A split second of hesitation as she looked up. "No."

"Who would want to harm him?"

"How do I know? I'm not his mother. I was just screwing him, all right?"

Gray had enough experience to recognize true grief when he saw it. Tears welled up in her eyes, but they weren't the tears of a lover. Customers walked past and stared before leaving the café.

She turned and hurried back to the counter. He followed, just as his phone rang.

Vivienne spoke quickly on the other end while he watched Kate wipe down the granite counter. She missed most of the stains. Mumbling a reply, he ended the call.

"We've had a complaint," he said. "You burst into Simon's office a little while ago, accusing him of killing Jimmy, and you threatened him."

"So the little weasel complained?"

"Yes, the 'little weasel' as you call him, complained. He wishes to file formal charges."

"For what? I didn't hit him. I wanted to, but I didn't. Jimmy's mom took it out on me, so I took it out on Simon. The idiot probably had nothing to do with the poisoning, but it's hard to be rational about your lover's murder."

But why accuse Simon in the first place, Gray thought? Of all the personnel at HealSo, why focus on the least intelligent, the most clueless? Simon's mother would have seemed a better candidate for Kate's rage. Unless Kate knew something Gray didn't, or else Jimmy had told her about the startup's tainted past, perhaps even about the faulty code.

"Why did you accuse anyone of murder?" Gray asked. "How do you know Jimmy didn't die of a bleeding ulcer?"

"He didn't bleed out from an ulcer."

Gray stilled. He opened his mouth and closed it.

A movement across the road caught his eye. Holly stood next to her car in front of HealSo's office building. She stared at her phone, and then looked around. Seconds later, she practically jumped into her car and whizzed away. The tires shrieked from across the road. Something had happened. And she was running.

That likely meant one thing. Her former identity had come to light, and with it her other secret since the two were inextricably linked.

"What are you looking at?" Kate said, turning to look out the window. She must have caught sight of Holly as well.

He mustn't lose his focus. Facing Kate, he said, "Where were you all of last night?"

She looked up, her expression now inscrutable. "Here, 'til five. After that, I went home. So, I have no alibi. What about you? Were you on your own, like me? If so, that's a shame." She motioned for another employee to take her place and headed to the kitchen.

Maybe she knew she didn't need an alibi. Anyone could have laced the coffee after it arrived at her café and before Jimmy drank it. The murder weapon had sat under her nose, at her easy disposal. Either Kate had killed Jimmy in a very sloppy way, or someone was trying to frame her. Or there was a third explanation.

His stomach growled. His eyes automatically fell to the delicacies in the display case, and the Peruvian beef sandwiches looked fresh. He narrowed his eyes, bought two, and left the café.

CHAPTER 21

April 4, 10:30 am

GRAY TOOK THE STAIRS to the basement after leaving Étienne's room. Every slam of his boot against the metal steps echoed his frustration through the hollow bowels of the stairwell. His hands fell to his sides, clenched into fists.

Why the hell couldn't the killer leave the boy alone – or was it killers? Gray didn't damn well know anymore, but if he couldn't get the boy out of the Institute, out of this hospital soon, who knew what awful thing might happen?

The stairwell steps reeked of strong antiseptic. Étienne's proud words rang in his ears – telling Gray how he'd single-handedly taken on the assailant and driven him away. He'd yelled and bitten the intruder's hand, causing the man to flee out of the room.

And it had been a man. The masked intruder had wanted information, information he should logically already possess.

So why risk entering the hospital at night, performing what must surely be an act of sheer desperation?

Gray's feet pounded down another flight, and then another. A sheen of sweat coated his back. He saw only two possibilities. The first involved only one masked intruder who feared the child would remember and reveal something he'd seen – something Gray hadn't yet uncovered. If so, why not just kill the witness? Why risk an interrogation?

The second possibility was more complicated and involved two assailants – with the second one wanting information about the first.

And he had two men dead by two separate modus operandi. What did it mean?

He reached the basement level, where Doug had spent many hours examining Norman's hospital charts after finally getting Judge Rodeau's permission.

Their assigned room lay somewhere in the morbid bowels of an older hospital wing left undemolished. The administration obviously didn't want the SPVM to get too comfortable and settle in.

He opened the fire door and left the stairwell, immediately wishing for the antiseptic instead of this heavy, musty odour. Dust irritated his nose, and he felt an urge to duck the low, domed ceilings while walking the narrow, poorly lit halls.

After two wrong turns, a plaque marked B13 hung on his right, and inside the open door Doug punching away at a computer. He looked up when Gray sneezed, giving a brisk nod.

The cubby hole of a room contained two computers, two old chairs, and an overhead light missing its shade – all completing the atmosphere of institutionalized gloom. The detective's gunmetal eyes followed him inside the room, thin lips pressed into a hard line.

"I see you're all ready for me," Gray said. He felt the hairs on the back of his neck stand erect. Doug's jacket hung behind his chair, and even from here, the bulge of the revolver was visible. Keeping one ear alert to any noises from the hall, he entered and lowered himself onto the chair opposite his detective, moving slowly in a mute showdown. He may need this man on the team, but he wouldn't let his guard down, even for a second.

The other detective clicked his tongue against the roof of his mouth. "Yup. Want me to start, Chief?"

Gray nodded solemnly.

"First of all, let me tell you that security on these hospital records sucks. Anyone with a password to enter the system and some IT knowledge could hack into it and change patient information – like their birth date, sex, even medical condition. Goes to show you, the government shouldn't be running healthcare."

"Noted," Gray said. "What else?"

"I've looked into the complaints filed against Norman with the medical board – both families say Norman put their kid into an experimental trial without permission. He forged the documentation."

"How did the parents find out about it?"

"The trial coordinators called them after their children died. Norman had shares in the biotechnology companies in the phase three trials, meaning he shouldn't have taken part in the testing in the first place. Conflict of interest, they call it. It gave him a peek at the drug's performance."

"An unethical peek." Gray leaned back in the creaky chair and crossed his arms. He hated a room without windows, especially a tiny one like this shared with a man he couldn't trust. Dust dried his throat, and he swallowed. "Norman would have to make certain his patients got the drug and not the placebo."

"I don't know how he managed that. Both those kids died, anyway."

"From the medication?"

"No. From their underlying diseases."

Gray rose and paced the small space. His heart raced, the regular pounding a sign that he was on the precipice of discovery. It was imperative to stay focused on the right clues and not get distracted by the others – such as this research angle, perhaps?

He spoke softly, despite his growing excitement. "What about PAS?"

Doug turned to the computer and punched the keys. "Forty-five deaths over the past year. Nine were directly under Norman, but he supervised the other cases too. It's gonna be tough to tell who died specifically because of PAS, and which ones we should focus on."

"We need to pare down the list." Something about the original scene of the crime nagged Gray, and he itched to put his finger on it. It hovered just out of reach, a single loose thread, elusive, unreachable – yet related to the original crime scene, the park, and its slides, swings, and frigid eastward current.

"What did the adult patients die of?" Gray asked.

"Two were post-op. One had..." Doug scanned his notes, "...pneumococcal pneumonia."

"And the other?"

"An eighty-year-old woman, Joan Beaumont, who got a bypass and contracted septicemia; that's a blood infection. She had a DNR, meaning do not resuscitate — so they didn't. Apparently, the family didn't know Norman put the DNR order into her chart."

"Must have made them angry," Gray said. "Although I can't see taking off a man's face over it. Anyone else?"

"Only the father of that kid who died. I looked into it like you said. He was a doctor and an athlete. Caught the infection from a patient and gave it to his son."

"Dying for the job. What else does his chart say?"

"Heshmatolosis. It hits the lymphatic system, and both father and son got it."

"Look into it in more detail. Get Vivienne's help if you need to."

Doug stiffened, his thug-like features grim. "I can manage. I won't need any help."

They reviewed the rest of the adult charts before discussing the children who had received PAS.

Gray said, "I remember a girl named Susan George."

"Yeah." The junior detective clicked onto her chart. "Her parents refused to immunize her. When she caught measles, it gave her encephalitis — a brain infection — but the customized antibiotic couldn't reverse all the brain damage. They had to turn off the life support. Parents got away Scot-free, too, since so many nutters don't immunize their kids."

They reviewed the remainder of the forty-five charts, but nothing set off intellectual fireworks. An overwhelming amount of medical detail stared back at them, making it impossible to tell if a faulty antibiotic had killed anyone.

But Gray knew it had.

The room began to get to him — the hundred-year-old plaster, linoleum flooring, and dusty air — all made him want to bolt up the basement stairs and out the front entrance of the hospital.

Another part of his mind raced and stayed focused on the obvious hurdle. That they couldn't blindly trust details documented in electronic charts which tech-savvy individuals could hack. That hospitals possessed the most outdated informational security protocols out there.

Breathing in and out only made the air feel thicker, harder to get in. He ran a hand through his hair. The other man's eyes were on him, intense and brooding.

Gray pushed the chair back with a screech, startling his detective. "We need a computational biologist to go over everything that went into making the customized antibiotic for each of these deaths and find the flawed one. Simon has the qualifications, but obviously we can't rely on his unbiased co-operation. Better get someone from the department."

"The Director's gonna flip over the cost. Forty-five deaths."

"We have to narrow them down somehow."

Again, Gray pictured Norman's body swinging from the branch – the theatrical setting, underscoring some need of the murderer. He let it go, trusting it would eventually come to him. It always did.

It was time to leave the basement. He motioned Doug to precede him. They strode up the stairwell, where the air improved perceptibly, and parted in the lobby.

Gray inhaled deeply and let clean air wash out his lungs. Somehow, he felt contaminated by more than that decrepit basement room. What was he missing? What had he just learned yet failed to understand?

The sinking feeling in his stomach remained and would later be justified. A vital flaw marred one of their assumptions

– one which, if discovered, could have blown the case wide open. His phone rang.

"You knew, didn't you? Why didn't you tell me?"

Gray covered the hospital lobby while listening to Vivienne on his phone. He couldn't blame her for being angry.

He needed a coffee, and after ordering it and paying the lady behind the lobby café counter, he slipped a tip into the appropriate container and gave her a wink. She playfully winked back.

The day of the shooting, this woman had knelt before him, handed him a bottle of orange juice and saved him from passing out. In gratitude, Gray bought a single long-stemmed rose from the lobby gift shop and handed it to her.

Reaching the revolving doors where only a few days ago someone had shot at him, he stopped and took in a deep breath. The sun shone over rows of neatly parked cars, coating them in a gold patina.

"Robert Black underwent gender reassignment surgery," Gray said, "and then he took on the name Holly Bradley. That has no bearing on the case, and it's her private business. I don't know if the outstanding fraud charges play into the murders either. They probably don't."

Her voice rose. Something was bothering her, something beyond the case. "How did you find out?"

"I brought her medical file to Dr. Seymour with a list of pre-admission medications. He explained the reason she took them." Gray gulped his coffee and pushed past the hospital doors, first looking to the right, then the left. Would he ever be able to go anywhere freely again?

Gray got into his car and spoke on the hands-free. The engine sputtered, and the feeble heating once again blew tepid air at his face, leaving his feet cold. The upholstery stank of old car. He pulled out of the parking lot, navigating to the freeway.

"What's wrong?" he asked Vivienne. "I can tell something else is bothering you. You're not yourself."

Silence. Then, he heard her sigh. "Saleem and I had a fight. I don't want to discuss it. When I came home last night, his things were gone."

"I'm sorry."

"Me too. Let's get on with the case, okay? It's easier that way."

He didn't miss a beat. "Where's Holly now?"

"No one's seen her. She's probably hiding out to avoid her fellow Board members. There's talk HealSo might have to return whats left of its last round of funding because of the embezzlement, but is she our killer?"

Gray turned onto the freeway. "She has no alibi for the night of Norman's disappearance. She tampered with a crime scene, lied about her identity, and has now disappeared."

He braked suddenly. A stalled car on the right forced traffic to merge into the left lane with little notice. What Gray wouldn't give to be in his Audi, zigzagging between vehicles wielding real horsepower, instead of having to drive this marshmallow.

"Would Holly have the technical knowledge to make concentrated arsenic?" he asked Vivienne. "Working in a health tech startup, she might have pharmaceutical contacts who could do it for her."

"I don't know. From what I've learned talking to Seymour, regular pharma can't get this stuff. It's experimental."

A thought – little more than a wisp of an idea – entered his mind, soon expanding and taking on enormous shape. He suddenly hit the brakes. The car behind nearly rear-ended him, blasted the horn, and then passed, the driver spewing expletives in French.

What Gray imagined seemed impossible. Or was it? He resumed driving.

"Seymour called me with fingerprint results," Vivienne continued. "The coffee packet at Jimmy's had his and Kate's prints on it. That's no surprise. SOCO found an interesting print at Jimmy's house, though."

The car jerked as he braked. You couldn't take a right turn on red on the Island of Montreal, despite multiple attempts by the mayors of various districts to make it legal, but why should the city or the police give up the regular income brought in by fines? Gray drummed his fingers; the idea in his mind continued to expand and light up the shadowy corners and crevices of the case. The street light seemed to take forever to change.

"Jimmy dusted and polished his place obsessively," Vivienne said, "so SOCO can be fairly certain of the timing of the prints. You'll never guess who they belong to."

Finally, the light changed, and he made a right turn. The road suddenly became smoother, the sidewalks new as he entered Westmount. He'd anticipated the owner of the print before receiving these results.

"Gabi," he said, pulling into a spot across her house. "Gabi visited Jimmy on the afternoon of his death."

He could picture Vivienne's mouth hanging open. "How did you know?"

"Just a hunch." Gray scanned the empty street. No kids played outside today. The snow had melted, leaving the street looking surprisingly naked and exposed.

"What does this mean? Did Gabi poison the coffee? And if so, why aren't her prints on the packet?"

"Exactly. I'm at her house now. She's got some explaining to do."

Gray put away his phone and tried the front door. No one answered. He returned to the car, prepared to wait.

Her Mercedes sedan pulled up a few minutes later, the diesel engine softly churning. She unfolded out from the tan leather seat slowly, shoulders hunched, as though older and more worn down than the last time he'd seen her.

Gray sprang out of his car. Hearing his approach, she turned and groaned. Mascara stains ran down her cheeks; she must have been crying. The bruise on her forehead still looked fresh.

Now, her lips pressed together, and she wiped the dampness from her face in one harsh movement. Last time he was here, he'd accused her of being a child murderer. He was about to accuse her of something again.

Gabi said, "I don't want to talk right now."

"I can come back tomorrow."

She seemed to register this as a threat and strode up the paved steps. A thick set of keys jingled until she unlocked the front door.

"You heard about Holly?" he asked, following her inside.

"Yes. We all have. So much for making millions. That's not why you're here though, is it? Get to the point."

Today, the corner fireplace in the living room was pristinely clean, any previous ashes cleared. A chill permeated the room and sank into his bones, despite the warming temperature outside. She motioned, but he didn't take a seat; didn't mince words. "We found your prints in Jimmy's apartment."

Gabi dropped the keys on the sideboard with a clang.

"Jimmy dusted and cleaned every day," Gray added, "and you had to be there the day he died. Withholding information is an offense. Now, I have to ask myself why you wouldn't mention it. The obvious answer is you went there to poison him. That you did poison him."

Her mouth hung open. "I didn't."

"You laced his coffee with arsenic, just like you did to your childhood neighbor. Only Jimmy died more painfully, didn't he? He bled all over the sofa and floor."

"You don't understand."

"Did you even stay to see your neighbor die, all those years ago? Did he bleed too?"

"Stop it. Stop it!" Gabi yelled.

"I have your prints at the crime scene. You misidentified your husband's body. Possibly tortured and killed him at HealSo, later transporting him to the beach." Gray crossed his arms and stood with his feet apart. "You inherit Norman's money. Give me one good reason why I shouldn't arrest you right now?"

"Because I didn't do it." Sweat beaded down her brow; her face gave nothing away.

"I don't believe you. You've been lying from the start, conspiring with the killer."

She didn't answer.

He moved closer, his face inches from hers. "I know you were there, and I want the truth."

Her heavy breath touched his neck; he heard the rasping of each inhalation in the background silence.

"Jimmy drank the coffee in front of me," she said. "Hell, he even offered me some, and I refused. Cardamom always makes me gag."

"Why did you go there?"

"To talk to him. Only talk." Gabi pulled away, her back nearly against the wall. The cords in her neck jutted out under the collar of her blouse. "Norman told me about the death at HealSo last year. He got drunk and confided the entire cover-up to me – told me a patient died because of Simon's alteration of the program. Norman could have prevented it; but he didn't. He said Jimmy might spill the beans. I knew if it came out, Simon would lose everything. I only wanted to persuade Jimmy to stay at HealSo, to... to... keep quiet."

Gray turned and paced the room. "What time did you go to his apartment?"

"Ah, I don't know. Maybe four in the afternoon?"

"Did you see anyone else coming or going? Did Jimmy mention meeting anyone else after you left?"

"No, and no. I don't know what happened to him. And neither does Simon."

Gray felt the cold air go in and out of his lungs and continued to pace. His legs needed to move.

"Holly's behind this," Gabi said. "What if Jimmy knew about her previous embezzlement and threatened to tell the Board?"

"I'll tell you what I believe," Gray said. "That Norman told you more than you're revealing. That you're being threatened. I can protect you."

"Thanks for your concern." Her tone sounded wry. "I don't know anything else. So, unless you plan to arrest me –"

He wasn't getting anywhere, and the clock was ticking. Gabi looked relieved when he moved to the door, yet she lingered at the doorway. Any second now, the door would slam, but for the moment, uncertainty played across her face.

"Evelyn Cane heard her son's agonizing cries."

Gabi's eyes flickered. She looked beyond him at the road. "In your job, you can't afford to make any assumptions, can you?"

Gray hesitated. "No, we can't."

"Not even the first thing you notice when you meet a person?"

"You mean whether they're a man or a woman? Are you referring to Holly's surgery?"

She looked at him and clicked her tongue. "Technology and advancement make life sterile, organized. I don't trust them."

"I'm afraid your riddles are too complex," he said.

"Oh, but you are very, very smart, Chief Inspector. You'll get there in the end."

She stepped back and shut the door in his face.

CHAPTER 22

April 4, 10 pm

THAT NIGHT, GRAY went to bed with the vague discomfort that comes with being overtired, yet unable to relax. His mind seemed awake; his body didn't. He felt at the edge of a precipice, on the brink of being able to solve the case; something restrained him. Lethargy, maybe even ambivalence about catching the killer. The entire thing made no sense. Best to stop thinking about it and call it a night.

He stripped and got under the crisp sheets and felt them slide across his bare skin. The moon glimmered through spaces between thickening clouds and jeweled the surface of the river, highlighting each watery spoke as it rose and fell on a gelatinous surface.

Breathing in stale, warm air, Gray got up to open the sash window; it always stuck. The breeze cooled his bare feet and blew the curtains. Tonight, the king-sized bed loomed large and empty. He'd go down to the studio and sculpt.

Each descending step felt arduous. Century-old pine planks, splintered and discolored, creaked as he walked. The banister felt cold under his hand, and the belt of his robe dragged behind his feet.

Opening the studio door, Gray stood. Each bust depicted Craig a few months older than the last, a row of imagined noses, ears, and high foreheads representing what the boy might have looked like had he lived past nine. Gray hadn't given him the chance and could never quite capture that quivering lower lip, no matter how many nights he spent working under the stars and sky.

Craig's trembling lower lip came to mind – on that last day when he had stood by the marina, clutching a handful of wildflowers picked from edge of the water to present to his father: bedstraw, bee balm, and creeping bellflower.

"For you, Daddy."

His small arm held out a present while his eyes darted to the thirty-five-foot diesel cruiser, then slowly back at Gray, aiming for a bravado his trembling lip betrayed. Craig preferred the safety of land, studying code, even knitting the red, white, and yellow winter scarf he'd given Gray for Christmas – but sailing in the open ocean off the East Coast – that frightened the small boy.

"Are the flowers enough, Daddy?"

What had Gray thought at the time? That his nine-year-old son wasn't man enough? That despite his wife's protestations, he had to toughen the boy up by taking him on a three-day father and son trip?

Everything on that trip had gone wrong. The first day was calm, but by the second, the clouds bore down on them with a moaning of sea and sky. The receiver and navigation system on the new sailboat weren't working properly.

By mid-afternoon, the clouds burst, and rain slammed their faces like marbles shooting through the air. Thirty-knot plus winds tore through their clothes and jostled the boat. The high waves poured in and flooded the cabin.

The rest was a series of nightmarish images: Craig sitting in the cockpit huddled and pale in the careening boat, the metal fitting snapping under the creaking strain and slamming Craig's temple; Gray lurching forward under the ten-foot wave and the crunch of the mast pinning down Gray's right arm and ripping the tendons and making blood spurt out as if from an open mouth. And those teasing lights of the approaching Coast Guard vessel, glinting in the distance – if he could hold on, a little longer, just a little longer.

But the boat capsized, and he went down over and over and groped in the darkness for Craig, again and again. And Gray screamed. He screamed. He screamed.

And Craig still rested underneath the water. Without anyone to protect him. Alone.

Tonight, the sculpting wasn't giving him the usual relief. Had something changed after his last interaction with Étienne?

He had to get out of the house. Not wanting to cart the large set of keys, he quickly grabbed his phone. Downstairs, pulling on the sleeve of his woolen coat, he pushed the front door open and stepped onto his porch. The cold night air kissed his face.

A walk would clear his head, and instinctively he knew his legs would take him to the nearby beach park, to the spot of the original crime.

Gray stepped onto his porch and pulled the door shut behind him. A rustle sounded from the bushes. He froze. His heart skipped a beat. Who'd be waiting here at night, expecting him to leave the house? It was probably a cat or a raccoon.

Time to get a grip. Gray blew out a breath and headed up the sidewalk.

The street lay quiet, lonely, with only the strengthening breeze rustling through the dancing leaves and grasshoppers rasping on the front lawns. The pungent smell of a damp and mulchy spring filled his nostrils. By the time he reached the empty beach park, a sheen of sweat had coated his entire body.

He finally reached the spot where the faceless corpse had hung so recently, and yet a lifetime seemed to have elapsed. An air of expectancy hung over the river. The first drops of rain made his coat smell of wet wool, and the heavy black sky loomed low overhead as if angry and obscuring the moon.

The beach park was black, ominous. Colorless shadows of chains and rectangles twisted and gyrated, sounding soft metal clangs from the nearby swings. The ghostly howl of the wind was different from any child's playful laughter. Another cold drop hit his face, then another.

Gray closed his eyes. Strange how unafraid he'd become when there was nothing left to lose, and how accepting of life and other people – where once he'd failed to accept his own son. Perhaps this response to loss defined him as a man better than anything else possibly could.

Norman had hung from a branch, a faceless entity, stripped of dignity and life, but he'd died somewhere else, exposed to the cold.

Exposed to the cold. Before death. Seymour's words resounded in Gray's ears.

Frozen before death.

How very simple and how very stupid of him. Clarity descended; the skin on his neck prickled.

He dialed the forensic pathologist's home number, knowing the call wouldn't be welcome this time of night yet unable to wait.

"Don't you ever sleep?" Seymour said, his voice slurred and heavy. "We're not all insomniacs you know. Some of us might even have company."

"Do you?"

"As a matter of fact, no, but that's not the point."

Gray shook his wet hair and felt it splatter his cheeks and neck. He strode to the water's edge with his cell clutched in his right hand. "Sorry. Something you said has sparked a thought."

"God forbid."

"Norman's body was exposed to the cold before death. What if the drop in body temperature induced death itself? Not the torture as we assumed, but the cold."

Gray waited through the silence on the other end of the line. The implications were clear, and Seymour linked together what they both should have considered much earlier – the pieces slipping into place – the doctor possibly slapping his head with his palm in a eureka moment.

Seymour finally spoke, all grogginess gone. Gray heard a creak of bedsprings. "Induced death through the most likely mechanism, an arrhythmia – provided DNA evidence matches Norman to the corpse?"

"Oh, it'll match. I'll have DNA results by tomorrow at the latest." Gray pulled the wet woolen lapels around his neck. Water slid into his collar and down his neck. Legs he couldn't control paced back and forth on the river's edge with shingle crunching under his boots. "Put identification aside. If he died of arrhythmia from the cold –"

"The killer didn't need to be there. They could be fairly confident about timing the death. John Doe's tissues were frozen, and cold can speed up the onset of an arrhythmia in someone predisposed to it. First comes sinus bradycardia, then slow atrial fibrillation followed by the terminal rhythm, ventricular fibrillation or asystole." Seymour went on for a while and then whistled. "All your alibis are useless, Gray."

"Utterly useless. But would Holly have that kind of medical knowledge? Would she know about Norman's heart meds? Would any of them?"

"Norman's wife would."

"Knowing Norman had a heart condition and knowing how to kill him with it reliably are two separate things. Meaning —"

"Your murderer had medical knowledge. Maybe even expertise. A doctor, perhaps one of Norman's colleagues who knew him at the hospital?"

Alarm bells rang in Gray's mind. He slapped his wet, denimed thigh. Facts linked together with sharp, distinct snaps, leading to one inescapable conclusion. Yet the last piece didn't fit. None of his suspects fit the profile. So where did that leave him? He recalled what Étienne had said during their first meeting, his desperate pleas to leave the Institute. Remembered Doug's findings from the hospital charts. Then, Vivienne's report on the early PAS antibiotics. But no, that didn't make sense. Or did it?

"What about the blood and acid found at HealSo?" Seymour said. "We found Norman's blood in that server room. The test came back positive. So, it has to be where Norman was tortured. Are you saying he was killed elsewhere?"

"Someone left blood and acid at the startup for us to find, John, to implicate the company. That isn't where Norman died; that isn't a crime scene at all."

"Clearing Holly Bradley, no? She cleaned up the blood, tried to protect the startup. Look for someplace cold as your crime scene."

"Our murderer is resourceful and intelligent. If the startup isn't the crime scene, the case opens up."

He heard the pattering of rain on water and ground; the thumping of his heart in his ears. Gray swung around, his eyes whiplashing to the nearby slide and then the swings.

One swing lay tangled in the other as the chains rattled with the wind and the metal seat banged against a supporting pole.

"A father and son died," Gray said, "Under PAS. The father was a doctor, and Étienne told me he's been waiting for his former doctor for a year – a doctor who was going to help him get transferred out of the Institute."

"That explains the puncture in the groin, Gray – a femoral stab for blood. The killer needed that blood to leave at the startup."

"Again, requiring medical expertise."

"My God. Do you think Norman's alive, and the body you found on the beach is someone else after all? That changes everything, every assumption you've made."

Rain dribbled into his eyes. His arms and legs moved on their own like cold and numb mechanical limbs programmed to take him home. The multitude of clues and suspects sprang upwards in his mind, swirled, fell into allotted slots forming a pattern. Someplace cold enough to freeze skin – that was easy. A father who had once been a doctor – the symbolic hanging by a child's playground.

Over the line, Seymour was still talking. "If Norman's alive, where would he go –"

Gray had momentarily forgotten he was holding his phone. He had to be alone to think. Mumbling a reply, he pushed end call, and Seymour's voice abruptly stopped, but the rain now pounded louder, beat in rhythmic force onto his head and neck. The soaked jeans tugged on his leg hair with each purposeful step.

His mind went down one avenue. No, that wasn't right. It can't be.

He breathed in damp, thick air, trying to snag that last thin thread – too thin – he kept grabbing and missing it at the edge of his imagination until he found himself crossing the beach road and heading up a residential street, his boots splashing black puddles and stumbling over uneven paving stones.

"She's Always a Woman" played on his mobile phone. Damn. Not now. Not when he hovered on the brink of identifying the killer.

"Céline."

"Where are you? It's the middle of the night, and you're not home."

Home? Whose home? Was she at his house? "I'm on my way back. What's the matter?"

"I need you. Séverin is going crazy. He won't leave me alone, and I'm not safe in my apartment, so I came here." Her voice broke. "When are you getting home?"

He sighed and kept walking. "I'm on my way." Gray remembered he hadn't bothered to lock the door on his way out. She must have found it unlocked and let herself in. "I'll be there in a few minutes."

He received no reply and subsequently heard a harrowing shriek, followed by a click.

Fat raindrops bounced off the sidewalk like countless ping pong balls. He swallowed, trying to get words out of his parched mouth.

"Céline? What's going on?" The line disconnected. He dialed, and her recorded voice said: "Okay, you have me. Now, what are you going to do with me? Tell me after the beep."

He shoved the cell in his pocket and ran, houses reeling by to his right, his legs and feet pounding the pavement. Séverin was jealous, but this? Gray hadn't expected this.

Finally, Leeson Avenue came into view. A quick turn to the right brought him before his house – the lawn, the porch – yet no lights shone from within.

And he'd left one on, he was certain. An elastic band snapped within his chest. Imagined screams filled his ears, but they weren't real, and he saw what he'd expected and most feared.

The front door stood open.

CHAPTER 23

April 4, 10 pm

ÉTIENNE LAY IN BED and clutched the old spy novel in his sweaty fingers. Reading it, he imagined the hero looked like the Inspector – except the Inspector didn't carry a Beretta 418, or have jolie girls hanging off his arms. Or maybe he did?

Reality descended with a sinking of the stomach. The book shook in his trembling grasp and the page blurred. He didn't live in any glamorous penthouse; he lived here: under a cracked ceiling and between old plaster walls, smelling the stink of the black river outside his window. They'd sent him back to his old room at the Institute.

Director Leblanc had come to his hospital room and explained that these things took time, that a convicted murderer, even one twelve years old, couldn't expect a quick transfer. Étienne was grateful the Committee was willing to transfer him to a hospital psychiatric ward, and he knew he had the Inspector to thank. Space would open up soon; in the meantime, he'd remain at the Institute.

The return had been a nightmare. His first day back, so far he'd gotten away from Carl trying to corner him in the yard, but after nightfall it was every boy for himself. And they mainly came at night.

Overhead, a buzzer sounded, indicating bedtime. He pulled the comforter up to his chin, inhaling the bad fabric softener smell. They'd trimmed down his meds at the main hospital, and he could think again, like before his arrest, before the psychiatrist forced all those pills down his throat – although thinking clearly made him more frightened of what might happen.

He moved the dresser to block the door.

The floor was cold under his bare feet; he ran to his secret place in the alcove – the one he'd shown the Inspector. Prying open the three-foot high door, he got on all fours and crawled inside, huddling under the musty blanket. Dust scratched his eyes, and he blinked. The tiny space smelled like mice and mold; he didn't care. It was better than what waited outside.

He pulled the object hanging from his neck out from his flannel shirt and clutched it in his hand – the alarm the Inspector had given him – hidden from the nurses at the Institute so they couldn't take it away.

In the small space, his raspy breathing bounced off the walls, and the air grew hot and thick from his sweat. Wiping it with the scratchy blanket, he fought off panic. Only a little air came in from the gray rectangular crack under the door, and Étienne huddled into a ball, and softly sang a Quebecois lullaby, Fais do do, meaning Go-beddy-bye, which he'd often sang to Claire when she was a baby: *Fais do do, mon petit, Claire. Maman est en haut, Elle fait des gâteaux; Papa est en bas, Il fait du chocolat. Fais do do, mon petit, Claire.*

A noise awoke him a while later. There were voices echoing down the hall, calling his name. Sitting up, he hit his head on the overhead beam.

They banged on his door. No neighboring boys would dare intervene. Now a deep screech like nails on a blackboard sounded.

"Keep pushing," Carl said.

Étienne sat riveted before the gray strip of light under the crawl-space door. The screeching stopped. He pictured them squeezing through the opening. The gray strip suddenly lit up with the sound of the lights being clicked on. He blinked and scurried further back until the wall pressed into his back. The blanket scratched his face, and his whole body shook.

Carl called out to him. Another boy did the same, their sneakers shuffling against the floor.

"Where is he?" the second boy said.

"He has to be here," Carl replied. "Come out, freak. We won't hurt you."

Étienne's teeth chattered; they must hear that. How could they not hear that?

Carl's grainy voice grew louder. "Now, runt. Get out here, or else."

Footsteps approached the crawl space, and a shadow hovered over the light under the door. Étienne's heart jumped into his throat.

"There's something here, Carl," the other boy said. "It's a door, and it ain't sealed like the one in my room."

A tapping against the wood. They were trying to pry it open.

He'd waited too long to call for help, and now it might be too late.

***

Gray stood on the sidewalk before his house, listening, rain slamming his face. No one hovered behind the bushes or hid behind parked cars. Looking overhead, the windows of his house were dark. No shadows lurked; no curtains shifted.

Water streamed into the collar and down his back. Someone watched – he could feel it – but from where?

Putting one foot before the other, he approached the low iron gate, opened it, and pulled it closed behind him, feeling the vibration of the latch as it locked. Covering the ten-foot walkway, he quickly climbed the porch and stepped inside the darkened threshold.

Wafts of Céline's favorite perfume lingered in the foyer, and all was silent save the slashing of the rain outside and his boots squeaking against the pine floor. The long hall, living room, and stairs were empty. He left trails of dripping water in his wake and headed to the kitchen.

Nothing. A quick glance out the window revealed no one in the back yard or by his car. The curved maid's stairs to the right lay shrouded. He'd take this way up.

Somewhere outside, a dog barked. Gray took the spiral steps leading up to the second floor – no banister to grip here – only the steady squeak of hundred-year-old planks, worn down by generations of subservient maids and butlers carrying meals to their employers.

The pounding of his heart was almost painful. He didn't call out Céline's name, expecting the worst, reviewing what she's said before her cry: that she had to get away from Séverin, that she feared for her life.

A cold wind howled up from the front door, obliterating her scent. But on the second floor, her presence enveloped Gray, and the air smelled stale and sour.

Instinct made him bypass the rooms on this floor. He crossed the hall and looked up the narrow central stairwell to his third-floor master bedroom. Gray walked up, the air more still here, laced with another stench he recognized.

Gray shot up into the waiting darkness, fists up, muscles ready to dodge an incoming punch or bullet, and reaching the threshold of his bedroom, he screeched to a halt.

Light streamed in from the nearby street lamp. Nothing could prepare him for Céline lying on her back, draped at the edge of his bed with one arm over her head, the other tucked under her body. Her neck fell over the side of the mattress, backward, eyes accusatory.

No amount of professionalism could save him from this. He'd been inside this woman in this very room only a few nights ago. Bile came up from his stomach. He swallowed it, knowing he mustn't contaminate the scene any further.

A droplet of blood from her mouth trailed down her cheek and forehead and into her hairline. The long amber strands hung upside down and brushed the pine planks. His attention had shot instinctively to her face, but now, the crimson-stained sheets registered, all soaked and tangled around her. A large patch of blood continued to expand on the white cotton, still streaming. Was she still alive?

He shot beside her and felt for a pulse; there was none. The urge to hold and comfort her overwhelmed him. She'd done nothing to deserve this, except wanting him, and that had led to this.

Gray fell to his knees and leaned his head in his hands. Did death follow him everywhere? Would he be a curse to everyone who tried to get close? He lifted his head and tried to connect with her eyes. They stared ahead coated with the film of death, making his heart pound louder than the smashing rain outside. A lightning flash momentarily blinded him. Instinctively, he held up a hand against the reflection and saw it.

He saw the familiar Japanese kitchen knife; it had an engraved picture of a dragon on the layered stainless steel blade – a Hagane blade made using sword-making techniques – sharp, efficient, ruthless. Once a wedding present, now something foreign and obscene lying on the floor of his bedroom. The dragon was streaked with viscous red.

Events shot through Gray's head like from a cannon: Céline in danger; someone following her here; the fatal stab, the intention to frame Gray.

Why kill your enemy when you could frame him instead? But who had killed Céline? Séverin or an accomplice? And would either stick around to watch Gray discover the body or stay nearby to make the arrest?

Gray looked left, then right. No one. He checked the bathroom next door and the closet. No one there either. He mustn't disturb the scene further, and already his dripping boots had left evidence everywhere, possibly at the expense of destroying other prints. It occurred to him that a greater danger existed than being arrested for Céline's death.

Gray ran to the window and scanned the front garden. The blue-gray night looked soaked with death. No shadows lurked in the downpour, and nothing moved under the misty haze, but his front gate now stood open.

He'd closed it behind him when he'd arrived and made certain it latched. Whoever passed after him hadn't latched it.

Every cell in his body wanted to bolt, but that would be suicide. Better to ring the police and then Cousineau. Tell them about Céline's terrified phone call and the attempt to frame Gray for her murder. If his adversaries had expected him to panic, they'd underestimated him. He wouldn't be gunned down on the street like a fleeing criminal.

Pulling out his cell, he dialed 911. The line connected and Gray spoke to the dispatcher.

"This is Chief Inspector Gray James of the SPVM. I've just returned home and found a woman stabbed in my bed. I know her. I've checked for signs of life, but she's dead."

Several questions were asked and answered. Gray felt lightheaded, from the stench, from breathing in the heavy wet air. He moved to the third-floor landing.

"Stay in the house, Chief Inspector. Don't touch anything and don't leave."

"I think the killer is waiting outside. I have no intention of leaving the crime scene."

"We'll send a squad car and an ambulance right away," the operator said before hanging up.

Only a few minutes to go. The sound of his heavy breathing filled the small landing. Mud and water from his boots dirtied the floor beneath him. Gray had stupidly obliterated all evidence of the killer's footsteps in his haste to find Céline. He had three minutes, possibly four before he'd hear the police siren or the wail of an ambulance. His hands hovered over the phone, ready to call Vivienne and give her instructions based on what he'd figured out speaking to Seymour.

A ringing startled him – the programmed ringtone on his cell from Étienne's alarm shrilled across the enclosed space.

No. Not now. He switched it off and gripped the handrail. The boy was back at the Institute, in trouble. He wouldn't have sounded the alarm otherwise.

To run from a crime scene would make Gray a marked man in more than one way. He glanced out the window to the road outside, leading toward the Institute. His muscles flexed; he shot down the stairs. All hope of surprise was lost after that ear-piercing ring. Down one flight. Then the other.

Gray steeled himself for an assault which could come from anywhere: the bottom of the steps; outside the front door; the middle of the street.

He made it across in living room like a shot. A creaking of the old floor sounded from ten feet back, and he turned to catch a dark form in his peripheral vision, hovering, then shooting toward him.

Gray stormed out the front door. Jumping the four porch steps, cutting through the garden and swinging gate, he risked another look backward.

The familiar face of Detective Doug Green snarled, and fists and legs pumped towards him. But Gray was quick, too. As fast as this assailant who had installed the car bomb at the beach park, who had murdered Céline, who planned to frame and kill Gray.

Rain stabbed at his face and eyes, making it hard to see. The wet pavement silvered under each passing streetlight, then blackened and bubbled like thick tar in the dark patches. His thighs cried out with each leap as he ran.

Not to escape Doug – who Gray would gladly fight – but to get to Étienne in time. To get to Westborough Psychiatric Institute before the unthinkable happened.

A shard of lightning lit the sky, bringing the Institute into view. The nine-storey addition seemed to melt in the rain, with its brown rectangular lines blurring and bending into a moribund abstract painting. He covered the deserted road, getting closer and closer, and half expecting a shot before he got there.

On cue, a crack passed by him, drowned by a roar of thunder, and Gray ducked and jumped behind a band of trees on the right, stomping soggy grass and slashing through puddles – still he ran. Another shot rang out and hit a passing maple. Now a dozen meters from the Institute door, he gave it all he had. No light shone in the entry ahead.

He raced up the path, covered the few steps and pushed through the Institute's heavy wooden door.

The same guard as before sat behind the desk and looked up – Doug only a few seconds behind – and Gray flew past him, yelling that Étienne was in trouble. He took the stairs two at a time, the guard close behind. They reached the boy's room together, and Gray scanned the empty bed and the corner by the crawl space. The small door of Étienne's hiding space stood open, the inside vacant. But a smashed guitar and a toppled dresser spoke volumes about what must have happened.

Gray faced the guard. "Where would they take him?"

The guard's stared back, blank. His mouth fell open. A muted cry made them turn.

"The stairwell," the guard said. "It's coming from the main stairwell of the extension."

***

He swung upside down like a pendulum, his neck swaying from side to side, and the muscles pulling and ripping along the sides of his head and shoulders. The thick rope tying his ankles dug into his skin tight enough to make his toes burn. He tried to work off the thin tape around his wrists.

"Non, Carl, non."

Étienne hovered with his head inches above the industrial tile, Carl's worn and smelly trainers on his left and the other boy's on his right. They held him by each leg and moved fast towards the addition, ignoring his moans and his cries.

They flew down the hall, past a door, and into the dim stairwell. His hair skimmed the top of each step, and he flexed his neck to stop from hitting the back of his head on the cement edges. Carl rapped a song off-tune. Sweat beaded off of Étienne's forehead, and snot hung from his nose as they went up and up, until he tasted vomit. They reached the top landing, and a metal door stood before them.

Carl turned the handle and pushed the door open with his shoulder. The frigid air hit Étienne's face and body before the rain began to seep into his clothes. The boys turned him towards the pellets of water shooting across his face and up his nose. He wanted to close his eyes against the sharp stabs and open them to find this all gone, only a nightmare. Instead, angry clouds hung overhead, and lightning tore open the sky releasing a flood.

He looked back, the swinging roof door getting farther and farther away, his heart throbbing in his throat. It was so hard to breathe. Arms and legs flailing, he tried to jerk free, but their hands clamped on his legs hard, so hard that he shrieked.

Then they pulled him towards the edge – where the railing was gone for six feet with nothing except yellow caution tape cordoning the crumbling barrier. The beach park and river melted into the distant darkness.

"Non! Non!"

Carl ripped the yellow tape, and together they held Étienne over the edge of the nine-storey drop.

Below, the cement sidewalk blurred and cleared. The wrist tape finally gave way to Étienne's fervent yanking and pulling.

He clutched the bricks at the edge of the roof. They broke under his nails and cut his fingertips. "Non, Carl. Please, you gonna kill me!"

"That's the idea, runt." Carl's wild face looked down at him.

The other boy finally spoke. "We can't. You promised we'd just scare him. And he's scared. Now, let's go back."

Carl yelled, "Go if you want. Get out of here. I'll do this alone."

"No, you can't. The runt's throwing up, and plenty scared."

"Get out of here, or I'll push you over, too," Carl said.

The other boy let go and ran, and Carl grabbed both of Étienne's legs. "Keep fighting me, and I'll let go."

"Non!" Étienne saw the other boy's retreating figure. "Come back and help me. Please." The world shifted, and blood pounded through his head. He heaved again.

"That's it. Keep doing that. My grip's loosening, runt."

Everything blurred. *Claire, where are you? I need you. Everything is lost.*

Until a familiar voice called out his name, and a man ran towards them.

***

Gray and the guard pounded up the steps. Reaching the roof, the swinging door shot open in their faces, and a boy ran through. The guard grabbed him.

"Where is he?" Gray asked.

The boy pointed outside. "Carl has him." He got out of the guard's grip, bolting down the steps.

"Let him go." Gray ran out into the pounding rain. He blinked, frantic to make out blurred shapes. One small bulb by the stairwell lit the entire roof, and beyond that, distant windows and streetlights dotted the backdrop in wet bleeding blotches.

A cry sounded from the left. Two squirming figures momentarily melded into one writhing form. Then Gray made it out. A large boy held Étienne upside down at the edge of the roof at a spot with no supporting rail. The boy's thick neck arched up as he laughed, and his victim screamed and wailed.

Gray flung forward, covered the fifteen feet in a flash, and yanked Carl back so that both boys fell onto him. Carl scrambled to his feet and ran off like a shot across the roof while Gray held onto Étienne. Gray saw the guard waver, unsure if he should follow Carl or help, until another man entered the roof behind them.

He moved fast; action blended into one continuous motion: of Gray fumbling to untie Étienne's feet in time; Doug bludgeoning the guard from behind, the guard going down; and Doug then racing to Gray, jaw tight, fists clenched.

The knot sprang free as Gray felt the slam, felt himself and the boy fly back and swing over the ledge, and he grabbed the small hand blindly, his right thumb and two fingers making contact with a small palm, his left clutching and gripping wildly at the roof's edge.

Pain shot through his wrist. Étienne swung from his fragile grip. Gray was hanging off the edge by one hand while holding Étienne with the other. Their skin, wet and slick, began to slip. The small voice cried out. Gray chomped down on his teeth, tightened every muscle, every inch of his arm and shoulders, because he couldn't let it end like this, with his crippled hand... his witness plummeting to the ground... a second death tonight, because of Gray.

Rain stabbed his eyes. Above him, Doug stood, feet apart, arms wide, dark hair flying in the storm. Another shot of lightning appeared overhead. Gray's grip on the small hand slipped another inch, and Étienne cried out. "Mama!"

He screamed it again. And violent spasms of realization shot through Gray like rounds from a machine gun. *Mama.* Was that why poor Jimmy had to die? Why Norman felt needles in his eyes before being frozen to death? *Mama. Yes, my son. I'm here. But you're not. And I'm so very sorry.*

Doug's eyes were wide, his mouth in a snarl. Framed by the smudged city lights, the sole of his foot lifted and hovered above; it came down and crushed Gray's fingers against the crumbling brick, sending shards of pain through his joints, up his arm.

"Courtesy of Cousineau," Doug said.

Gray's breath caught in his chest and his eyes squeezed shut. He opened them and another shadow moved in the background like a drunken dancer moving unsurely. The injured guard struggled towards them, his moan nearly drowned out by the thunder, but Doug heard it. He turned, his foot inadvertently lifting off Gray's knuckles.

Gray whipped the boy upwards by his right hand, high enough so that when the grip slipped, Étienne caught him by the waist and hung on – leaving both of Gray's hands free to pull them up, secure one elbow on the roof, and swing a leg upward – only possible for a man accustomed to mountaineering. His arm went up fast, then a leg.

Doug lifted his sole again, over Gray's head. The guard was too far away to help.

Gray raised his right hand to fend off the blow; his thumb and small finger gripped the other man's ankle, twisted, and Doug teetered, losing balance, his arms flailing before that final outcry.

Doug fell backward off the edge, the whites of his eyes visible and his mouth wide open, now growing farther and farther away until a thud sounded below. Shards of rain shot downward towards his twitching body, making shallow puddles in the indents of his black leather coat and the surrounding asphalt.

The guard reached their side and helped Gray and Étienne onto the roof. Gray turned towards the boy, who gave a thumbs up. Time was of the essence.

"I'm sorry," he said, "but I have to ask you a critical question. It's about your doctor from last year."

The answer confirmed what he'd expected. Swallowing the lump in his throat, he turned to the guard. "Call an ambulance for both of them, right away. And keep the boy with you while you wait. The other boy is still around, so don't leave him alone for a second." Flying down the steps, he punched Vivienne's number, each stab sending a knife through his hand.

"Come to the Institute at once. Doug's injured, probably dead. He tried to kill me and Étienne on the Institute's rooftop. And he murdered Céline and bombed my car, all under Cousineau's orders." Gray descended flight after flight. The call went in and out.

"Cousineau?"

"I mistakenly thought it was Séverin, but Cousineau's behind all this. I need you to confirm it fast. Wake up anybody you have to."

"How? What do you want me to do?"

"Call the HealSo investors, Vivienne. Find out if Cousineau is behind a dummy corporation; if he's invested in the startup."

"I don't understand. He assigned you to the case in the first place."

"I was next in line on the roster. He didn't want me on the case from the beginning."

He had more to tell her. She wouldn't be happy about it.

"I found Céline's body in my bedroom and phoned the police. Call uniform and explain I had to leave for an emergency. They're at my house by now."

Vivienne's mind always worked fast. She didn't let him down. "Doug tried to frame you? Leaving the scene looks bad, but we can justify it if you go back now. Maybe even take the boy with you."

"I'm sending him to the hospital; I won't be returning to my house yet."

"What? Are you out of your mind? You discovered the body; you'll be the prime suspect."

Gray reached the ground floor and flew out the main doors. He took a sharp right, and ahead on the pavement; Doug lay unmoving. "Hang on a minute," he told Vivienne.

His detective had a faint pulse. Unbelievably, this was the man who had so recently helped on the investigation, who had unearthed so much while working under two opposing forces – though in the end, Doug had made his ill-fated choice, and he'd spend a lifetime living the consequences.

Gray didn't dare move him, knowing the detective's spine would be fractured in multiple places.

An ambulance raced towards them, sirens blaring, lights blazing in the downpour.

Vivienne shouted on the other end of the line. "I just got the call to your house."

"I'll be there later."

"But–"

"Hold on," Gray told Vivienne. He waved the ambulance over. The large tires skid to a halt on the flooded road, sending up a muddy spray onto his already soaked clothes. The two attendants jumped out to examine the injured man, and a third accompanied Gray inside the Institute.

Gray spoke briskly, and after handing Étienne to the ambulance attendant, he exhaled, all the steam going out of him. He hovered outside the Institute door, sheltered from the rain under the awning. They'd take the boy to the hospital and away from this terrible place. At least, he was safe for tonight.

But that one moment of rest cost Gray. His hand throbbed; every muscle in his shoulders and back cried out in pain. Crouching down, his head forward, his arms swaying, he wondered how he would finish all that remained to be done.

He knew who had killed Norman and Jimmy, and why.

Vivienne was waiting on the other end of the line. Gray straightened and felt the wind rip through his soaked clothes, chilling him to the bone. His cramped hand was blue. He spoke softly into his phone. "Cousineau is behind this. We need Doug to live to testify."

"Oh God."

"First, I have to bring in our murderer."

"You have to come in first," she said.

"No, the investigation comes first. We shouldn't have taken the most basic information on those medical records for granted. Can't make the most basic of assumptions. Gabi tried to tell me that. And only one setting fits the mechanics of this killing. Jimmy's death bought us time, but the next murder could be imminent. Go to my house and organize things with SOCO. I've contaminated the scene, but there's no getting around that now. I'll bring our killer in tonight."

Gray ended the call. A police car pulled up. He spoke to them and borrowed their vehicle. Tires skidding, he sped out onto the road and away from the Institute.

CHAPTER 24

April 4, Midnight

HIS DESTINATION WAS before him, and he hesitated in his car, dreading the upcoming interrogation.

Lightning shot overhead, a firecracker in the sky, but it had stopped raining. The gray and magenta clouds spoke their own story, captive and restrained. Any time now, the storm would resurface.

Chilled and injured, he got out of the car. His hand felt broken in several places; it continued to discolor and swell. He walked the path where cut-back rose bushes lined either side, and small hydrangeas shimmered with droplets of water.

Gray made steady progress to the front door. It wouldn't budge. He pounded on the glass, and a backlit silhouette moved forward in the dimly-lit interior, posture relaxed but arms crossed.

The door opened, and Gray stepped inside, looking into subdued eyes. He said, "You know why I'm here."

"Yes. Your face makes that plain."

Gray inhaled the familiar scent, comforting and robust. His wet clothes dripped and stuck to his skin. "It didn't have to be like this."

"Of course it did."

He accessed his official voice. "Kate Grant, I'm arresting you for the murder of Dr. Norman Everett. You do not have to say anything, but it may harm your defense if you do not mention when questioned something which you later rely on in court." Reciting the remainder of the caution, he glanced behind her towards the open double doors leading to the kitchen – the gas oven and stove, and the industrial fridge.

He moved past her; their shoulders grazed. She smelled again of cinnamon and flour. The industrial refrigerator sat to the left, the stove and oven to the right. The fridge had a solid steel door and a make-shift timer, and he noted that the mechanism locked from the outside. The inside safety looked like it had been tampered with.

The soft shuffle of her footsteps approaching from behind made him turn. Lifting his hand, he moved the long swatch of red dyed hair from her cheek and touched her scar. Kate flinched. "From the early antibiotic," he said. "It caused a non-healing rash." She didn't reply.

"The killer stabbed Norman with a sedative," Gray continued, "tortured him and left him in a cold room with a timer set to lower the temperature – enough to bring on Norman's arrhythmia and subsequent death at a time when the killer had an alibi. A doctor could have managed that."

"I'm a barista, Sherlock."

"And I'm the tooth fairy."

She turned and left the kitchen. He kicked the wheel of a trolley on his way out. So that's how she'd carted Norman's body out of here. The lab might still be able to recover some DNA. "Who did you plan to kill next? Holly or Simon?" he asked.

Kate stopped before the café window and stared out, frowning. The rain had resumed. Fog, creeping up the sides of the window, continued to isolate them from the world. A couple outside rushed to their car and hurriedly got inside. He heard the screech of their tires but kept his focus on Kate's profile – the rigid jaw, the nose ring now purple instead of red in the dim light, her absolute stillness. And her continued silence.

Gray said: "The killer then planted Norman's blood at the startup because why should the company profit after what they'd done? Did you recognize Étienne at the beach park?"

She finally turned. "I don't know anyone by that name."

"He remembers you from last year. In a way, he's still waiting for you to save him. And Holly will recognize you from the stairwell."

"Unless her attacker wore a mask. Did he? All circumstantial, Chief Inspector. Good try, though."

Gray leaned in. "You can change your name, your life, and your appearance, but you can't change who you are – and that's Dr. Catherine Lapointe. I mistakenly began looking for a male physician who had lost a son. A doctor who can falsify her death can falsify her gender in a medical chart. You're Henri Lapointe's mother. You contracted the infection, and Henri got it from you."

She shook her head, turning so that he couldn't see her face. She must know there was no escape.

"What was your first clue?" she said.

"You told me Jimmy didn't bleed out from an ulcer. Baristas don't generally speak that way. The phrase stuck in my mind." He sighed. "It's over, Kate. Now that we know your real identity, everything falls into place. If your son died from the infection, was it fair to blame Norman? Was it fair to torture him?"

Kate lurched forward. Her eyes blazed; her mouth hung open. "Henri didn't die from the infection; he died from the goddamned antibiotic. His skin came off. His eyes bled. He cried, blind, begging me to make the pain stop." She slammed a fist against the glass. "Do you know what that's like? Dr. Catherine Lapointe is dead. I killed her with every jab, with every scrape. Felt her die with every scream for mercy out of Norman's mouth."

She continued: "He brought PAS to the hospital unit, knowing the technology was flawed, but he wouldn't risk losing his precious clinical trial." She reached out and touched Gray's two rigid fingers above the scar. "I know about this. If you could set this right, would you?"

"Nothing sets it right. Nothing brings them back."

"You could have this broken hand fixed and choose not to. It's all you have left to keep you company. Like my anger."

All emotion had drained out of him, from dealing with crisis after crisis, from the stench of failure. When he'd completed the case, he could go home and rest. She would never go home again.

They left the café together. Buckets of rain beat down onto the overhead canopy; thick air made his lungs heavy. The lightning and thunder had grown fierce, and rain slashed sideways across the deserted street.

They passed several empty cars, with his marked police car just around the corner. The sound of an ignition, then nothing. No crunch of tires on wet asphalt, no accompanying backsplash. Instead the wind howled down the road as though through a narrow tunnel, and somewhere in the distance a faint humming lingered.

The two of them hurried in the downpour, their eyes shut against the debris flying in the street. Gray's mind was weighted by the upcoming interrogation and Céline's death. The long night stretched before him. Rain dripped its icy fingers down his neck and back, the already clammy clothes peeling back from his skin as he walked.

He motioned towards his car up ahead. Kate passed him and stepped onto the road.

Two blinding high beams came upon them. Events registered at once: the lights, the deafening screech of the tires, a burst of thunder overhead. And images moved in slow motion with Kate's body stiffening under the headlights; his surge towards her after that split-second of indecision; the black sedan coming towards them at lightning speed.

He covered the distance to Kate a moment too late, the car making contact at the level of her hips, her arms spread outwards and legs spread-eagled in the air. She flew forward, pellets of rain bouncing off her body – until she landed on the road ahead.

The car braked. It came to a complete stop just short of its front tire crushing her ankle. He'd fallen on all fours, and jolts of white light flashed before his eyes from the excruciating pain in his hand. For a second, all went black before the rain stabbed his face and the outlines of buildings and cars returned.

Lightning lit the scene like a stage – with Kate lying on her side in front of the car's lights, facing away from Gray. He struggled to his feet, and even as he ran over to her, he feared the worst. She wasn't moving.

A puddle of blood widened. Rain thinned it and spread it across the pavement. The driver of the car jerked open the door and screamed.

"You killed him! You bitch, you killed my Jimmy!" Evelyn Cane faced Gray. "She did it! You were going to let her get away with it, weren't you? She took my Jimmy from me!"

Gray reached Kate's side. Punching 911 into his phone, he shouted the relevant details to the dispatcher. Looking at her pale, drenched face, he didn't know what to do. He didn't risk moving her. In the torrent of wind and rain, he couldn't tell if she was breathing. He touched her wrist to feel for a pulse, his fingers clumsy and numb, and he could just detect a faint beat.

Behind him, Evelyn still screamed in between sobs.

Gray cursed and rushed over to the driver's side of her car and pushed her aside. Another peal of thunder drowned her protests. Swiftly, he turned off the ignition – silently berating himself for not having done it earlier. It was sheer luck Jimmy's mother hadn't run them both down in her distress.

"Calm down, Mrs. Cane. The ambulance is on its way."

"Ambulance? I don't want an ambulance. She killed my boy, and I want her dead."

She began screaming again. The rain glued her long hair around her head, a witch's halo framing fierce eyes and bared teeth. Gray grabbed her by the arms. She'd presumably followed him, seen him arrest Kate, and assumed Kate responsible for her son's murder. He understood her reasoning. And no two people could better understand her grief. But her logic was flawed. Even over the hammering in his chest, his heavy, uneven breath, and her loud wails, he had to make her understand.

"Mrs. Cane, listen to me," he said. "Kate Grant didn't kill Jimmy."

"What? She poisoned him! She did it! Jimmy screamed in pain, begging me to help, and she did it. I know she did!"

"No, Evelyn." He looked her directly in the eyes, willing her to understand. She stilled, the muscles of her face hanging limp as water streamed down her pale cheeks.

"Kate didn't poison your son. Someone else did."

CHAPTER 25

April 6, 10 am

GRAY STEPPED OUT of hospital room 2B on the East Surgical ward and nodded to the police guard stationed outside.

Vivienne approached him from down the corridor, her body rigid, dark circles around her eyes. She hadn't smiled in days, and he knew why.

The surgical floor bustled around them with doctors and nurses busily occupied; the white noise of machines ringing and beeping echoing off the pristine white walls.

He wiggled his left hand, heavy from the cast and damn itchy. At least his ear had healed.

"How is she?" Vivienne asked, motioning towards the room he'd just left.

"She remembers nothing of her previous life."

"How do you torture a guy, burn his face off, and then forget?"

"Don't worry," he said. "Kate will remember soon enough. Her mind won't give her a permanent reprieve. Any news?"

Vivienne rested one hand on her hip. "You're reinstated. Congratulations. And cleared of any involvement in Céline's murder. Doug killed her under Cousineau's orders – all with the express purpose of framing you and getting you out of the way. He also planted the car bomb – sneaky bastard, none of us saw him there. He's recovered enough to point the finger at Cousineau for fear of facing the charges alone."

Gray's hunch had proved correct. Some financial digging had unearthed Cousineau's silent involvement with Norman and the startup. He had millions (ill-gotten millions at the taxpayer's expense, no doubt) at stake with the company's success. It turned out Cousineau and Norman were old schoolmates, accustomed to collaborating in shady business dealings.

"Cousineau had tried, unsuccessfully, to get in touch with Norman the previous night," Vivienne said. "By the time he received a description of the body – which described his associate to a T – you had assumed responsibility for the case. He didn't want you to identify Norman and connect him with the startup, for fear it would jeopardize the estimated two hundred million dollar sale. Your unblemished record for solving cases worked against you."

Gray said: "Cousineau attempted to take me off the case – even asked if I'd leave it alone if he assigned it to another detective."

"It's never an advantage to be too competent when you work for the city."

Vivienne's face relaxed, but she still didn't smile.

"How are you?" he asked.

She straightened and raised her chin. "Saleem moved all his furniture out over the weekend. He won't talk to me, just gives me cold, one-word answers." An orderly came by pushing a stretcher; she waited for him to pass and kept her voice low. "I told him about the abortion. Didn't tell him you helped by carting me back and forth from the hospital. He says it's the worst thing I've ever done to him, and that I'd never fully understand why. He's right. I don't. That's my failing I guess — putting my career first. What am I supposed to do? Take a part-time desk job at the department and give up detective work?"

"Other officers have kids and work full-time. I don't know how they do it, but they manage."

Strong antiseptic wafted towards them. Down the hall, a cleaner pushed a mop in their direction. They moved towards the elevators.

"Maybe he'll cool off," Gray said. "Give it time."

"He won't. There's something he isn't telling me, I know it. But enough about that. Are you sure you don't want to charge Kate with Jimmy's murder?"

Gray looked down at Vivienne's short tresses, her swollen red eyes. She hadn't been sleeping, only living and breathing two cases at once.

"Kate used the engineer for information, but she wasn't the one who poisoned his special order of hazelnut-cardamom coffee."

"Then who?"

"Someone higher up at the hospital, someone involved in experimental trials and known to operate unethically within those trials. Seymour claimed the arsenic was pharmaceutically concentrated, so I had to ask myself, who had access to that type of drug?"

Vivienne's eyes widened. "You think it was him?"

"I know it was. Before he became a faceless corpse."

"But when did Norman doctor the coffee, no pun intended?"

Gray resumed walking, and Vivienne followed. They reached the elevator, and he pushed the button. "While it sat at the café waiting for Jimmy. Perhaps even on the very night Kate killed Norman. Jimmy had threatened to reveal the startup's secret and had to be silenced. I spoke with Norman's pharmaceutical contacts. After some pressuring, they confirmed supplying him with the arsenic, off the record.

Vivienne shook her head. "So, Evelyn Cane ran down the woman who unknowingly avenged her son's death."

"Yes."

The elevator arrived empty, and they silently stepped inside. It trundled downward to the main floor, where Gray could now walk without looking over his shoulder. He took a deep breath and exhaled.

As he crossed the lobby, he thought of Jimmy and Céline. "This case hasn't been one of our successes."

He stopped short of the revolving doors. Vivienne followed his gaze.

Outside, Étienne was getting into a car with a man and woman seated up front, and a little blonde girl beaming in the back.

"You helped him get transferred out of the Institute and into a regular psychiatric ward, didn't you?" Vivienne said.

Gray shook his head. "His good behavior did that. Étienne's case was under review, and they noticed he never fought back during Carl's first attack. His earlier conviction, at the tender age of ten, will be overturned in time."

"With your help, I'm sure it will. Looks as though he has a weekend pass with his sister's foster family."

Vivienne smiled for the first time in days, like her old self – but she'd forgotten something vital and as yet unexplained. He hoped she wouldn't remember; his hopes were dashed.

"There's one thing I still don't get," she said. "A man entered Étienne's hospital room, pretending to be the killer – not Kate – a man. Who was that?"

Gray thought to himself: if the intruder knew Kate killed Norman, he might have interrogated Étienne to make sure the boy couldn't identify her – to protect Kate.

Avoiding Vivienne's eyes, he merely shrugged. "It may come out in the trial. We'll see who comes forward to support Dr. Catherine Lapointe."

He knew what Vivienne would ask next, even before the words left her mouth.

"Then, who was Henri's father? Kate's dead son – who was his dad?"

CHAPTER 26

April 6, 10 am

IN A GUARDED hospital room at Westborough, Kate lay in bed, observing the blackened sky outside her window.

Across the road, she could just see the beach park and the throbbing St. Lawrence River, its rippling waves partially lit by lamps on the boardwalk. The wind rustled the branches of the darkened oaks, making them appear alive, as though they were reaching long arms out towards her. Cars left the beach parking lot, their headlights floating down the road.

The room itself was stark, foreign. Kate remembered that she worked in a café, though the details remained foggy. A hollow ache rested in her belly, a sharp yearning for Jimmy, while everything which existed beforehand remained blank; yet this felt natural. As though she'd never had memories of her own before, never needed them. Maybe her past would come back to her, the doctors had said. Maybe it wouldn't.

She lay back, nestling her head on the pillow, snuggling under the sheet. A sigh escaped her lips, as though it had been a long time since she'd had a rest. It felt peaceful, regenerative, with her thoughts blissfully blank.

A knock on the door made her turn. A tall stranger stood in the doorway, his face dark, all lines and angles – an unbelievably handsome face. Something in her chest jumped, the present moment shaken and invaded.

Kate opened her mouth to speak; nothing came out. She heard a familiar name.

"Hello, Catherine. It's me, Saleem."

He closed the door and came into the room.

"I want to talk to you – about Henri."

***

Gabi took a cleansing breath and let it out slowly. The party had moved to Simon's house – specifically into his backyard beside his saltwater pool – and would probably go on until the early hours.

The charges against Holly were cleared, and quicker than Gabi thought possible. It turned out that Robert Black hadn't embezzled all those years ago, and Holly had little difficulty in proving it. She had only wished to escape her former identity, begin a new life with Melanie and the baby.

HealSo's executives and the investors had signed on the dotted line and sold PAS to Juva Pharma as an asset sale. After the killings, they were lucky to manage that. They'd carry all the liability for HealSo for the rest of their lives, their names recorded somewhere as the shareholders of an empty shell that no longer did business.

Simon had purchased a three thousand dollar, fifteen-litre bottle of champagne the size of a suitcase, and five dozen champagne flutes in preparation for the impending celebration.

Smartphones clicked and recorded the event: the popping of the enormous cork, the pouring, the overflowing of glasses, the resultant giggles.

Fifty people spread out inside Simon's Outremont residence situated in the most affluent French area of Montreal.

Three drunk engineers came towards Simon. Within seconds, they lifted and threw him fully dressed into his pool. He hit the water and came up soaked, laughing, and holding his now dead electronic Tesla key up in the air.

***

The days passed slowly for Jimmy's mom. She sat quietly at her kitchen table. The chirping of the birds and the sounds from the nearby river greeted her like they had every morning for the past twenty-eight years.

Two cappuccinos sat on the table, one just the way Jimmy liked his, along with two plates with toast and jam, and his favorite crunchy peanut butter.

Her tangled hair stood up in clumps, but her mind remained clear.

She knew her baby would never share a coffee with her, ever again. He lived in her mind, omnipresent, in her every breath and every thought. Each morning, she put on her grief like a set of clothes and wore it throughout the day.

Evelyn Cane sipped her coffee, finishing it, and then she drank his.

***

Dusk fell by the time Gray reached home. The April evening was mild, and the grapevine and hydrangeas in his back garden swayed in the gentle breeze as he passed and entered by the back door.

Inside, the air was cool, crisp. Gray switched on the kitchen lights, had a drink of water, and poured three fingers of single malt scotch into a crystal tumbler.

Cradling the glass, he approached the studio door, opened it, and stood at the threshold.

Everything remained where he'd left it, the air still and heavy with the smell of clay, moonlight streaming in like shards from a broken mirror.

Gray lifted his drink and swirled the golden liquid, edges of the cut glass reflecting the light, and inhaled the sharp aroma brought out by sixteen years of meticulous care. The first sip touched his palate, smooth and smoky with a long finish before trailing a line of heat down his throat.

He'd solved the case, yet it left him raw.

Jimmy and Céline remained dead. And Étienne – there, at least, Gray could find a semblance of comfort and satisfaction: his young witness would start a new, more promising life.

Gray didn't need to sculpt tonight; instead, he stepped out of his studio, closed the door, and locked it, removing the key from his keychain.

Moving to the kitchen, he pushed it to the back of a crowded drawer he rarely opened, where it might soon be at least temporarily forgotten. His hand shook.

He might finally be ready to tackle lonely nights without the sculpting; the ground beneath him seemed to have grown firmer.

Calm slowly washed over him as he built a fire in the living room hearth. Forsaking the driving obsession of the sculpting was a small step towards absolution, but a step nonetheless. He couldn't mold his son back to life. He couldn't give Craig a future.

The living room lay quiet, like the street outside, save the crackling from the fire. A log shifted and sparks flared. He felt wafts of hot air caress his face.

Picturing Evelyn Cane alone in her house, he wondered how she'd get through the rest of her days. The same way he did, probably. The empty room and the hypnotic swaying of the flames provided no other answer.

Gray sipped the whiskey, already priming himself for the next case. A couple of days of rest, and soon, the next investigation would begin, the next chase — although for tonight, he welcomed something else.

Nurse Dubois's number was still in his jacket pocket, penned in a slanting, elegant hand. Gray brought out his cell and dialed. The conversation was brief and predictable, with her taking the lead: Adeline would join him within the hour.

Restless, he moved to the window, twirling the crystal tumbler.

A long way down the darkened street, a curved, amoebic form shifted, barely distinguishable from the abstract shadows of the night. Was it the form of a woman carrying a child? The apparition receded and faded into the background, and he blinked, uncertain if he'd seen or imagined it.

He plopped down on the couch, anxious for Adeline's arrival — when a knock sounded at the door. She must have been very close by to have reached his house so quickly.

On aching legs, he moved to the front door. Opening it brought in a gentle breeze, carrying with it a familiar scent.

The woman under the porch light, her jet-black hair shimmering like silk, looked the same — yet oddly changed.

Gray's wife, Sita, who had disappeared three years earlier, stood at the threshold – holding a small girl.

"Hello, Gray. It's been a long time."

He knew his mouth hung open; no words formed.

She rocked the girl, who looked to be about two years old, in her long and slim arms. Arms which he remembered rocking Craig.

"This is Noelle," Sita said. "Your daughter."

Gray said nothing; felt nothing.

Outside, a car approached and shrieked to a halt.

The squat tumbler of scotch slipped from his hand and crashed to the ground.

THE END

Find out what happens to Gray next in Book 2.

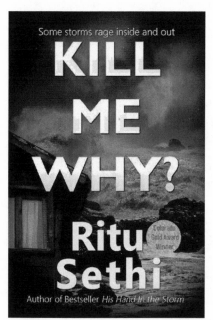

Gray is on Christmas vacation, sort of. Something is brewing in the quaint and peaceful coastal town of Gray's youth – edged between the Pacific Ocean and the Rocky Mountains near Vancouver. The town where it all began – where he had a hand in his son's death.

But healing has to wait because THE STITCHER is back after a fifteen-year absence. And the victim – lips sutured shut with medical nylon – disappears within minutes of being found at a Body Farm.

With threats launched against Gray's family, he must solve the case before a storm blasts the village, before his estranged wife takes what matters most, before his guarded secret is unleashed to the world.

EXCERPT OF BOOK 2, *KILL ME WHY?*

ON SATURDAY, December 23, Chief Inspector Gray James unknowingly drove towards the Stitcher's third crime scene.

"Tell me where we're going," he said to his passenger.

"No, not yet."

"Why?"

"I'm afraid you might say no. And you're needed on this case."

"Then I may as well turn this car around now."

"No, you won't. Your curiosity would take you off the edge of a cliff. Don't worry. That won't happen today."

Driving across dark mountainous roads, jostling headlights flashing upon moss-covered boulders, towering pines, and occasional startled feral eyes in the bushes, Gray kept his meditative calm, held at bay the gloom which threatened to consume him in those unguarded moments.

Moments when Gray remembered.

Ordinarily, his passenger, forensic pathologist John Seymour, was a proverbial fountain of bubbling information. He liked nothing better than stepping past the confines of his job and accompanying Gray on cases – and yet now he sat stolidly in the passenger seat of the Lotus Exige, his round silver-rimmed glasses sitting below thick blond brows resembling caterpillars trying to jump off his face.

The thrashing Pacific and the quaint village of Searock lay miles below, as did Gray's family seaside cabin, just three hours north of Vancouver along British Columbia's ironically named Sunshine Coast.

Christmas in coastal Searock epitomized charm. The historic downtown was decked with illuminated sleighs, decorated trees in the town square, and lights adorning quaint shops: the local butcher, the elegant bistro-cafe, Rusty's pie and home decorations, and Stone Art Gallery, frequented by tourists and featuring local and national sculptors and painters.

With every passing kilometer, Gray travelled further from that charm and up into the wild BC Mountains he adored. Wafts of birch and pine brought back visceral teenage memories – of hiking these trails with Dad, making coffee on the camping stove, hungrily ripping home-dried beef jerky with his teeth. Yet he knew that something sinister and unnatural awaited – as it always did with his job.

"It's not my jurisdiction," Gray said, swerving on a hairpin turn. The cliff's edge was only a meter to the right.

"Won't matter, James." The doctor always called him by his last name, a habit from years of working together on the force. "Just wait and see."

"Remind me never to invite you over for the holidays again. Why are you grinning?"

"I've just never seen you without your thousand dollar suit. You seem almost human."

"Others might not agree with you."

A few tricky turns, directed at the last minute by Seymour, brought them to their mystery destination.

No sign adorned the iron gate which autonomously opened and shut behind them. No intercom voice greeted their arrival.

The Lotus's wheels rolled over grass and spat mud while edging along a claustrophobic, winding trail barely wide enough for the car. Branches scratched against the custom teal finish, grinding at Gray's insides.

He gave Seymour a dark sideways glance – to which the doctor merely shrugged.

Finally, the trail ended, and they reached a dimly lit patch of ground, flanked by a border of trees to the left, and low-lying mist to the right. Only a single, beat-up pickup rested in this makeshift car park. Gray pulled up beside it.

The drenched ground squished and slid under his feet as though it were alive.

He pulled together the collar of his black leather jacket against the keen wind and inhaled the cold, wet air – tinged with the smell of something else... something very wrong.

Seymour stepped out of the car. He was tall but not as tall as Gray. "What do you think?"

"I think my loafers will never be the same."

The doctor pointed towards the right, where, within a clearing patch of mist, an amorphous form was taking the shape of a rustic cabin. Smoke spiraled upward through the crumbling brick chimney, and a back-lit silhouette paced at the paned window.

"Alright," Gray said. "If this is the crime scene, where are the Scene of Crime Officers? I need more information before we proceed."

"I'd rather the lady inside tell you."

"Why the secrecy?"

"I'm not quite sure how you'll react to the details."

The doctor moved forward alongside Gray, their familiarity a balm against the storm. Although Gray mainly lived in the eye of that storm – calm, at peace – and watching the cyclone all around him with detached interest. He'd moved past loss to that sweet place where nothing that happened mattered because he had nothing left to lose.

Until recently.

"You can't solve your problems in an instant," Seymour said, in his usual ironic tone.

"Three years isn't an instant."

"But you've just returned home to this –" he gestured with long, tapered fingers, "wilderness of yours."

"I hid these last three years in Montreal; licked my wounds after what I did. And I didn't know I had a –"

"Daughter?" Seymour completed. "Must have been a shock. How do you feel?"

That was the problem. He felt as though someone had ripped apart his chest and the life he'd built, while offering him a dazzling prize. But this wasn't the time or place for this conversation. What the hell was this place?

"Did you see the tracks going up the mountain?" Gray said. "Before we turned into the gate?"

"What? No, I didn't see anything."

"Someone must have come out this way after this morning's rain."

The slamming of Seymour's car door must have announced their arrival because a tall young woman with streaming, almost witch-like, hair ran out the front door, then paused to take them both in before motioning them to follow her towards a darkened path to the right.

Seymour acknowledged her with a wave.

She'd moved so fast that Gray, who had, since childhood, categorized impressions into flavors, had only a fleeting impression of licorice (her hair), strawberries (the red lipstick on full lips), and vanilla (from her impossibly pale skin).

The woman evaporated into the murky blackness.

No introductions; no preliminaries. Only getting down to business, which suited Gray fine, since all he wanted was to get back to his Dad's cabin, put up his feet by the hearth, and have a drink – a single malt scotch to warm his chilled bones.

He scanned his smartwatch: it was just past ten.

Mud gripped his heels with each step. After about fifty feet, his nostrils screamed.

"That smell –"

"Try and ignore it," Seymour said, walking alongside him.

Now well past the cabin, Gray hesitated before entering the pitch dark – afraid of meeting that void within himself which made it hard to move from one moment to the next, from one breath to the next. Especially this last week of being back in his hometown – where the greatest tragedy of his life had happened. What if he stepped into that darkness and never came out? His heart slammed his ribs; breathing became a struggle. A panic he'd never known before threatened to consume him.

Gray shoved past it, arms outstretched, feet crunching over uneven ground, not knowing what lay before him, with only Seymour's raspy breathing by his side.

"Doctor –"

"Just a little further."

Seymour must also be feeling the claustrophobia, the perceived lack of oxygen in the saturated, dense air.

A click preceded a series of lights turning on, suddenly blinding, revealing a large rectangular patch illuminated by three oblong beams.

The woman had reached a spot adjacent to a wired fence on the far right, where a blue tarp covered the ground. It looked flat, as though covering nothing but dirt. Certainly no dead body lay under it.

She stood against the wind, the silk hair jetting behind her, fists on hips, and legs apart. Now Gray noticed that she appeared to be of mixed heritage: part South-Asian, part Caucasian? She was also gorgeous.

"I found it here," she said in a surprisingly melodic voice.

Thick, cold droplets touched his cheeks. The full sky was giving way, having concealed the last of the overhead stars with low-lying clouds.

Seymour introduced the woman as Dr. Emerald Kaur, who responded with a firm handshake and eyes which couldn't quite meet Gray's.

Accustomed to a certain response from women, Gray noticed the unshielded resentment in her eyes with interest. He didn't mind; perhaps she distrusted all policemen.

"Sergeant Slope didn't believe me," she said.

"Slope's been here?"

"Yes. Earlier today."

Seymour had mentioned the word 'murder' to get Gray to come with him, but little else.

No signs identified the site, save brown, individually numbered markers placed close to the ground. He opened his mouth to ask, when Seymour said:

"Tell him about the corpse, Emmy."

Emmy?

"It's gone," she said.

Gray had already pieced that together by SOCO's absence. No Scene of Crime Officers likely meant the lack of a corpse. And with the local sergeant not believing "Emmy," that implied she'd seen something no one else had.

"Am I correct in assuming that the body disappeared when you went to go for help?" Gray said.

"Of course." She turned to Seymour. "Haven't you told him anything?"

"I thought this would be more fun."

Emmy sighed and began a robotic recital: "Every day at 3 pm, each body gets assessed by one of my student staff, or me. Today, I noticed a change at site 144 right away — a change in color."

"Color? I'm having difficulty following you." This place...this peculiar place — at once familiar yet foreign, with that awful smell —

She pinned him with a stare a professor might reserve for a not very promising student.

"Do you live or work here?" Gray asked. "You mentioned students and a site —"

He took in the scent, the seemingly scattered debris and site markings. And suddenly, without having ever visited one before, he'd knew where he was.

"Is this a body farm?"

"We don't call it that," Emmy snapped.

Seymour jumped in. "She's right; that's an ignorant layman's term."

"I'm only an ignorant policeman." Gray faced Seymour. "Why didn't you tell me this was a forensic research facility?"

"I'm a forensic pathologist. You could have worked it out yourself. Besides, curiosity got you off that chair by the fire and out here on a cold night, didn't it?" The doctor ran a thick-knuckled hand through his thinning hair. The caterpillar eyebrows rose a fraction and fell in conciliatory appeal. "A lot rides on you taking the case, unofficially."

Emmy unceremoniously pushed Seymour out of the way. "If I can continue?"

"Go right ahead."

"I found a specimen lying spread-eagled, long brown hair sprawled out in a fan, the neck bent at a peculiar angle. The bright pink underwear initially caught my attention from afar, and, of course, I didn't reposition the corpse. I know better than to interfere with evidence."

She painted quite a picture. Gray took in his surroundings: the rusting dilapidated car with the closed trunk; the recycling bin resting against a towering maple with branches arching on either side as though anxiously guarding the contents; the irregularly lumpy garbage bag casually tossed by the nearby fence.

Each section of this so-called body farm possessed a sequential number. He didn't want to look too closely at what was numbered.

He approached site 144 with a quickened pulse and a healthy amount of dread, his new shoes squishing in the soaked, rotting earth. Wetness seeped into the stitched seams and drenched his socks.

Emmy began a recital. "We observe and record the decomposition process in various circumstances. We study and form an understanding of the decompositional changes that occur in the human body and use that research for medical, legal, and educational purposes."

"And this," he pointed to a mannequin-like leg sticking up from the ground at site 144, part red, part glistening purple and looking impossibly bright in the relative darkness, "is forensic anthropological research?"

"From the fresh to the bloated, and finally the dry stage."

A clang sounded to the left. Seymour had moved to the nearby rusty car and stood wide-eyed looking inside the trunk. What could make the eyes of a forensic pathologist go that wide?

When Gray turned back, the glistening leg moved, and he jerked back and fell — hard, onto his behind and right onto a rock.

END OF SAMPLE
Purchase *Kill Me Why?* for just 99 cents on Amazon

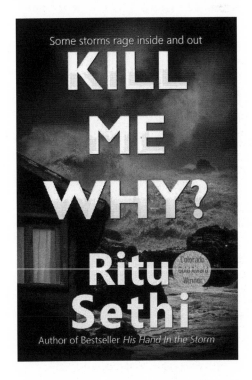

ABOUT THE AUTHOR

Ritu Sethi needs coffee, beaches, and murder mysteries to survive – not necessarily in that order. She won the Colorado Gold Award for the first in the Chief Inspector Gray James Murder Mystery Series, *His Hand In the Storm*. The book was also a Daphne du Maurier Suspense Finalist and an AMAZON BESTSELLER.

Right now, she's fulfilling her lifelong desire of becoming a mystery writer. Many thanks to all the readers who are making that possible.

SUBSCRIBE NOW.
SAMPLE CHAPTERS and EXCLUSIVE CONTENT
SUCH AS THE SAILING SCENE WHERE GRAY'S SON
DIES can be found at her website:

www.rituwrites.com
Facebook: @ritusethiauthor
Twitter: @ritusethiauthor

Made in the USA
Middletown, DE
22 January 2021